The Star Warriors

Other works by this author:

Final Flight of the Ranegr
The Starlight Lancer
The Awakening
Path of a Hero
The Cursed Jewel
Metanoia

Find them online at
https://www.cscooper.com.au/books

The Star Warriors

C. S. Cooper

ISBN: 978-0-6451753-9-4

For Chiaki.

CONTENTS

Acknowledgements

It goes without saying that I owe a lot to the artists, upon whose work this book is based. But I also express the greatest appreciation for everyone who read my other books and were so excited to see this story come to this epic point. I cannot state enough my gratitude to my friends and family for their encouragement and support.

The Story So Far

Seeds of great change have been planted in the world in the last few years alone.

Until a few months ago, Nathan Grant lived a regular life in the dormitories of Warrawul Boarding School in Wollongong, Australia.

What he thought was a nightmare, in which a mechanical snake killed him, turned out to be a chilling reality. An Alchemic Warrior named Astrid Rachelle saved his life by implanting an Alchemic talisman, known as a Kakugane, into his chest. According to her, his town was infested with homunculi: malicious man-eating beasts that disguise themselves as trustworthy people. Immortal and immune to conventional weaponry, they could only be destroyed by an Arms Alchemy: a human soul, manifested in physical form by an activated Kakugane.

Having realised that his sister Ariadne and his friends were at risk of being hunted, Nathan decided to harness his new powers under Astrid's tutelage. Upon activating the Kakugane in his chest, he summoned a lance into existence, with which he helped Astrid destroy the homunculi in their town.

As they investigated, the duo learned that a rogue Alchemist, codenamed Papillon for the butterfly mask he wore, was creating the beasts. They determined that Papillon was a reclusive student at Nathan's school, named

Koushaku Chouno. When they confronted him, they learned that he suffered from a terminal disease and would soon die. But if he were to turn himself into a homunculus, he would be cured and live forever.

Nathan attempted to stop Papillon from succeeding in his final experiment, but failed. He reluctantly killed Papillon, ending his rampage of carnage. And yet, despite Astrid's best efforts to keep secret the existence of homunculi and the Arms Alchemy, she couldn't stop Nathan's best friend Klein finding out. Rumours started to spread across Wollongong of the Starlight Lancer, defending the people from the beasts in the shadows.

Those rumours continued to bother Nathan for months, along with memories of his encounter with Papillon. And then, two months after leaving him with little more than a simple fist bump, Astrid returned to Warrawul. Not only that, but one of the teachers revealed himself as another Alchemic Warrior, codenamed Captain Bravo.

Bravo trained Nathan as an Alchemic Warrior, in anticipation of a confrontation with the League of Extraordinary Elects, or L.X.E., a nefarious homunculus society. They plotted to revive the rogue Alchemic Warrior, Victor Powers, who terrorised the world before his defeat decades earlier.

During their hunt for the L.X.E., Nathan learned that Papillon was still alive. His grandfather turned out to be the leader of the L.X.E., Doctor Butterfly. Fearing Victor's return, Papillon defected to Nathan's side, and warned him of spies at Warrawul.

Meanwhile, Astrid grew closer to Nathan's friends and sister. However, two of those friends, Tao and Shu Wu, were soon revealed as the L.X.E. spies. After defeating them in battle, Nathan and Astrid learned that the siblings were victims of tremendous abuse as children, and longed to become homunculi to live together forever. Nathan took pity on them, and convinced Bravo to take the siblings in. Grateful, the siblings informed Bravo of the location of the L.X.E. base and their plans.

By that time, it was too late, and the L.X.E. had begun their attack on Warrawul, the richest source of nourishment for Victor. During the battle, the homunculi were defeated, but Nathan, Astrid, Bravo, and Papillon could not stop Victor's revival. The being was neither human nor homunculus, but a life-sucking monster armed with a Black Kakugane. Victor easily bested Bravo and Astrid, and killed Nathan. But that only cracked the shell of Nathan's Kakugane, revealed to be another Black Kakugane in disguise. Nathan became the same beast as Victor, who was forced to retreat.

Astrid's words allowed Nathan to return to normal, but Papillon suggested that he is merely in an intermediary state, and activation of his Arms Alchemy might cause him to revert to that monsterous form.

Daunted by his experiences, chastised unfairly by his parents, encouraged by Klein, and overwhelmed with frustration, Nathan publicly activated his Arms Alchemy, right in front of a crowd of journalists and live cameras, proclaiming his identity as the Starlight Lancer.

Meanwhile …

Death City, the hidden fortress of the Grim Reaper, sat in Death Valley, Nevada. At its centre stood the Demon Weapon Meister Academy. DWMA had, for centuries, trained and honed the power of Demon Weapons: people who can shapeshift into weapons. These people were paired with Meisters, who have the ability to wield Demon Weapons. These pairings were dispatched by the Grim Reaper to hunt and reclaim the dark souls of evildoers, known as Asura Eggs.

Not all graduates of DWMA were drafted into this war. Most, in fact, went back to their normal lives after learning to control their powers. Those were called NOT graduates – standing for Normally Overcome Target. And they made for a juicy standing army for those inclined to mind control.

Death the Kid, also known as Kiddo, the son of the Reaper, discovered that NOT graduates were being brainwashed into an army. Knowing he could not handle this threat alone, he asked his father to recruit his elite warriors. Those were the prodigy Maka Albarn and her weapon, Soul Eater; and the rock-star ninja Black-Star and his weapon, Tsubaki Nakatsukasa.

The team discovered that Masamune, a rogue Demon Weapon, was leading the army. This troubled Tsubaki tremendously, as Masamune was her elder brother. However, he was not the brainwasher.

The brainwasher revealed herself as Shaula Gorgon, a Witch thought killed millennia ago. She attacked DWMA, using her braid-stinger to control students into fighting Maka and Soul. Then, with that as a distraction, she stole the Shining Trapezohedron, an artefact holding the destructive spirit of Nyarlathotep. In the attack, Maka's students were killed, which grieved her terribly.

Shaula unleashed Nyarlathotep upon DWMA. While Kiddo battled the monster, Black-Star and Tsubaki took on Masamune, defeating him and vindicating Tsubaki's regret over his downfall. Maka and Soul engaged Shaula, slicing off her braid-stinger. Losing control of Nyarlathotep, Shaula was attacked by the monster and thrown toward the horizon.

The team joined forces and destroyed Nyarlathotep once and for all, much to the joy of the citizens of Death City. The friends reconciled their differences, and vowed to work together again in the future.

That wasn't the only alliance formed. Shaula was rescued and nursed back to health by the remnants of the L.X.E., led by Moonface, Doctor Butterfly's second-in-command. He excitedly offered her another chance at revenge.

Meanwhile …

A year ago, the life of Tokyo middle-schooler, Sakura

Kinomoto, was an average one, and she loved every second of it. She had her best friend, Tomoyo Daidouji, her Dad, Franklin, and her older brother, Touya. Touya's best friend, Yukito Tsukishiro, often spent time with the family, and Sakura was absolutely smitten with him.

That all changed when Sakura discovered the magical Clow Cards. She unintentionally awakened them, and they scattered across the city. The Guardian of the Clow, Kerberus, bestowed upon her the Shadow Key, which she could use to find and seal away the Cards before they caused a tremendous calamity.

Along for the ride was Tomoyo, who recorded her exploits capturing the Clow Cards and uploaded them to the Internet. This made them instantly famous, and served as a perfect cover for their true activities. Seriously, who would've thought that videos about magic entities would be anything but CGI?

It did, however, incur the wrath of Xiaolang Lee, a descendent of the Clow Cards' creator. He declared Sakura an unfit Master of the Clow, and demanded she return the Cards to him. But when he later saw she could be a good Master, he decided to train her in magic.

Lee wasn't the only one Sakura impressed. Upon obtaining all the Cards, Yukito revealed himself as the alter ego of Yue, Kerberus' counterpart. Yue carried out the Final Judgement on Sakura, in which she proved herself worthy. Yue reluctantly announced Sakura as the Master of the Clow, to the joy of Tomoyo and Kerberus. Even Xiaolang was happy, having confided in Tomoyo that he'd always had feelings for Sakura.

Barely a day after the summer holidays, Sakura woke to find the Book of Clow changed into the Book of Sakura, and the Shadow Key transformed into a Star Key. The key wouldn't respond to her activation spell, and the Clow Cards felt cold and inert.

A huge deluge threatened to drown her friends, until she realised new spells were necessary. She activated the

Star Wand, transformed the Watery Card into the Aqua Card, and used it to calm the storm.

Thus, she created the first Sakura Card. This endeavour drained her stamina tremendously. Kerberus and Yue warned her not to change too many Cards at once or it might kill her.

At school, a new English teacher arrived from Scotland. His name was Eriol Lamperouge. Sakura immediately made friends with him and helped him practice his Japanese. He was a delightful friend, much to Xiaolang's fury.

Compounding Xiaolang's irritation was Sakura, beginning to think that he and Tomoyo were a couple. His patience broke when Tomoyo teased too much about the situation. He confronted Tomoyo about her romantic feelings for Sakura. Emboldened by Xiaolang's words, Tomoyo came out to Sakura, who was completely taken off-guard and very rattled.

At the same time, Yukito was disappearing. Sakura's magic was not enough to sustain him and Yue. Touya, desperate not to lose Yukito, gave up his own magical powers to keep him alive. When Sakura learned of this, and her own evident powerlessness, she received another blow.

Fearing that she wouldn't have another chance, Sakura confessed her love for Yukito and her desire to be his wife. He turned her down, explaining that he felt for Touya, and that he would not be able to make her happy.

As a final blow, Sakura learned that if she didn't change the Clow Cards into Sakura Cards in time, they would die. Devastated and terrified, Sakura tried to change all the Cards at the same time. She nearly died.

After recovering, Sakura's life seemed different. She was happy, but saw the world differently. She grew closer to Xiaolang, who indicated his feelings for her. But before they could pursue it, a calamity brewed over Tokyo. A great darkness took the skies and put everyone in the city in a coma. The culprit was Eriol, who revealed himself as the reincarnation of Clow Reed, the Cards' creator.

In order to undo his spell, Sakura had to change all the remaining Cards, including the Light and Dark Cards. She managed this with Yue, Kerberus, and Xiaolang's combined strength.

Delighted, Eriol explained that he was part of Clow's plan to have Sakura become the master of the Cards. He said that Clow's soul split in two, one half being him and the other being someone else in the world. At Eriol's request, Sakura cast a spell to transfer some of his magic to the other, alleviating the burden of all that power upon him.

With the completion of Clow's plan, Eriol returned home. Sakura looked forward to a bright future, only to find Xiaolang was leaving too. Discovering her true feelings, she caught him at the airport and professed her love for him. Xiaolang promised to migrate to Japan to be with her.

Franklin soon learned of Sakura's magical powers, having mysteriously been bestowed his own. Not long after, he was whisked away to Australia, where Bravo showed him the Silver Key he'd long sought. He immediately set to work to unravel its mysteries.

Behind the veil of the cosmos, agents unknown and ancient extend their feelers and antennae, across space and time, searching … fearing … hunting …

1 | It begins

Even in summer, the Australian outback is chilly at night. The sun falls below the horizon, blasting out rays of red light as if clambering to stay in the sky. Then comes the bluish darkness of night, which pushes the day off the ledge and stands at the top of the sky. And the land becomes cold.

Though cold, it was the night that gave the Kunja people a magnificent view of the stars. Those Kunja people, who lived in regions of Southeast Queensland, saw the Magellanic Clouds that orbit our galaxy, and thought them elders watching over the red Earth. They had names for the white, the blue, and the red stars pockmarking the celestial tapestry, its light woven into myths by the spiritual loom known as the Dreamtime.

"That, at least, is what I've read," said the man as he gazed up at the night sky.

"That sounds amazing, Dad," said his daughter's voice, carried all the way from Japan through his mobile phone. "I'd love to see Australia someday."

"Well, once you've finished high school, we'll go on a trip," said the man. "Your brother too. Maybe even Tomoyo and Yukito would like to come."

"Don't forget Kero," said the girl excitedly. She added softly, "And Xiaolang too." The girl's sigh reverberated through the phone. "You've been on this dig for weeks," she moaned. "When are you coming home?"

The man grit his teeth. He eyed the guard nearby, who tapped his watch impatiently.

"Soon," said the man. "There's a really difficult passage this faculty needs me to translate. And only I can do it."

"Well, hurry up and finish it soon, okay?" asked the daughter.

"Will do, Sakura," said the man. He ended the call, and followed the guard back into the unmarked building. He slipped through the doors with a sigh, knowing he was going back into that wretched underground facility. He took his access card from the front desk, bearing the name 'Doctor Franklin Avalon.' He would have preferred the surname of his wife, Nadeshiko Kinomoto.

Franklin swiped the card and the elevator opened for him. The guard didn't notice the woman waiting inside for them. Only Franklin could see the ghost of his wife, and it was all that had kept him sane for the last few weeks.

"Don't worry, Dear," she said, though only Franklin could hear her. "You'll be seeing Sakura soon enough."

Franklin smiled at that. His elation was only hampered by the fact that he couldn't respond, on account of the bulky, emotionless agent standing beside him.

That agent escorted him back to his office, filled with papers, drawings, and photos of an artefact. That artefact — the absolute bane of his existence for decades — sat infuriatingly still on his desk. He hunched over it, and glared at the intricate metal carving. He ran his finger over the text engraved upon its surface.

"You managed to translate the writing," said Nadeshiko. "Remember what it says."

Franklin nodded. Amid the fires of his frustration, he saw the words hanging in his mind.

"Two into one, space and time re-sown," he recited. With a shake of his head, he plonked down on his chair and stretched. "What does that mean though? And why does this Alchemic Regiment care? They need to know how it works, he said. But … it's a plank of metal. Beautiful, of course, and significant to history … but it's just a metal carving."

Nadeshiko chuckled, "You thought that about our daughter's wand until a few months ago. Thanks to her, you have some magical abilities now. Perhaps this Silver Key is another wand."

Franklin huffed, "I can see you, sure. But I doubt I can fly."

Nadeshiko leaned down and looked at him fixedly. She smiled warmly and said, "You could only see me because you still desperately wanted to. It's all about intention." She directed his gaze to the artefact. "If you focus on what you want to know, perhaps it will tell you."

With a sigh, Franklin rose to his feet. Of course, he would have. Nadeshiko never steered him wrong when she was alive. He approached the rod, touched his hands to it, and closed his eyes. He breathed in slowly, and breathed out with increasing force. Every time he exhaled, he uttered the same question, "What are you?"

An infinitesimal flash burst through his mind. He saw a technicolour tapestry of threads, woven and overlapping each other in tremendously diverse combinations. He gasped at the overload of information, which brought to the fore lessons he'd forgotten when he was a teenager: quarks, electrons, and the energy fields that bound them together.

He gazed down at the artefact, and perceived wisps of cyan puff outward from its surface. They mesmerised him as much as they terrified him. He came to a realisation that almost made him laugh.

"There's another," he murmured.

"Another what?" asked Nadeshiko.

Before Franklin could respond, an explosion hit him like a tornado. His ears rung, and his vision was blurry. He couldn't get a fix on what was happening as half a dozen burly hands pulled him out of the rubble. He shook his head furiously as he struggled to get a bearing on his surroundings. He could feel heat on his skin from nearby fires, and his lungs burnt from the smoke. He managed to open his eyes, and look at the person in front of him.

The woman's irises, cyan in the middle and blood red at the edges, emanated the pungent stench of pure crazy. Her head was crowned with deep magenta hair cut at neck-length, and she wore a leather outfit that left nothing to the imagination.

"Doctor Franklin Avalon, I assume," said the woman with a strident voice. Franklin didn't respond, so she slapped him so hard his jaw almost broke. "I don't have all day, Brit-shit! Are you Franklin Avalon?"

"Yes!" barked Franklin. He struggled against his captors, but their vice grips were stronger than steel. The men who held him thrust out their chins in hostile sneers. Their thick, leathery skin contorted as they grunted, especially around their foreheads that bore helical tattoos of purple ink.

The tattoo elicited memories from within Franklin's concussed mind. He recalled his briefing with his current employers, and knew exactly who they were.

"Homunculi!" he exclaimed.

"Moon!" bellowed a high-pitched, jovial voice. Through the wreck of the laboratory strode a tall, lanky man with a yellow face. He held the collar of his double-breasted suit, and carried himself with sophistication that was not reflected in his wide, psychotic smile. "This ardent archaeologist knows of our carnivorous kind, Shaula," he chirped as he looked right into Franklin's face.

"You've come to eat me, then?" spat Franklin, doing

everything he could to hide his terror.

"Pshaw! Not at all," said the yellow-faced man. "Your utility yields adroit advantage."

"Moonface, enough with this crap," snapped the woman. "Just make him a homunculus already."

Franklin's chest stung with horror. "Don't you dare!"

"Of course, not," exclaimed Moonface. "You'll remain just as you are, my fretful friend. You'll yet pursue pertinent purpose." To his men, he chimed, "Take him."

The brutes dragged Franklin, flailing and yelling, toward the exit. The woman named Shaula growled, "I can't brainwash him, so how do you propose we make him do as he's told?"

Moonface was too busy looking at the box containing the Silver Key. By now, the wisps of energy signifying the artefact's activation had dissipated. And yet, Moonface knew it was the real thing. He closed the box and hefted it off the desk. To Shaula, he said, "He'll do it, because it's his constant compulsion – his furious fixation, fuelling him to find the fundamentals." He dumped the box in Shaula's arms and motioned her to leave.

But Shaula wouldn't go.

"Then, why did you bring an embryo?" she asked.

Moonface's grin widened with perverse excitement. He motioned for his subordinate nearby, who carried a metal cylinder with as much reverence as a priest would a holy relic, or mother a newborn. Moonface's tiny eyes darted around, looking at all the corpses their bomb left behind. His nostrils, highly attune to the scent of live meat, smelled a body. He hopped over the rubble and upended a bulkhead, under which writhed a woman in a Regiment security uniform.

The woman saw Moonface loom over him, and panic burst from her face. She fumbled for the hexagonal talisman strapped to her chest. Glimmering tendrils of black light wrapped around her wrists and held her down. The woman looked over in dismay to see Shaula, her hands waving to direct the magical bonds with tremendous strength.

Moonface took the canister from his subordinate. When the captive woman saw it, she knew instantly what it was and started to thrash and scream with horror. The canister cracked open with a hiss of cold air, and Moonface withdrew a creature from within. The tiny thing, no bigger than a garden lizard and made of both metal and pale flesh, flailed and squealed. Moonface held it in front of him, cooing it as it swung by its tail.

The woman wriggled and screamed in Shaula's magical vice grip. The Witch snaked a black energy ribbon around the woman's neck to subdue her further, and another to wrest her mouth open. Slowly and affectionately, Moonface lowered the creature into the woman's mouth, then forced closed by Shaula's magic.

The woman thrashed, cried, and screamed as her body started to morph and contort. Shaula released the woman, who flopped around like a fish out of water. Her head smashed against the floor, her limps pounded the rubble around her, until she fell still. She looked dead by all accounts.

Then she gasped back to life. She robotically looked at Moonface, her gaze no different from that of a mindless zombie.

"You will soon have the memories of your host," said Moonface. "Maintain membership here, supplant your symbiote's service, and avail us of these arrogant Alchemist's aims."

The woman nodded mechanically. Shaula then flipped her onto her front, and Moonface covered her with rubble. The subordinate who had held the canister looked confused.

"My lord," he said. "You don't intend to take her Kakugane?"

"And tip off the shrewd shysters?" retorted Moonface. To Shaula, he intoned, "That's why I brought the embryo."

Shaula chuckled as she gazed around the mess they'd made. The scent of death never ceased to arouse her, and she drew deep of it. Then she and Moonface re-joined their group on the surface. They climbed into their escape craft, and, as it took to the skies, Shaula looked at Moonface with a maleficent grin.

She proclaimed, "Let's change us some history!"

They did not see the Japanese woman on the roof of the building. Only their hostage could see her. She wore a pained, worried expression, which was tempered by foreknowledge and the certainty that everything would be all right.

"Clow," she murmured to the skies. "It's begun."

2 | Anzacs

A sweet, dry scent wafted upward from the box. The security guard opened it, and his grin widened.

"Careful, they're dangerous," joked the young woman. Her facetious grin wrinkled the scar that crawled across the bridge of her nose. She noted the gleam in the guard's eyes and snapped, "You're not allowed to have one."

"Sorry, Warrior Rachelle," said the guard. "I haven't had breakfast, and you're making me hungry."

"Too bad, they're for him," said the girl.

With a growl of disappointment, the guard pushed the box through the X-ray machine. The woman then placed a paper bag, her wallet and phone on the conveyor belt, and strode through the metal detector. She pocketed her things, grabbed the box and paper bag, and eyed the technician behind the scanner. The technician reported, "All clear. Have a nice day, Astrid."

Astrid nodded and strode down the brightly lit corridor. She had a bit of a spring to her step, though it mystified her as to why. All she'd done was bake some Anzac[1] biscuits, and it was at his request. Had it not been

---

[1]   ANZAC, Australia New Zealand Army Corps, was a branch of the Mediterranean Expeditionary Force in World War One. The biscuits named after them were invented during that time as a snack that would

for him, she wouldn't have lost her Kakugane, wouldn't have been suspended from active duty, and wouldn't have had to babysit him. On the other hand, this idiot, his sister, and his friends had become such a wonderful part of her life. It at least put a damper on her traumatic past.

Of course, the stupid stunt he pulled to get him in this mess had also landed her in hot water. Hence, the suspension.

It made her marvel, *Then why the Hell am I bringing him biscuits like a schoolgirl?*

Astrid reached the end of the corridor, where another pair of guards waited. The Kakugane holstered to their chests glistened as she approached, betraying the guards' heightened nerves upon seeing her. It was understandable, given who – or rather, *what* – they were guarding. The doors slid open and she passed them, revealing a laboratory full of jittery scientists, overseen by an impatient supervisor. Astrid edged toward the supervisor and mumbled, "What're they worried about, Commander?"

"What do you think?" retorted the Commander. He nodded to the boy in the isolation room, playing a Nintendo Switch furiously.

Astrid scoffed, "He's playing *Smash Brothers*. He's not going to go Victor over that." She nudged the Commander. "You should go and play with him. He'd love a visit from Captain Bravo."

Bravo glanced at her, the slightest sliver of irritation present in his eyes. In the next instant, it was gone. With a sigh, he moved toward the science team and said, "That's enough. Stop the IV, draw some blood, and re-run the analysis." One of the scientists protested, but Bravo insisted. They carried out his orders, and moved their work to another lab, leaving only Bravo, Astrid, and a few remaining overseers.

Astrid and Bravo went into the room with smiles.

---

last a long time and were easy to make with the limited ingredients available at the time. They are still very popular today.

Astrid's was far more genuine than Bravo's. The boy's eyes brightened when he saw Astrid. She presented him the box.

"Baked 'em this morning," she chirped. "Be grateful, it's my first time cooking."

"You're a disgrace to your gender stereotype," jibed the boy.

"Oi, Nathan, make sure you say 'thanks,'" chided Bravo.

Nathan rolled his eyes and said, "Thank you very much, Astrid."

Astrid chewed her lip nervously as Nathan took a bite of a biscuit. He leaned back and savoured the taste.

"God bless those Anzacs, eh!" he exclaimed as he took another bite. Astrid found herself sighing with relief.

Bravo curiously reached forward and nabbed one. He too found them delicious.

Astrid eyed the screen. Nathan, playing as Cloud Strife, once again stood the loser, while the victor was Solid Snake. She chuckled, "Still can't beat him?"

"That bastard, *Hellhound99*," grumbled Nathan. "I swear, I meet that dude in real life, I'll wring is neck." He swallowed another biscuit and sighed, "That said, only so many times I can replay every game on the net. Any chance on a day pass, Bravo?"

"No can do, Grant," said Bravo. "That last test didn't work."

"No duh," spat Nathan. "I was sitting here for an hour, waiting for those drugs to knock me out. Nothing."

"So, we can't anaesthetise you and remove the Black Kakugane," said Astrid. She rubbed her nose scar, which tended to tingle when she was stressed. She turned to Bravo. "What about Newton's Apple? Where I found the Black Kakugane."

"Already checked," said Bravo. "Sent teams there twice

to scan it up and down. ASIO[2] investigated quietly too. Nothing. Whatever was done to disguise it as a regular Kakugane, it wasn't done there. And according to the head priest, it'd been there since the school's founding. The one who donated it died ten years ago, with no relatives."

"Damn," growled Astrid.

"Back to my first point, could I please have a day pass?" asked Nathan. His brow furrowed with stress and boredom. Bravo's response only frustrated him more. "It's been six months, Bravo. I've been in this room for *six months!*"

"Well, you should've thought of that before you pulled that stunt at Warrawul," snapped Bravo. His hair stood on end, and his breathing quickened as he glared down at the boy on the bed. Nathan's glare returned the same hostility Bravo radiated, and the Commander forced himself to calm down. "Look, I'm sorry," he sighed. "I don't want you to be stuck here any more than you do. I don't want that thing in your chest anymore than you do, okay?" The boy gazed away, his shoulders shaking. Bravo huffed and decided to throw him a bone. "I might be able to arrange a visit for your sister and parents. But until we figure out how to reverse your condition, you're staying here. Understand?"

Nathan let out a long sigh. The thing in his chest clanged, and he could hear its rumbles echoing up his spinal column. As much as he wanted to be out of the room, the creature inside him also wanted out. Because of that, he had to stay put.

That didn't stop him from haggling.

"Klein, Jessie, and Paul too," he said.

"Just your family," said Bravo firmly.

"Then a video chat with my mates too," blurted Nathan. He slowly added, "Please."

Bravo eventually agreed. His eyes turned to the TV,

---

[2]   Australian Security Intelligence Organisation, the Australian equivalent of the FBI.

and he said, "Haven't played this in a while. Think Jessie's online?"

"I'd message him if you gave me a phone," said Nathan. He offered Bravo one of the controllers.

They were partway through setting up a game, with Nathan as Cloud Strife and Bravo playing as Kirby, his favourite character. Bravo's phone buzzed, the calling number he clearly recognised. He took the call by the door. Nathan waited patiently, while Astrid sat down beside him.

"Wanna play too?" asked Nathan.

"No, thanks," said Astrid. She patted him on the shoulder, sensing he still missed his friends. The cabin fever was clearly getting to him. She recalled the contents of the paper bag, and showed it to him. "Ariadne sent me this," she explained. "She said it was from her and your parents."

Curious, Nathan reached into the bag and pulled out a shirt made of light fabric, not unlike a gym shirt. The shirt was predominantly green, with gold stripes running diagonally upward. The stripes met at a central point on the chest, where there was a gold, five-pointed star. The design made him laugh.

"What's this? My superhero costume?" he chuckled.

"Don't be mean," chided Astrid. "Ariadne designed that herself."

"I'd look like Captain America," said Nathan.

"Well, more like Captain *Australia*," replied Astrid.

Nathan checked the bag, and found another shirt. He pulled it out, revealing a dark blue design, with similarly oriented stripes of silver and white. On the chest, instead of a star, there was a crucifix. The more slender shape indicated it was for a woman.

"Looks like you've got one too," he chimed. He held it over her chest and chuckled, "You'll look like Bible Man."

"Hey, don't diss that show," said Astrid. She held up the shirt and couldn't help but smile. It had the same colour scheme as her Newton's Apple uniform, which Ariadne had clearly remembered. She gazed into the bag and said, "There's something else in there from me." Nathan looked into the bag and found a folded length of red cloth. He unravelled it, revealing a long scarf in the same colour as the sash that had once hung from his Arms Alchemy.

"Oooh, nice," he chirped.

"I figured it really suited you," said Astrid. "Back when we were fighting the L.X.E. at Warrawul, you looked cool with that sash wrapped around your neck."

Nathan beamed, "Thanks, Astrid."

"Don't try to kiss me," warned the battle-scarred girl.

Nathan poked his tongue out facetiously. He then turned to the door, wondering if Bravo was finished with his call. He saw the man, hunched against the doorframe, pale faced and panting heavily. Nathan stood nervously and approached the man.

"Bravo, what happened?" asked the boy.

Astrid drew near. "Commander, what's wrong?"

Bravo finally noticed they were looking at him. His eyes shifted and he fidgeted. He blurted, "There's been an emergency. I have to go."

Nathan grabbed him, and Bravo found himself unable to move out of the boy's grip.

"What's going on? You look freaked out," said the boy.

Bravo huffed irately and said, "Moonface attacked a Regiment facility at Cunnamulla. And it looks like he had help from a Witch." His eyes darted between the pair, before falling on Astrid. "Warrior Rachelle, I need you to come with me. You're the only one who fought with the L.X.E. who isn't being held in custody."

"And what, I stay here?" exclaimed Nathan. "I can help catch him. Especially if he's still working with Victor, or knows where he is."

Bravo pulled out of Nathan's grip and thrust his finger in the boy's face. "You're staying here! Got it?" Nathan stepped back from the man's advance. Bravo's eyes were roaring for his obedience, which he gave out of respect. Astrid gave him an apologetic glance as she left, leaving Nathan alone in that cursed observation room.

He plopped on the bed with a sigh. His hand brushed against the shirt his sister sent. Not caring that people were watching from behind the one-way mirror, he pulled off his hospital shirt and donned the new one. It fit to his well-built form, showing off the six-pack bestowed upon him by the Kakugane in his chest. The golden star, an insignia of his heroic epithet, glistened in the cold hospital light.

He couldn't wait to wear it in public.

3 | An Unexpected Prize

A girl with mid-neck-length chestnut hair strode out of a convenience store in Tokyo. Her school uniform was well kept, despite the time being well into the afternoon. She fumbled a little with the wrapper on the popsicle she just bought, just in time for a few passers-by to notice her.

"Excuse me," said the blonde. The girl looked at her and assumed she was an American tourist. She held up a camera and said, "You're that Cardcaptor girl from YouTube, right?"

The girl beamed, "Yep. Sakura's my name."

"Oh, you speak English too," exclaimed the blonde's black friend. She pointed to the rest of their group and said, "Any chance you could do a selfie with us?"

"Sure," Sakura chirped. She held her popsicle behind her back and stood in the middle of the group. The girls were delighted with the photo.

One of them stepped forward and asked, "There's rumours going around that you can do real magic. Is it true?"

Sakura just giggled, "Unfortunately, no. Would be really cool if I could, right?" The girls clicked their tongues with disappointment. They thanked her for the selfie and moved on down the street.

Sakura gave a contented sigh, and went back to her

popsicle. She was in an especially good mood, hence the decision to spoil herself. The reason for her mood: her boyfriend in Hong Kong was going to call her tonight, and she couldn't wait. They'd been doing long distance for two months, and it had been a week since they'd spoken. Even though it was so she could study for a test, the break in their contact was driving her crazy. But the exam was finished, so she could talk with her beloved Xiaolang.

To augment her good mood, Sakura donned her earphones and hit play on her phone. The song streamed through her ears, and she danced her way down the street. She drew the attention of many onlookers. Some of them frowned and their discomfort spurred them away. Others joined in with the dance, infecting bystanders with laughter and merriment.

God, I love having this power, thought Sakura.

Just as the song finished, she felt a tap on her shoulder. She turned and saw a dark-haired girl that made her smile.

"Tomoyo!" she exclaimed. "You got out of choir practice early."

"I never went," said Tomoyo. She brandished her camera. "I simply had to record you on the eve of your call with Mister Lee. I think I'll call this 'Sakura dances to Owl City.' Sounds wonderful, right?"

Sakura face-palmed with dismay. "Seriously, Tomoyo! I'm sure your girlfriend doesn't appreciate you obsessing over me."

Tomoyo's gleaming eyes went to the sky and she proclaimed, "My partner appreciates the true amazingness that is Sakura! As does everyone else here!" She held her arms wide to encompass all the onlookers. Most of them had been dancing along to Sakura's beat, and still wore smiles from it. "Ah, Sakura is the source of all joy. Why would my beloved partner stop me from showing the world your amazingness?"

Sakura put her fists on her hips and sassily jibed, "Well then, why won't she introduce herself to me? I want to meet the one who has stolen my best friend's heart."

Tomoyo smirked, and hooked her arm around Sakura.

"Sakura," she began slowly. "My partner is still trying to sort things out with her family. It's important to me that she comes out on her own terms. Like I did, remember?"

Sakura pursed her lips, recalling the awkward moment. She pondered how moment that nearly wrecked her relationship with her best friend, among many other things. If it were that bad for her, she could only imagine how it would be if Tomoyo's partner's family was less understanding. She patted Tomoyo's arm and said, "Well, I understand that. And I hope that her family is understanding too."

Tomoyo nodded and smiled with relief. She then said, "Enough about me. What about Lee?"

Sakura immediately chuckled and her heart fluttered at the image of her boyfriend. She recalled the moment when they kissed for the first time, at the airport before he left for Hong Kong. Blood filled her face and her body shook with excitement. She clamped down on her popsicle to cool herself, lest she appear a little too excited in public.

Beside her, Tomoyo just giggled. She looked over and saw a raffle being held in the middle of a nearby mall. Excitedly, she dragged Sakura over to the line-up.

"Tomoyo, I can't use magic in public," Sakura whispered in her friend's ear. "I can't rig the raffle, and I won't."

"I don't mean that," said Tomoyo. "I was joking that one time. But maybe you can win a nice prize." She pointed at the prize list. The top prize was a Tesla Model X. But it was third on the list that caught Tomoyo's eye. "Third prize is a trip to Hong Kong."

Sakura's eyes brightened at the prospect. She quickly got in line, and procured some coins to participate in the prize draw. It was soon her turn, though it felt like a lifetime's worth of waiting. She paid the two-hundred-yen fee, and turned the crank on the ball box. Out popped a dull yellow ball.

Every eye bugged out in amazement. Taken aback, Sakura looked to the board, and saw the prize that corresponded to yellow. Her jaw dropped in shock.

* * *

"Ya won!?" exclaimed the living teddy bear with a Kansai accent. He sprayed a hail of cookie crumbs from his mouth, almost covering the prize packet in Sakura's hands.

"Kero, that's gross," moaned Sakura.

Kero, whose full name was Kerberus, swallowed his cookie mouthful. He then floated into the air and studied the prize more closely. "Five days and four nights in Hong Kong." He pointed a stubby hand at Sakura and yelled, "Take me too! Take me! Take me! Take me!"

Sakura backed away and exclaimed, "Okay, hold your horses. Of course, I'll take you." She looked a bit closer at the ticket. "It's only for two, so I'll have to pick someone to go with."

"Go with me!" screamed Kero.

"You can disguise yourself as a plush toy," replied Sakura. Kero returned to his plate of cookies with a harrumph. Sakura meanwhile counted all the people she could invite. "Tomoyo would be first to invite … but she may be busy with her girlfriend. Maybe Yukito could come." She thought a bit. "He mightn't want to come without Big Brother. Plus …" She recalled the moment when Yukito reluctantly broke her heart. She decided it might be a bit awkward if they went on an overseas trip alone together. "Who else?" she thought aloud.

A familiar tone blared from her open laptop. She sat down at the desk and saw the incoming call.

"Xiaolang's calling!" she exclaimed. "He's gonna be so excited when I tell him!" She clicked the answer widget and the face of her beloved Hong Kong boyfriend appeared on the screen. His eyes lit up and he waved.

"*Nǐ hǎo!*" he chirped. He shook his head and blurted,

"Sorry! Hello, I mean!"

Sakura chuckled, "Been too long speaking Cantonese?"

"Switching languages is hard," said Xiaolang.

"I hear you there," said Sakura, her grin widening despite her effort to stay nonchalant. "Last time I got back from England, it took me a day to switch back to Japanese."

Xiaolang giggled. His smile softened with longing and he said, "I miss you."

Sakura's grin burst into full blown laughter. Xiaolang looked almost hurt, but didn't have a chance to protest before Sakura bellowed, "Guess what? I got into a raffle today, and won the third prize. You know what it is?"

"No, what?" asked Xiaolang. Sakura held up the prize pack to the camera. Xiaolang frowned. "I can't read it."

"It's a trip to Hong Kong!" exclaimed Sakura.

"No way!" yelled Xiaolang. "You're coming to Hong Kong? What're the odds?"

"I don't care!" retorted Sakura. "I finally get to see you again."

Xiaolang laughed with joy and he gripped his camera. "When are you coming?"

Sakura checked the prize pack information.

"Next Saturday," she said. "I've got a week to decide who's coming with me."

"I'll inform my parents," said Xiaolang. "They'll be really excited to meet you. Especially, my mother. She's wanted to meet you ever since she predicted you'd become Master of the Clow."

"Master of the *Stars*, now," said Sakura, touching the Star Key hanging from her neck.

"I'm gonna be seeing stars when I see you in Hong Kong," chortled Xiaolang, winking flirtatiously.

Sakura's heart raced again, and she bit her lower lip. She could almost feel his lips on hers, and longed to feel his presence again.

"I can't wait," she said.

Kero butted in to chide her for being too flirty, and then left the lovers alone to play video games. Sakura and Xiaolang talked a while longer, listing all the things to visit in Hong Kong. Sakura noted them down excitedly. Then, they chatted a little more about home life, and Sakura's father's long absence on work. They ended the call when Sakura heard her older brother call her down for dinner.

Sakura invited Kero to come down, but he was too enthralled in his game.

"I just love kickin' this Aussie's butt," growled Kero as he knocked the blonde swordsman out of the park. "Wahoo! Suck it, *Grant734!*" Sakura just rolled her eyes and trotted down stairs. A pale-skinned, light-brown haired boy set the table for four places, while another darker haired boy sharing some of Sakura's features stirred the spaghetti sauce.

"Hi, Sakura," said the pale boy with a kind face.

"Yukito!" chirped Sakura warmly.

Yukito glanced around her and asked, "Is Kerberus not joining us?"

"Nope, he's too busy bullying kids in games," chuckled Sakura.

"Tell that Kansai puppet he's a butt-head," snarled the other boy at the stove.

"Big Brother!" chided Sakura.

"That's not nice, Touya," said Yukito.

"Facts are facts," retorted Touya. He glanced over his shoulder at Sakura. "Ain't you got some good news, Kaiju?"

Sakura almost burst a blood vessel. She raised her dukes in a show of vehement retribution and bellowed, "I am not a kaiju!"

Yukito tried to chide Touya further. And yet he couldn't help but laugh at Sakura's over-the-top reaction. He took a seat at the table and motioned for her to do the same.

"What's this announcement then?" he asked.

"Oh, I won the third prize in a raffle," Sakura announced. "I won a trip for two to Hong Kong!"

"Wow! How lucky!" replied Yukito. "So will it be you and Daidouji, then?"

"I don't know," said Sakura. "She said she might have prior engagements she can't get out of. She said she'd talk to her mother about it tonight."

Yukito grinned facetiously.

"Well, Miss Sakura, you know how I'm like, totally, your bestest bestie in the whole wide world?"

Sakura gave a bewildered chortle at his brown-nosing. Of course, she knew it was a joke, and that made it all the more hilarious.

The chef put the pot of spaghetti sauce and a bowl of pasta on the table. The trio sat down and said the customary Japanese phrase, "Itadakimasu[3]," before tucking in. Yukito took the biggest helping by far, and dug in quickly. Sakura took a more modest mouthful and said, "Delicious, Big Brother."

Touya looked right at her and droned, "You got sauce on your nose." That earned him a nudge from Yukito, which was much less than the kick Sakura would have given him.

"Meanie," snorted Sakura.

"Careful, Sakura," said Yukito. "You might have to get him to come with you to Hong Kong."

Touya cut them both off. "No can do. I've got two college exams week after next." He looked at Yukito. "You should go, Yuki. At least so the other guy's got her back."

Sakura pursed her lips as she thought of Yue, Yukito's alter ego and the counterpart of Kero. They were both her guardians in magic, and they always looked after her. Yukito gazed downward at nothing in particular, and remained that way a while, before he said, "Yue would be fine to go. He says, 'If it's to protect the master.'" He

---

[3]   Literally translated, "I receive." This is similar to saying "Grace" before meals in Western cultures.

made a faux impression of the stern man's voice that was so unlike the real Yue it was comical. It even made Touya chuckle.

"Well, Kero's coming too, in my backpack, of course," said Sakura.

"But I'll only go if Miss Daidouji isn't," said Yukito. "She's your best friend, so she should go."

Touya nudged him. "I wanted you to go so that creep doesn't try anything."

"He's not a creep," snapped Sakura. "And he's my boyfriend now, so you need to be nice, Big Brother."

It was then that Kero floated into the kitchen, drawn by the scent of Touya's Bolognese sauce. Drool trickled from the edge of his mouth as he approached the table in a hypnotic state.

"Good of you to finally join us," said Touya snidely.

"I had to teach that kangaroo a lesson," retorted Kero, no longer afraid of the boy from whom he'd hidden for so long. His eyes fell on the nearly empty bowl of pasta and cried, "Why didn't you save any for me?"

"I was hungry and you didn't come down," said Yukito.

Kero outstretched a stubby hand and bellowed, "You're just as bad as Yue. You're greedy! *J'accuse!*[4]"

Sakura rolled her eyes and dragged Kero into the kitchen. She brought some more water to the boil for more pasta. Meanwhile, Touya's foul mood persisted. Yukito leaned in and said, "You should probably be nicer to Lee. He might be your brother-in-law one day."

"Never," growled Touya. "He's a creep and a woman-beater."

Yukito grinned and put his finger to his ear, as if listening to a fake earpiece. "This just in, Touya Kinomoto has cornered the market on the sister complex."

"Shaddup," Touya snarled facetiously.

---

4   French: "I accuse!"

* * *

Sakura received a call later that night. She pulled away from her math homework to answer the phone, displaying Tomoyo's number. The girl's voice carried a small amount of disappointment.

"I'd love to go to Hong Kong with you," said Tomoyo. "But, unfortunately, Mom and I were planning a three day getaway that week. I'm so sorry."

"That's alright," replied Sakura. "It's important that you spend time with your mother. Give her my regards."

"So, who are you planning on taking?" asked Tomoyo.

"Maybe Yukito," said Sakura, though she felt strange about it.

Tomoyo could clearly sense her unease and said, "That might not be a good idea, since he's Touya's partner, and he did turn you down."

"That's fine, we're past that," said Sakura. "Big Brother wants him to go with me to make sure Xiaolang doesn't try anything."

"Lee would never," exclaimed Tomoyo.

"Of course not," replied Sakura. "Big Brother's just being silly." In her mind, however, she could not shake the giddiness of Xiaolang actually trying something. Her body quivered with excitement, for which she immediately chided herself.

Not very lady-like, Sakura, she thought.

"Anyway," she stammered. "I need to finish my homework. I'll talk to you later."

"Later then," said Tomoyo, and the call ended.

As Sakura put the phone down and went back to her homework, she pondered the last time her father had called. He'd been really busy on his archaeology trip, so much that he'd only been able to call on Fridays. Strangely, he hadn't called that particular day. That hardly worried her, since he sometimes missed a call when on an important dig. His work was important to him, and she supported him in that regard. Nevertheless, she still missed him.

"And I need to tell him about my trip, so he doesn't worry," she thought aloud.

Sakura forced herself to focus on her homework. She managed to finish two more problems before her laptop blurted an incoming call alert. It was Xiaolang again.

"Twice in one day," exclaimed the girl, though softly so she didn't wake Kero.

"My parents wanted me to convey a message," said Xiaolang. It was clear he didn't like the idea, but he said it anyway. "They asked if you would come to Hong Kong alone. Don't bring anyone else with you. Even Kerberus."

Sakura cocked her head. "Why?"

"They want to meet you and only you," said Xiaolang. "They don't want either of your guardians here. I'm not sure I understand either. But that's their conditions for meeting you."

Sakura frowned. She couldn't understand what problem the Lee family could possibly have with Kero or Yue. They were the former guardians of Clow Reed, the ancestor of the Lee family. So why would they not want them there? To be honest, she could think of many reasons why they would not want Kero there; but why not Yue at the least? She looked into Xiaolang's pixelated eyes and saw the same confusion. At the same time, she couldn't bear to not be with him much longer. And if she wanted to be with him – and even marry him at some point – she had to make a good impression on his parents.

"Okay," she said. "Kero will be disappointed, but I won't bring him, or anyone else."

"Thanks," said Xiaolang. "I'll make sure everything is ready for when you arrive. I'll even learn to make takoyaki for you."

Sakura beamed. "Thank you, Xiaolang. Love you!"

"You too," he said, blowing her kisses. Then he shut off the call.

* * *

The big day came.

Last time Sakura had stood in the Tokyo Haneda Airport terminal, it had been to see off Xiaolang. Now, she was finally going to meet him and his family. Her brother and friends were all there to see her off.

She gave Touya a hug and he said, "Be safe, ya hear? And make sure that creep keeps his hands to himself."

Sakura poked her tongue out at him. Then she embraced Yukito, who said, "Remember those Cantonese phrases I told you. Okay?"

"Will do," said Sakura.

Then Tomoyo butted in and threw her arms around her friend. Sakura felt some wetness on her shoulder, and realised Tomoyo was crying.

"It's alright, Tomoyo," she said. "I'm only going to be gone a week."

"It's not that," said Tomoyo. "I won't get to film my beloved Sakura!" Sakura face-palmed. Tomoyo's tears stopped in an instant, and she held out a paper bag. Her eyes glimmered as she bellowed, "If ever there's a Cardcaptor moment, make sure you wear this!"

Sakura warily looked into the bag and saw a scroll of pink fabric. Within the scroll, she was sure she could see armour plating of some kind.

"Another costume?" she asked dismayed.

"It is my magnum opus!" exclaimed Tomoyo. She grabbed Sakura's hands and insisted, "You must wear it if a moment comes. Promise you'll wear it."

"Okay, okay!" replied Sakura.

"By the way, there's another costume in there," said Tomoyo. Sakura fumbled through the bag and saw a green roll of fabric. "That one's for Mister Lee. Make sure he wears it and you get a photo together. Okay?"

The image made Sakura laugh. She nodded and promised to get the photo and send it to her friend straight away.

Sakura then eyed the head poking inconspicuously out

of Tomoyo's purse. She knelt down and said, "Thanks for understanding, Kero."

"Lee Clan don't like me, and I don't like them," said Kero. "Prob'ly good I ain't goin'. But you just make sure you're safe, ya hear?"

Sakura caressed the plush toy with a smile and said, "I hear ya."

The traveller then put her costumes in her backpack and headed for security. She waved to her family one last time, and started to feel homesick. Her overactive imagination concocted so many bad scenarios, such as being mugged on the Hong Kong streets. At the same time, her need to see her boyfriend again spurred her onward, through security, customs, immigration, and finally onto the plane.

"Here I come, Xiaolang," she said as the plane took off.

4 | Hunt in Rome

The skyline of Rome buzzed with the prayers of Sunday night mass. The sky above, pockmarked with clouds, reflected the orange light of the city. It made for an image reminiscent of Dante Alighieri[5] – ironic, given the holiness of the locale.

A blonde girl didn't think it so ironic as she gazed out over the ancient city.

"A city of predators," she murmured with a sneer.

"Save it for ya blog, Maka," said the albino boy crouched to her left. His deep red eyes glistened in the light as he gazed up at her. "Ya found him, yet?"

Maka closed her eyes and extended her senses outward. Her sense of social justice drew her immediately to Saint Peter's Basilica, to the priest presiding over mass. As the bedizened man administered communion to a young boy, Maka's skin crawled. She checked his soul, but found no corruption expected of an Asura Egg. She saw nothing in the parishioners either.

Too bad, she thought. She shook herself to focus her mind, and she looked elsewhere in the city. There was only one signature she should have been focusing on. And, like her albino partner, what she was looking for was best left

---

[5]   Author of *The Divine Comedy*, depicting a descent into Hell and then a journey to Heaven.

to her blog.

To the east, Maka sensed their quarry.

"There!" she said. "Let's go, Soul."

"That's what I like to hear," growled Soul, wiping away his drool. He and Maka leapt from the roof and cleared the street in one bound. They hit the opposite roof running. Soul eyed Maka, who cocked her head like a bloodhound honing in on prey. They leapt across rooftops with inhuman speed, while their souls resonated with each other across the unseen aether. Their strength augmented one another, amplifying Maka's senses so that she knew exactly where the fiend was.

"Soul, scythe form!" she yelled.

Soul's body flashed white, and morphed into a helical stream of energy. That stream came to rest in Maka's hands and took the form of a sharp black and red scythe. She gripped the handle of her weapon tightly as Soul's voice echoed in her mind, "Get him!"

Maka launched from that last rooftop. With her eyes, she saw what her soul had perceived ten blocks away: a gangly creature with lopsided posture, blood staining his white shirt. He stood in the middle of the alleyway, looming menacingly over his latest prey with a lascivious look in his lidless purple eyes. The terrified child threw his hands over his face, saturated with tears, and awaited the final blow.

The monster sensed an incoming attack from behind, and swivelled to block Maka's blow with his bloodied axe. His purple eyes flashed brightly upon perceiving the souls of his attackers. Suddenly, the kid was meaningless. The creature swung his axe, throwing the girl off him.

Maka flipped through the air and landed like a cat – a badass cat. She glared at the villain and proclaimed, "Sonson Jay, you have fed on human souls. In the name of Lord Reaper, I claim your soul!"

Sonson Jay snarled and lunged forward. With a single arm, Maka twirled Soul's scythe form as if it were weightless. She swatted the axe aside with the blade, and slammed the butt of the scythe handle against the beast's temple. He stumbled into a dumpster and ducked at the last moment, avoiding Maka slicing his head off. Maka leaned back to dodge the beast's blind axe swing, and then jerked the scythe. She locked the beast's underarm and his axe, wresting it out of his hand and sending him headfirst into the alley wall. Maka didn't give the creature a chance to recover, and with a loud roar, she bisected his back with the scythe blade.

Sonson Jay gurgled away his last and disintegrated, leaving behind a floating ball of burning matter. Maka released the scythe, which retook human form. Licking his lips, Soul grabbed his ethereal prize and shoved it down his gullet.

"Mama mia! That's a spicy meatball!" he exclaimed with a faux Italian accent.

Even that had to earn a chuckle from his over-serious meister. She quickly sobered and said, "C'mon, we need to report back." She swivelled and headed out of the alleyway. Soul glanced over at the flabbergasted boy and shuffled uncomfortably.

"Oi, Maka, what about the kid?" he mumbled.

"Send him home," said Maka.

"With what he's seen?" asked Soul. "Shouldn't we, ya know, make sure he's okay?"

Maka raised an eyebrow. "He'll just think it was a nightmare. He'll be fine."

Soul glared at her irately. "Maka, seriously. If it were a chick, you'd be all Mother Goose over her."

Maka put her fists on her hips and glared at her weapon partner. Soul didn't let up, even though he usually caved when his meister gave him that look. He held his ground, until Maka acquiesced with a sigh.

The boy didn't speak English, so Soul had to use the translator app on his phone. It was helpful enough. The boy especially warmed up when Soul explained that they protected people from evil monsters like that creature. Then they walked him home, during which they asked him to keep everything a secret. They left him with a promise that if ever monsters attacked, they would protect him. He waved goodbye with a smile, leaving them in a suburb of Rome at eleven o'clock in at night.

"Wanna go grab some food somewhere?" Soul suggested.

Maka was clearly in a foul mood after being side-tracked. Unfortunately for her, she didn't have a hardcover book to throw at him. Plus, she was hungry. So they went looking for food. They found a nice-looking pasta joint that was just about to close the kitchen before they walked in. Maka ordered the minestrone, while Soul ordered the largest Tagliatelle Bolognese dish on the menu.

"I'm hungry, and I want it," he retorted when Maka rolled her eyes. She continued to huff, but Soul couldn't have cared less. He started to sing 'I Want It All' in his best impression of Freddie Mercury.

"I can't believe you listen to Queen," exclaimed Maka, a bemused sneer on her face. "It's so last century … literally *and* figuratively."

"Oi, Freddy Mercury is awesome," retorted Soul.

"He wasn't that good a singer anyway," Maka went on.

"Hey, you gotta like Queen, or else you're homophobic," snapped Soul.

Maka scoffed, "What kinda logic is that?"

"Twitter logic," retorted Soul with a mocking smirk.

"It is a valid website for learning, Soul!" Maka growled, even though she knew she was full of it.

Before the argument could continue, they heard chuckles from nearby. The couple at the adjacent table was looking at them and smiling. They were an older couple. To Maka, they looked as if they'd been married for decades. They exchanged glances when Soul and Maka looked at them, and they joined hands.

"Sorry to intrude," said the husband with a thick Italian

accent. "You are such a lovely couple."

"We were just the same as you," said the wife. "Always bickering, but beneath it all …" She smiled lovingly at her husband, as if it carried the message across.

Maka started to stammer as blood filled her face. Meanwhile, Soul decided to mess with her and said, "Yeah, we're getting married next year." He reached across and caressed her hand.

"Oh, *molto bene*[6]," exclaimed the wife. The couple stood and departed, their smiles widening at their demeanour. Maka maintained her smile until the couple had left the restaurant, after which she mumbled, "You keep holding my hand, and you'll lose it."

Soul released her hand, but didn't stop laughing.

It took them an hour after dinner to finally find a secluded mirror. Maka drew an access number into it, which turned it into a portal back to the Demon Weapon Meister Academy, hidden away in Death City, Nevada. Maka strode quickly through the castle, squinting to avoid the late afternoon glare of the Nevada Desert. Soul kept up the pace, until they reached a door that looked like the very Gates of Hell.

Of course, that was just their boss's sick sense of humour.

They walked right through those gates and into the pale white room. They strode through the picket of black crucifixes and up onto the dais, where a figure in black stood in front of a large mirror.

"Lord Reaper, we are here to report," Maka announced. "Sonson Jay has been neutralised. One Asura Egg collected."

The figure – known only as the Reaper – raised his head. Then he swivelled, revealing a white, cartoonish skull mask, and a pair of cuboid white hands. He clapped them together and jovially bellowed, "Well done, Maka Albarn!

---

[6]　Italian: "So wonderful."

Soul Eater!"

"No prob, Lord Reaper," said Soul. "We managed to take it out, easy-peasy. And plus, we made sure that kid it attacked got home safe."

The Reaper clicked his tongue (if he had one), and said, "Good on you, Soul. That's really nice of you."

"It ain't cool to leave a kid high-and-dry," said Soul.

"Even though he exposed the existence of our organisation," murmured Maka.

"Ah, Maka, you lovely Asura hunter," said the Reaper. "You did an amazing job cleaning up that beast. As always, you're an excellent meister."

Maka beamed, and bowed reverently. "I am honoured to serve the will of Lord Reaper."

"Kiss-ass," muttered Soul. Maka shot him the evils.

"Well, provided there's nothing else to report," said the Reaper. "I think you can head on home."

"Reaper, should something not be done about the boy who witnessed us?" asked Maka.

"Ah, never mind that, my dear," replied the Reaper. "If anything, it'll be a rumour of guardian angels. I wouldn't pay it much worry."

Maka huffed. The Reaper's word was often final. Nevertheless, she still couldn't shake the need to address the problem. More and more, she'd been worried about exposure of their world. It had become especially more troublesome when a certain Australian boy pulled a viral stunt involving an Arms Alchemy.

She continued to fret over it all the way back to their shared apartment.

* * *

After Maka and Soul left, the Reaper sighed and turned back to the mirror. Things were about to get very stressful for someone such as Maka. He knew the girl was a stickler for protocol in certain matters, especially when it came to secrecy.

But she and Soul are still the best ones for this job, he concluded.

At that instant, the doors to the Reaper's chambers burst open. In strode a short boy with three white stripes encircling half of his head. Aside from that, everything about the yellow-eyed one was symmetrical. He walked in, but then walked back out. He walked in again, cursed under his breath, and then walked back out. He walked in a third time, and yelled, "How damn hard is it to land on my left foot when I am exactly three-point-one-four-one-five-nine metres from the door?"

"Kiddo! I need you here now," said the Reaper firmly. The boy glared at him with bloodshot eyes, which quickly softened when he realised the Reaper needed him. He pushed past the gut-wrenching tingle he felt when things didn't accord to his symmetrical designs, and stomped up to the dais.

"You sent for me, Father?" he mumbled. "And you asked me not to bring Liz and Patty, so I can only assume you have another diplomatic mission for me."

"Ever so astute, Kiddo, m'boy," said the Reaper. "It seems the Alchemic Regiment has pooped things up again."

Kiddo buried his palm in his face. "Again? First Restigouche, then Victor, and then Nathan Grant! What is it this time?"

"Well, this isn't entirely their fault," said the Reaper. "It's ours too."

"How so?" asked Kiddo, offended by the notion.

"You remember Shaula Gorgon?" asked the Reaper. Kiddo grit his teeth at the mention of the Witch who attacked their school and killed several innocent people, including two girls. He motioned for his father to continue. "It seems that, since we didn't catch her — what with, ya know, Ol' Nyarlie attackin' us and all — she went and teamed up with some old friends of the Regiment … You know, the L.X.E.?"

"The League of Extraordinary Elects?" said Kiddo with a raised eyebrow. "Witches hate homunculi. Why would one join with them?"

"To run a heist on a Regiment facility in Australia," said the Reaper. His shadowy form quivered as he added, "They stole a very important relic that the Regment was studying, known as the Silver Key."

Kiddo didn't recognise the name, having carefully studied every ounce of his father's lore.

"What is that?" he asked.

"Not sure," said the Reaper. "Might've been something humans created before my kind came to Earth. I do know that humans had some pretty amazing powers long ago, but lost 'em well before I found 'em."

Kiddo shrugged and returned to the issue at hand. "So the Alchemic Regiment messed up, and they want us to fix the problem?"

"Not exactly," said the Reaper. "They want to run a joint-operation, to find the Shaula and the L.X.E., and reclaim the Silver Key. I want you to meet with them and discuss terms of cooperation."

"Should I not take Liz and Patty with me?" asked Kiddo. "I could probably handle these flesh-eaters with ease."

"Nope, I want to keep you in reserve in case things go south," said the Reaper. "If the Regiment will cooperate, then I'll send in Maka and Soul."

Kiddo coughed nervously and muttered, "Aside from myself, they're your best meister and weapon. Perhaps one of the other meisters. Black-Star and Tsubaki might be a better team. Or even Kim and Jackie."

The Reaper waved a large cuboid finger at his son and said, "Tsk-tsk, Kiddo. When you take over the job from me, you need to always put your best foot forward. Understand?"

Kiddo pursed his lips and sighed, "Very well. Send the itinerary to me, and I will meet with these charlatans. If they are willing, I will inform you."

The Reaper snapped his fingers with delight and watched his son leave. As the doors closed, the Reaper hunched and moaned, "The ball really is rolling, isn't it?"

5 | A Shaky Alliance

A tense mood settled upon the conference room. The generals of the Alchemic Regiment took their seats, though they could not relax their tightly knitted brows. Even the usually flippant General Shantanu Vasuman of the Middle-East Branch couldn't keep a frown from his face. Each general and their aides fidgeted nervously as the appointed time approached.

About a minute before the briefing was supposed to begin, the doors opened, and three figures entered. General Piers Rodrigo of the Oceania Branch took a seat near the head of the table, and introduced the taller of his two companions.

"Ladies and Gentlemen, this is Commander Tristan Costable of the Australian division," he said. "Call sign: Captain Bravo."

Bravo stepped forward and addressed the leadership. "Thank you for allowing this meeting at such short notice." He referred to the young woman behind him. "This is Warrior Astrid Rachelle, call sign: Spartan Valkyrie."

The Chinese general sneered at the girl's salute.

"So you're the one who put us in the mess with Nathan Grant and Victor," she muttered.

Astrid grit her teeth but said nothing.

"Nobody is here to assign blame," said Rodrigo firmly.

The other generals nodded resolutely, though some still shot the evils at Astrid. Rodrigo motioned for Bravo to sit, and Astrid took her place behind his seat as an aide. The other generals moved closer to the table, with their aides behind them at the ready.

There was something odd about the arrangement of the conference room, Astrid noted. There were an equal number of men and women, separated evenly across the table. The genders and numbers of people were identical on both sides of the room.

Two seats, at the end of the table, were conspicuously empty.

Before anyone could complain about those who were tardy, the full-length mirror adorning the nearby wall lit up. It outshone the lights in the conference room, before fading out. In front of it stood the son of the Reaper.

"Death the Kid, thank you for coming," said Rodrigo.

Despite her excitement at meeting this legendary meister, Astrid leaned down to Bravo and mumbled, "He's shorter than I'd expected." Bravo shushed her.

Kiddo pursed his lips to hide his distaste for present company. He then moved toward his seat at the head of the table. His yellow eyes scanned the room, and went bloodshot when he saw the empty seat to his left.

"This is unacceptable!" exclaimed Kiddo. "Why is there an empty seat?"

"We are waiting on one more speaker," said Rodrigo. "I must ask that you be patient."

Kiddo, however, refused to begin the meeting until the seats were filled.

"What is your problem?" scoffed Astrid.

Every eye turned to her with dismay, and she immediately chastised herself for her outburst.

I've spent too much time around Nathan, she concluded.

The son of the Reaper stood up and marched right up to her. His nostrils flared and he bellowed, "My problem is with your organisation's absolute disrespect of order and symmetry. Do you not understand that? You are careless, so much that you let a homunculus get away, only to join forces with a Witch –"

"That *you* let get away," interjected a Scottish voice that made Astrid's hair stand on end. Both she and Kiddo glanced over at the source of the voice: an eighteen year old with a reddish tinge to his hair. He wore a grin that Astrid well knew meant trouble. The young man addressed the table, "Sorry for my being late, eh."

"Eriol Lamperouge," Rodrigo announced. He worked hard to hold his own bile back. "Thank you also for coming."

Eriol motioned to the woman following him. "This is my personal assistant, Ruby Moon. I hope it is acceptable for her to be present also." The young black-haired woman bowed.

"Of course!" exclaimed Kiddo to the exclusion of anyone else. "Now, there is symmetry." And he promptly returned to his seat at the head of the table.

"Oh, Kiddo, you really should get that issue looked at," said Eriol as he sat at the table. He glanced around with a giddy look. His gaze fell on Astrid. He shot up and yelled, "Oh, Triddy! Been a while, girlfriend!"

"Do not hug me," snapped Astrid. She glared at Bravo. "Why didn't you tell me he was going to be here?" Bravo feigned ignorance.

"He contacted us," said Rodrigo.

"And I freely offer my services in finding the Silver Key," said the Scotsman.

Rodrigo drummed his hands on the table and said, "Then let's begin." He addressed everyone. "We are facing a crisis. Never before have the Witches joined forces with homunculi, until now."

"You are certain it is Shaula who has joined with these L.X.E. remnants?" asked Kiddo.

Rodrigo motioned the woman behind him, who saluted the generals. She spoke with a loud voice and said, "I am

Warrior Hannah Peterson, previously stationed at the Cunnamulla research outpost in Southeast Queensland. At approximately twenty-two-hundred hours, three days ago, the outpost was attacked. They used high explosive to break through security and breach the underground lab. Then they stole the Silver Key and the lead researcher, Doctor Franklin Avalon."

Eriol gasped, "Do you mean, Franklin *Kinomoto?* As in, the father of Sakura Kinomoto?"

"We did not refer to him by his married name," Bravo interjected. "We used his original name in our system, so that nobody could connect him to the Cardcaptor without a lot of digging."

Eriol looked right past him to Rodrigo. "I told you to leave her out of this."

"No, you said, *almost a year ago*, she wouldn't be able to assist us with Victor just yet," Rodrigo insisted. "Besides, we didn't recruit her. We recruited her father."

The Chinese general leaned forward. "I feel as if I should have been informed of this. Japan is under Asian jurisdiction. One of its citizens being recruited without my knowledge is serious breach of protocol."

"We needed him to decipher the Silver Key," Bravo put in.

"People!" bellowed Kiddo. "I'd like to know what you intended with the Silver Key in a minute, but could we get back to the issue at hand, please?" The conference room settled down, but still simmered with heightened nerves. Kiddo motioned for Hannah to continue her testimony.

"I was buried under rubble, and luckily the homunculi didn't sense my presence," said Hannah. She stammered as she fought down her resurfacing trauma. "I clearly saw a woman with blue-red eyes and purple hair. It was short, and a bit stumpy at the back. She utilised magic to restrain the researcher."

"Shaula Gorgon," Kiddo concluded. "Maka Albarn sliced off Shaula's braid a few months ago. It was through that she was able to brainwash people. I assume then that she lacks that power now, otherwise she'd not have needed to restrain him." He raised his eyebrows at Hannah, asking for more.

"I saw another man," Hannah went on. "A homunculus, with yellow skin. He liked to say 'Moon' a lot."

"That's definitely Moonface," said Bravo. "He managed to escape Warrawul when Victor incapacitated me."

"When response teams reached the site, the hostiles were already gone," said Rodrigo.

"Do you have any intelligence on where they are now?" asked Kiddo.

"We've compiled a list of L.X.E. safe houses across Australia and New Zealand, but none of them are occupied," said Rodrigo.

"Same in the Middle-East," said Vasuman.

The other generals were similarly empty-handed.

"I will speak with my father," said Kiddo. "Perhaps the other Death Scythes supervising Oceania will know something."

Rodrigo voiced his appreciation.

Eriol raised a finger as if he was in kindergarten. "Question: how did you get the Lee Clan's approval to study the Silver Key?"

Every face in the room lit up in shock.

"What do you mean?" asked Vasuman.

"We found the Silver Key in Antarctica, right where Doctor Avalon said it was," said Bravo.

At that, Eriol's eyes widened with horror, amazement, admiration, and resentment, all at once. "You found the other one?" he intoned. Not even Kiddo knew what he was talking about. "The Silver Key is in two parts," Eriol explained. "It's a device that only works when the two parts are combined. I ... or rather, *Clow Reed*, found one half in the Gulf of Bothnia."

The room suddenly erupted into a chorus of screaming and fingers pointed at Eriol. The Scotsman just shrugged and waited for them to quiet down, being well acquainted with such treatment.

The Reaper's son slapped the table loudly and hollered, "Hey! Everybody calm the Hell down!" The room quieted down, giving Kiddo a chance to ask, "What does this Silver Key do? Not even my father knows of it."

Eriol shrugged cryptically as he turned to Rodrigo. "Why don't *you* tell us, Rodrigo?"

Rodrigo opened his mouth, but choked on his words and closed it again.

Bravo quickly interjected, "We don't know what it does either. That was why we were researching it."

The Scotsman gave a look partway between a sneer and a knowing smile. He finally gave another shrug and said, "Well, if Clow knew, I didn't get those memories. But I do know two things. One, you got one half of the key, you can locate the other half pretty easily, 'cause they're connected."

"We studied it for months and didn't detect any connection," exclaimed Bravo.

"That's 'cause you don't have magic, ya bawheid," retorted Eriol. When asked about the second thing he knew, he said, "The Lee Clan has the other half of the key. They keep it in their compound in Hong Kong."

The group immediately moved to discussion of contacting the Lee Clan. It wasn't long before an argument broke out over jurisdiction. Some wanted to go and take the Silver Key fragment by force, others wanted to bring the Lee Clan into the fold. Eriol spoke against either action, but his own suggestions fell on deaf ears. Kiddo remained silent, and started to feel as if he'd been invited only as a courtesy. He stood from the table and walked toward the mirror, drawing the gaze of all the generals.

"This is why you never work," growled the Reaper's son. "You spend less time fighting homunculi and more time bickering amongst yourselves." Then, he activated the mirror portal and disappeared through it.

The conference room went back to arguing after he left. The discussion went to tabulating votes for different courses of action, and then eventually devolved into lumping all the blame for the situation on Rodrigo and Bravo. That only led to more arguing and yelling.

Eventually, Eriol rose from the table and sauntered over to Astrid, who had remained silent throughout the meeting. The Scotsman could see the irritation mounting on her face, and rested a hand on her shoulder. She almost jumped three feet in the air when he touched her, but maintained her calm in the presence of the infuriating Scotsman.

"Bunch o' tadgers, jockeyin' for position," he mumbled. "It'd be much better if you had a leader who just said, 'We're doin' this!'"

Astrid glanced at him, wondering what he was insinuating. Of course, Eriol hid his meaning behind that smile of his. He beckoned Ruby to follow him out of the room, offering a wink to the survivor of Moonface's attack.

Astrid turned back to the rabble of generals, who had been arguing for at least ten minutes and had gotten nowhere. She rested her hand on Bravo's shoulder and said, "I don't think you'll need me here. I'll go and see Nathan."

"Keep outta trouble," mumbled Bravo, irritated that he couldn't run from the meeting.

Astrid left the room. As she departed, she brushed past Hannah. She caught a whiff of something that made her hair stand on end. She looked back at the woman, who offered a smile and asked if she was all right. Astrid reached out with her senses a second time, but felt nothing out of the ordinary.

Just my imagination, she thought as she exited the room.

6 | The Great Escape

Nathan had paced so much, there were wear marks on the floor beneath the one-way mirror. He'd done little more than that since finishing Astrid's Anzac biscuits. Occasionally, he asked the supervisors if Bravo had organised the visit from his family, as promised. He always met with a negative answer.

Astrid entered the room to see the boy in a fretful mood. He threw his arms around her and bellowed, "Tell me, you're gonna get me outta here."

"Not yet," sighed Astrid. Nathan saw her agitated mood and inquired. "I just came from a really annoying meeting, so I'm obviously a little miffed."

"What happened?" asked Nathan.

Astrid explained what happened at the meeting. She glossed over Death the Kid and Eriol, not wishing to sidetrack Nathan with more exposition about the strangeness of their world. When she finally finished, she found herself sitting on Nathan's hospital bed. The boy sat next to her and took her hand in his.

"You know what might make you feel better?" he asked lasciviously.

Astrid tried to pull her hand away.

"Not a chance," she snapped.

Nathan held her hand and whispered, "Didn't mean *that*."

"Then what do you mean?" asked Astrid suspiciously.

"I meant escape!" exclaimed Nathan. He leapt onto his bed and bounced on it. "Let's bust outta here and go to Hong Kong. We'll get the Silver Key and kill Moonface and this sheila chick before anyone knows what's what!"

"Oh, Nathan, don't be an idiot!" snapped Astrid.

Nathan leapt off the bed and stood in the middle of the room.

"I ain't being an idiot," he proclaimed. "I think we should break out and save the world, just like we used to. Remember you and me against Burrumering? And, of course, kickin' arse against the L.X.E. and Tao and Shu, and all that? Let's go!"

Astrid rose to still him. She tried to hold him down by the shoulders and chided him. But he was too strong for her, thanks to the Black Kakugane and his own cabin fever.

"Come on, Astrid!" he yelled. "It's you and me! Starlight Lancer and Spartan Valkyrie! Let's be badass!"

The room's intercom whined, and a voice trickled through it.

"Ahem, I'm afraid you won't be able to bust out of here, Mister Grant," said the supervisor. "You don't seem to realise that I can hear everything you say."

Nathan nodded facetiously and chimed, "Well then, since I'm busted, I might as well break out anyway."

"Nathan, don't do it!" exclaimed Astrid. "I am begging you, don't do it!"

"Too late!" screamed Nathan as he launched himself at the one-way mirror. The glass caved inward, as if it were water and Nathan were an Olympic swimmer. He landed in the control room and was greeted by half a dozen flabbergasted faces. He upended a table on three of them, smacked two of them unconscious, and hurled another across the room. Then, he saw the guards at the entrance to the lab. The two men placed their hands to the Kakugane strapped to their chests and bellowed, "Arms

Alchemy!" The guard to the left materialised a pair of jutte[7], while the other summoned a halberd.

Nathan sighed. Then he put his hand under a nearby desk and flicked it at the men. They slashed through it easily, but didn't see their enemy in the downwind. Nathan laid out the halberd wielder with a single punch. The other thrust one of his jutte at the boy, who held up his hand without looking. The thin blade stabbed through his palm, much to the wielder's horror and amazement. Nathan looked at him, red-faced with the pain searing through his hand and wrist. He painstakingly closed his hand over the hilt of the jutte, twisted it out of the man's hand, and slammed its handle against the man's temple.

The weapons reverted to inert Kakugane beside the guards' still forms. Nathan waited a moment for his hand to heal, before he picked up one of the talismans. He saw one of the lab technicians struggle toward an alarm switch.

"Hey, mate, could you not?" he asked earnestly. The technician regarded him as he would a hungry lion ready to pounce. "To be honest, you're a nice guy, and I'd rather not hurt ya. So, if you could just fall down, that'd be beaut." The man's lip quivered with fear, and he let out a shriek as he reached for the switch. Nathan loosed the talisman, which hit the man squarely on the back of the head. His hand missed the button and he crumpled to the floor.

"Oh! Howzat, motherfucker!" bellowed Nathan. Part of his mind wondered whether he should be so proud of that. At the same time, he was finally out of that infernal lab, so who cares? He waltzed down the corridor and sauntered through the doors.

Astrid stood in the remains of the lab. She was absolutely dumbstruck by the chaos and the ease with which the boy did it. Part of her was terrified that the Black Kakugane was asserting itself. Another part

---

[7]   A Japanese dagger.

wondered whether it was just sheer boredom. She gazed over at the alarm switch, and considered triggering it.

Eriol's voice came to mind, and it said, *It'd be much better if you had a leader that just said, 'We're doin' this!'*

She couldn't help but agree, albeit very reluctantly. She looked upward to the Heavens and whispered, "God, why do you hate me?" Then she gave chase.

* * *

The internals of the Regiment headquarters had not yet been alerted to the destruction of Nathan's holding cell. The escapee scampered through the building as fast as he could, as if he were a streaker at Buckingham Palace. He did his best to walk nonchalantly through the halls, hiding his face with his hand whenever he saw people in the distance.

He eventually found a locker room full of Regiment uniforms. As he scoured for one that fit him, he heard footsteps outside the room. He pressed his back against the wall, his heart thumping from excitement of escaping and the fear of capture. His hand drifted to his chest in anticipation of a fight. He heard the footsteps approach a nearby corner, and his gaze darted in the direction of the assailant. He found himself looking at Astrid.

The boy had never seen a woman look so angry. Nevertheless, he relaxed considerably.

"Do you realise what you've done?" exclaimed Astrid.

"Broken out of prison," said Nathan as he peeled off his hospital gown. Astrid diverted her eyes as he pulled on the uniform he'd found.

"You also assaulted eight Regiment officers," snapped the girl.

"That last one wasn't my fault," said Nathan. "I asked him not to hit the switch, and he didn't."

"Oh, so not your fault," replied Astrid sardonically.

"Actually, it's all your fault," said Nathan. Astrid glared

at him, but he didn't care. "I'm an idiot from the 'Gong[8], and even I can see it. They all blame you for my situation, since you were the one who put the Kakugane in my chest."

"I did it because I thought your life was worth saving," retorted Astrid. "I wouldn't've needed to if you'd not been a show-off with a messiah complex."

Nathan grabbed her shoulders and held her firmly. He looked right into her eyes and said, "And I'm grateful. You won't hear any complaints from me. But *they* ... the Regiment, the scientists, even Bravo lay this all at your feet." Astrid shifted uncomfortably. "So you got one of two choices," Nathan went on. "You can alert them to me breaking out, and prob'ly never get your Kakugane back. Or, you can help me bust the Hell outta here, and we can go do some good while they all argue and carry on." He regarded her with raised eyebrows, awaiting her answer.

Astrid pursed her lips as Eriol's voice resounded in her head once more. She even remembered words Nathan had yelled to an eagle homunculus: *Some things we have to do, even if it kills us.*

Of course, she'd already made her decision. She held up a Kakugane, taken from one of the fallen guards.

"Let's go," she said defiantly.

* * *

An officer entered the meeting between the generals. The room was still the site of an ongoing screaming match, over which the officer could not be heard. The officer finally caught Rodrigo's attention and informed him of a situation in the containment lab.

"Everyone, shut up!" he bellowed. When the room was silent, Rodrigo turned to Bravo and said, "Grant has broken out of custody."

The generals left the conference room and charged into

---

[8]   An Australian slang word for Wollongong, Nathan's hometown.

the security control room. They barked orders to lockdown the building and post security to every access point. Bravo marched over to the surveillance cameras, where a technician sat with an embarrassed look on her face. The feed from the lab showed the place in utter shambles.

"Why didn't you sound the alarm?" barked Bravo.

"Well … Commander, I was distracted," stammered the technician.

"By what?" exclaimed Bravo. "Too busy watching TV or something?"

"No, sir, I was watching the conference room," said the technician sheepishly. The other technicians around them did everything they could to conceal their grins.

Bravo glared at Rodrigo and the other generals.

"Death the Kid might've been right," he grumbled.

One of the technicians spoke up, "We have an unauthorised launch." She pointed out the feed that displayed the hangar of Regiment headquarters. A small jet was already out of the hangar doors, and it was too late to close them.

Rodrigo hit a communications widget on the panel in front of him and yelled, "Pilot, identify yourself."

A video feed appeared on the main screen of the control room. Nathan and Astrid were seated in the cockpit, with the latter piloting the craft. Nathan noticed the camera and waved to it.

"Mister Grant, we must ask you to return immediately for your own safety," said Rodrigo.

"Yeah, nah," replied Nathan. "I'm bored and want to go for a walk. We were thinking Hong Kong'd be a nice place."

Bravo butted in, "Nathan, don't do this. If you do, you'll be treated as a rogue, just like Victor."

"Hey, Bravo, I'll be back, don't you worry," said Nathan. "We'll just go, kill Moonface for ya, and bring back the Silver Key, all good and proper." He exchanged glances with Astrid, who nodded resolutely.

Bravo noticed a Kakugane fastened to Astrid's chest. "Warrior Rachelle, return to base immediately."

Astrid grit her teeth and steeled her nerves.

"No, Commander," she said. "Nathan and I will get the job done, jurisdiction be damned."

The jet accelerated away from the headquarters building, and veered into the sky. It disappeared from view before it hit the clouds.

"They've activated stealth mode," said the radar technician. "We won't be able to track them."

"We'll let you know once we've finished everything in Hong Kong, okay?" chirped Nathan. He reached for a panel to cut the feed, but stopped and asked, "By the way, you guys want some Szechuan or something?"

Bravo shut the feed off himself. He pursed his lips to contain his rage, as well as his need to laugh at the boy's antics. Few others weren't nearly as controlled, and the control room reverberated with soft giggles.

Vasuman, the only one openly grinning, approached Rodrigo and whispered, "Mightn't be the worst idea, really." Bravo heard him, and shot him a look of surprise. Vasuman added, "Think about it, ya! We'll be able to get more data on Nathan's powers. All the better to know him with, wouldn't you agree?"

Bravo only shook his head with dismay, and wondered what cat had torn its way out of the bag.

* * *

Six floors above ground, in the men's room, Eriol heard every single event that transpired in the secret bunker below. He even sensed the two rogue warriors who took flight without permission.

He chuckled with excitement, while shivering with fear.

Goddamn you, Clow, he thought.

Then he wove his hand in front of the mirror, and the glass lit up. The cartoonish mask of the Reaper appeared before him.

"What up, Eriol?" asked the Reaper.

"Send them in," said Eriol resolutely.

The Reaper chuckled, his interest piqued tremendously.

7 | Reunion in Hong Kong

The arrivals terminal of Hong Kong international airport was futuristic, to put it lightly. Sakura marvelled at the sleek architecture of the well-maintained terminal. It was a stark contrast to the brown-orange of Tokyo Haneda, which had a mood reminiscent of a sepia photograph, modest but wholesome.

Sakura nervously looked left and right. The terminal stretched seemingly forever in both directions, filled with people and occasionally marked with blue and red gate signs. She decided to follow the stream of commuters from her own plane. Eventually, she found the end of the terminal, which gave way to a two-floor complex of duty-free stores and restaurants. She looked around for the baggage claim sign, to which the push and shove of the crowd guided her.

Sakura found her bag at the turnstile, cleared customs, and emerged into the arrivals terminal. She looked around for a familiar face, but there were far too many in the terminal. They all seemed to blur together. Slowly, Sakura started to regret ever leaving home, and she almost wanted to race back onto the plane.

Then her eyes fell upon a sign held above the crowd: a pink shisa hugging a gold and green one. Through the forest of faces, she saw those yellow eyes, and her heart raced with joy. She advanced through the crowd, pushing toward the holder of that sign, and came face to face with her beloved Xiaolang. All self-control went out the window, and he embraced her.

"I missed you," mewled Sakura as she gripped him tightly.

"I wish I'd never left," replied Xiaolang. He stroked her cheek and kissed her softly.

As she savoured his lips on hers, Sakura thanked God for allowing her to win that raffle.

* * *

The Lee mansion stood in the mid-level of Hong Kong Island, just on Stubbs Street. It was a beautiful house unlike anything Sakura had expected. A structure of traditional Chinese architecture, it's brick walls were marked with areas of darker reds and lighter pinks. Its jade-green roof-tiles stood stark against the blue sky above, sculpted in intricate designs that could only have come from the greatest lover of his craft.

Sakura glanced down at her simple white blouse and jeans combination. Its crinkled, off-colour appearance – owed to a six-hour transit from Tokyo – seemed almost offensive in light of such splendour. She withdrew into herself as she smelled the slight muskiness of her clothes.

"What's the matter?" asked Xiaolang as he carried her suitcase from the car.

"I don't think I'm dressed quite right," stammered Sakura.

Xiaolang grinned and held out his hand to her. "I think you could spend a fortune and not look better."

Despite her blush at his complement, Sakura took his hand and let him guide her to the front door. A man, dressed in a fine grey vest and trousers, bowed reverently, and took Sakura's luggage from Xiaolang.

"Lady Kinomoto, it is an honour to finally meet you," said the man.

"Thank you, Mister Lee," said Sakura.

The man chuckled, "Begging your pardon, but I am not a member of the Lee Clan. I am Wei Wong, a butler to Master Xiaolang."

Sakura coughed nervously and apologised fervently. Xiaolang chuckled a moment, before placing his hand on the girl's shoulder. He issued some orders in Cantonese, prompting Wei to take Sakura's luggage inside. After he calmed Sakura, Xiaolang led her into the house.

The main entrance hall was breathtaking, and every step made Sakura feel as if she had defiled it. The floor was a mosaic of coloured tiles, in various patterns resembling lotuses and swastikas. The ceiling hosted a chandelier composed of jade, adorned with small glass Buddha statues. Opposite the entrance was a walkway into a garden behind the mansion. Two half-spiral staircases stood either side of the entrance, and led to the upper floors.

Wei carried Sakura's suitcase up the right staircase, and Xiaolang beckoned her to follow. The second floor was carpeted with red, lined with shimmering gold paint. Sakura was not required to remove her shoes, even though she really wanted to. She willed herself to follow Xiaolang and Wei down the corridor of the west wing of the mansion.

Wei entered the third door on the left, which was the guest bedroom assigned to Sakura. The poor girl almost fainted at the sight. The room was three times the size of her bedroom back at home. Against the left-hand wall was a queen-size bed, and a small lounge suite – complete with coffee table – occupied the right side of the room. Wei indicated an en-suite bathroom, which was twice the size of the bathroom at home. It was the bed that perturbed her the most; she felt as if the mattress needed its own area code.

Xiaolang dismissed Wei, who closed the doors behind him.

"I can't stay here," blurted Sakura.

Xiaolang looked horrified. "Is it not good enough?"

"It's too good, Xiaolang," replied Sakura. "I don't feel like I deserve something so nice like this!"

Xiaolang scoffed and drew near to her. He pulled her into an embrace, and stroked her cheek. His touch alone was enough to calm her nerves, and she looked into his eyes.

"For *my* Number One, Heaven's Palace wouldn't be good enough," said Xiaolang.

Sakura melted and she leaned into his chest. She thought about her earlier nerves, and giggled a little.

"The house just freaked me out, is all," she muttered. "I've been used to my small room for so long, I just …"

Xiaolang chuckled, "Hey, to be honest, I prefer your bedroom back in Tokyo." Sakura smirked and her eyes shifted nervously. Xiaolang quickly blurted, "I don't mean … *that*. I just meant that your bed is nicer … bed-*room!* I meant your *bedroom!*"

Sakura burst into laughter as Xiaolang stammered nervously. Before he could babble another apology, she silenced him with a fingertip. Then she leaned up to kiss him.

A loud bang startled them, and they turned to the door. A woman a bit taller than Xiaolang burst into the room and glared at the pair. Her odango[9] pigtails swung as she strode toward them. She ignored Xiaolang and glared right into Sakura's eyes.

"So, you're this Cardcaptor girl?" snarled the woman in English. Sakura nodded sheepishly, recalling the first time she'd met Xiaolang. The woman's expression then flipped, and she pinched Sakura's cheeks delightfully.

"Ain't you a cutie!?" the woman shrieked. She glared at Xiaolang and bellowed something in Cantonese. Xiaolang rolled his eyes as the woman cuddled a very befuddled Sakura. He stepped forward and broke the pair up.

---

9   A hairstyle in Asia, in which hair is organised into balls.

"Sakura, this is my elder sister, Meiling," he said.

"Oh! Sakura, you say?" exclaimed Meiling. "You two're already on a first-name basis. You might as well get married now."

Sakura shrieked, "What? Marriage?" She looked at Xiaolang with a mix of suspicion and confusion.

The flummoxed boy raised his hands in defence.

"I didn't invite you here for that," he insisted. "I wanted you to meet my family. That's all."

Meiling narrowed her eyes at Xiaolang, scratching her chin as if she were an art critic analysing a Picasso. She then leaned to Sakura and said, "See, that face means he's talking nonsense. He's totally gonna sneak into your room in the middle of the night."

Both Sakura and Xiaolang shrieked in horror at the comment. They broke into a paroxysm of stammers and babble as they tried to explain their true intentions. Meanwhile, Meiling stood back to enjoy the chaos. A fourth figure entered the room unheard by anyone, until she stood beside Meiling, who quickly lost her smile.

Though shorter than Meiling by half an inch, the woman's stern expression sapped the embarrassing mood from the room. Xiaolang straightened up and addressed the woman with all the discipline of a military cadet. He bellowed something in Cantonese, to which the woman replied in a soft voice carrying no more threat than seemed necessary. The woman then glared at Meiling, who bowed and left the room.

Sakura couldn't bring herself to look the woman in the eye. The woman kept her gaze fixated upon the girl. She held out her hand and, in fluent Japanese, said, "Lady Kinomoto, I am Yelan, Matriarch of the Lee Clan."

Sakura finally looked up into the woman's eyes. A warm sensation of kindness flowed from the woman's face. Spurred by that feeling, Sakura accepted the woman's handshake.

Yelan dismissed Xiaolang, who promptly left the room,

closing the door behind him. Then Yelan motioned Sakura to sit on the lounge. As she sat, Sakura studied the woman in more detail. She definitely had Xiaolang's determined gaze. She did not, however, boast his lighter hair colour. Hers was raven, tied into a high ponytail and held in place by two golden rods.

Her white hanfu[10] swished about her form as she waved her arms. A clay-pot tea set materialised, earning a surprised whistle from Sakura. The girl sheepishly apologised.

"No need," said Yelan as she poured a cup of jasmine tea for the girl. "It is no sin to voice your emotions." She took a seat beside Sakura and motioned for her to drink. "My son dearly loves you," she said. Sakura almost choked. "Does this fact embarrass you?"

Sakura shook her head fervently.

"Not at all," she insisted. "I just … I feel as if I should be accepted by the Lee Clan before I admit that."

Yelan cocked her head stoically. "That did not stop you from flying into the airport at Tokyo, risking discovery of your secret powers, to confess to him. I believe you called him your 'Number One.'" Sakura's cheeks reddened at the memory of her first kiss. She tried to hide it with a long sip, but Yelan could clearly see through her façade. "I am glad that you feel so fondly for my son," said Yelan.

Sakura smiled warmly at the thought. She set the cup down and turned to Yelan.

"Missus Lee," she began awkwardly. "I feel as if we've met before. I sense something from you that feels very familiar."

Yelan held out her hand and said, "Take a closer look."

Sakura edged her hand toward Yelan, and her fingertips brushed slightly against the woman's palms. She suddenly recalled a certain attempt upon her life at Tsukimine Shrine. Yelan's signature was very similar to that of Alice

---

[10]   Traditional Chinese dress.

Axilotl.

"I am not the same kind of Witch as that abomination," said Yelan upon receiving Sakura's shocked glance.

"So, are you a good Witch, or something?" asked Sakura.

"Good and evil are troublesome labels at best, Lady Kinomoto," said Yelan. "Suffice to say, some Witches have affinity for offensive and destructive magic. Others lean toward healing and regeneration."

Sakura recalled Xiaolang's healing magic. Her brain's wheels ground together when she also remembered her boyfriend's ability to control the elements.

"Are boys different?" asked Sakura after pointing out Xiaolang's magical proficiency.

"Not at all," said Yelan. "Some people have the affinity for both. But it is in what is done with those powers that the truth of good and evil lays. There are many Witches of Axilotl's affinity, who are well-meaning and mannered. And there are many of my affinity who are selfish and callous."

Sakura harrumphed and took a placid sip of tea.

"Guns don't kill people," she murmured.

"You are wise, Lady Kinomoto," said Yelan.

"I've tried to be, at least," said Sakura.

"I must confess, I have looked forward to this meeting for nearly twenty years," said Yelan. "I predicted your birth, but never knew where or to whom. I was truly excited to finally identify you, yet my trepidation paled in comparison to the fervour with which Xiaolang begged to meet you. My husband took a great deal of convincing to allow him to go to Japan."

"I know," said Sakura, a hurt smirk riding on her lips. "He'd wanted to get the Clow Cards off me before I collected them. It took a lot to convince him I was worthy."

"Hardly," said Yelan. "I saw the look in his eyes. He

had chosen you the moment he saw your photograph. It was no different from the gaze I saw in my own husband's eyes upon our first meeting."

Sakura's eyes bugged out in amazement. She recalled their first meeting in which he'd tried to deprive her of the Clow Cards. She couldn't believe that same boy harboured feelings for her as far back as then. Suddenly, every glance he'd thrown her way over the last year made sense. In those flashes of memory, Sakura saw his strong affection and desire to be with her.

How did I not see it before?

Then she recalled the Final Judgement against Yue, and all of Xiaolang's behaviour made sense.

"He was afraid I'd fail the Final Judgement, and he'd lose his feelings for me," she thought aloud.

"Precisely," said Yelan. Sakura beamed at the woman, who kissed her forehead maternally. Then she rose from the couch and strode to the door. She said over her shoulder, "There is a dojo in the basement. My husband would like to meet you when you have eaten."

Then she opened the door and disappeared down the corridor.

Xiaolang entered the room not long after, and Sakura threw her arms around him. She gripped him tightly, and captured his lips vigorously. She finished her kiss and looked into his bewildered eyes.

"I love you, Xiaolang," she said. When he said it back to her, she couldn't help but think, *Wedding bells're gonna chime!*

8 | Sparring

Sakura took lunch with Xiaolang in the garden behind the mansion. Meiling joined them, but was far more civil than she was before. She even apologised for her earlier jokes. Sakura suspected Yelan had compelled her to do so, but accepted the apology all the same.

"Trust me, Kero is worse," she said.

They discussed Sakura's experience with capturing the Clow Cards and transforming them into Cards of her own design. Meiling had a lot to say about Tomoyo's videos, particularly the sheer brilliance of disguising the hunt as a webseries. Xiaolang's sister then asked for details about their dates in Japan, of which there was little to discuss.

"We only went on one before Lamperouge's shenanigans," said Xiaolang.

"Oh, I hear the Scotsman is really annoying," said Meiling.

"He's not that bad," Sakura interjected. "He *is* quirky, but I like quirky people."

"Yeah, but he delights in torture," said Meiling.

"The airport was bad, but he was worse during that movie shoot. Remember?" said Xiaolang flatly.

Sakura thought about the film in which her brother had been involved. She tried to remember Eriol's behaviour during the shoot, but all she could recall was his encouraging applause when she emerged in Tomoyo's hand-made Meiji costume. He'd even praised that her life was more fun than she realised. Then again, that was when she thought that Tomoyo and Xiaolang were a couple, and she had a chance with Yukito.

"Aha, now that I think about it," she thought aloud.

Discussion went onto future plans for the couple. Xiaolang reiterated his intention to migrate to Japan. He smiled at Sakura as he said it. That only prompted Meiling to re-broach the subject of marriage. Sakura put that in the future, after she'd finished high school. But the glances she kept throwing Xiaolang stated, loud and clear, that it was a certainty.

When lunch was finished, Sakura recalled Yelan's invitation to meet Xiaolang's father in the dojo. Xiaolang guided her downstairs, into the basement of the mansion. As they descended the stairs, Sakura could hear loud clacks of wood striking wood. Upon entering the brightly lit dojo, she saw a man in a white shirt and black trousers, before a wooden dummy, practicing wing-chun drills.

The man soon finished, and turned to greet the new arrivals. He approached slowly, gliding across the dojo floor as he unfurled his sleeves, and stopped in front of Sakura. He bowed reverently, his smile warm and earnest.

"I am honoured to finally meet you, Lady Kinomoto," he said. "I am Feiwang Lee." His Japanese was slightly off, suggesting it was not his strongest language.

Sakura bowed and stammered, "Thank you for having me, Mister Lee."

Feiwang eyed Xiaolang, who stood at attention with just as much discipline as for his mother. His father's smile widened and he motioned his son to be at ease. Then he beckoned Sakura to follow.

"I am afraid I understand Japanese far more than I speak it," he said in English. "Would it be permissible to speak this language instead?"

"That would be fine," said Sakura. "Aside from my family on Sundays and your son occasionally, I don't get much practice."

Feiwang approached the altar on the wall opposite his practice dummy. He reverently lit a stick of incense and set it into the burner before the Buddha statue. Sakura studied the nameplates adorning the wall above the altar, all of which hung beneath the Chinese symbol of the Lee Clan. Feiwang pointed to an outlying name in the top-left corner.

"There," he said. "That is the nameplate of Clow Reed. Do you know why he stands alone on this wall?"

"Kero … I mean, Kerberus said he was incomparable," said Sakura. "He was the greatest magician in history. So, obviously, he'd be out there."

Feiwang chuckled, "Wrong. He stands alone on this wall because he stood alone in life." The man turned to face the girl. "Do you stand alone, Lady Kinomoto?"

Sakura glanced over at Xiaolang. Then she considered Kero, Yukito, Yue, Touya, Tomoyo, and her father Franklin. She turned to Feiwang and said, "I am not alone."

"Because of that, young one, you stand more powerful than Clow Reed could ever have hoped to be," proclaimed Feiwang.

The phrase sent shivers down Sakura's spine. But she didn't know whether to be proud or frightened. More than once, she'd failed her friends. She hadn't noticed so many important things. Recently, she had started to worry that she'd missed something about her father.

"You disagree?" asked Feiwang.

Sakura explained her concerns in a hushed voice, so that Xiaolang would not hear.

"There is no shame to be had there, Lady Kinomoto," said Feiwang. "Pity the person to whom friendship comes naturally. It is through making mistakes and learning that we truly become masters of our arts. Friendship is no exception. And it is only through struggle that we triumph. Would you not agree?"

Sakura considered her experiences in gathering the Clow Cards, and their subsequent transformation. She knew he was right.

Feiwang motioned to the floor of the dojo.

"I understand my son has given you training in wing-chun," he said. Sakura nodded. "Would you demonstrate for me?"

Sakura's eyes widened and she looked around nervously. "You mean, fight you?"

"Just a friendly spar," said Feiwang. "We shall not use our full strength."

The girl coughed and eyed Xiaolang. The boy looked worried, but motioned for her to proceed. Meiling clasped her hands giddily. Sakura removed her shoes and socks, and set them beside the door. Then she walked toward the centre of the room where Feiwang awaited. His smile remained on his face. Sakura reached for the key beneath her shirt, but Feiwang stopped her.

"No magic, please," he said.

Sakura almost backed out, but steeled her nerves and took position facing him. She jutted her knees inward, tucked her right fist under her shoulder, and held her left palm out in the starting stance. It was just as Xiaolang had showed her, and yet she felt awkward and out of her element.

Feiwang took a similar stance and his face became incomprehensible as he fixated upon her. He motioned for her to make the first move. She made several fault starts, before finally sucking in a deep breath and launching forward. She aimed for his face, only to find her strike diverted with lightning speed. Then, she brought her fist around to strike at his torso, but was blocked by the most gentle of swats. Feiwang's hand swung her arm around, exposing her back to him, to which he issued a palm strike.

Sakura stumbled away with a soft cry. She quickly swivelled and faced him. Her body trembled with the need to flee. Yet, she stood her ground, determined to prove her worth to her boyfriend's father. She advanced with greater speed. She levelled more blows, all of which missed their mark. Then she switched to her feet, and aimed a kick at Feiwang's stomach, which he nimbly evaded. He then hooked his arm under her knee and hurled her away. She hit the ground with a thud.

Cradling her shoulder, Sakura scrambled to her feet and winced.

"Are you alright, Lady Kinomoto?" Feiwang asked with genuine worry. Sakura waved him off and resumed her stance. "I'll go a bit slower this time," said Feiwang, assuming his own stance.

Sakura advanced again, but he caught her arm in a firm hold and touched his palm to her shoulder.

"Hit," he announced.

Sakura pulled back and swiped with her other fist, which he ducked before touching his elbow to her cheek, announcing another hit. He gripped her forearms, pulled her toward him, and pressed his palms to her temples. Then he issued a volley of punches, deliberately falling short of striking her torso, neck, and head.

Sakura fell to the floor in a daze. Though none of Feiwang's strikes had harmed or even touched her, she felt as if she were on death's door. She peeked out from under her raised arms, and saw Feiwang's hand held out to her. His smile had not wavered. She took the hand and rose to her feet.

"Lady Kinomoto, are you afraid of me?" he asked. Sakura nodded. "Why is that? I am hardly someone who can deceive your eyes, or lash out at you from the shadows."

"I just … I'm not used to fighting without magic," said Sakura. "I'm not a fighter, really."

Feiwang smiled, and motioned to Yelan, who had entered the dojo during the spar. The Witch waved her hand, and a translucent wall surrounded the combatants. Sakura's eyes bugged out in surprise.

"A barrier, to protect the house while we spar," said Feiwang. He held his hand out. "You may use magic this time."

Sakura glanced over at Xiaolang, who wore a nervous yet excited smile. He propped up her courage, and she withdrew the Star Key. She uttered:

Key of the Stars, Master of dreams,
Bequeath unto me the power ye deems.
Let us fulfil our vow in time's great streams ... Release!

The key flashed and transformed into her wand. The topaz star set within its pink metal circle glimmered as she held it before her. With much greater confidence, she faced her opponent.

Feiwang clapped his hands. As he prised them apart effortlessly, a Chinese jian formed between them. He took the blade and pointed it at Sakura. He advanced, and brought the sword to her right. The blade clanged against Sakura's shield. He twirled and slashed at Sakura's head, but she parried it with the wand, which had become a majestic rapier. She resonated with the Blade Card, and let it guide her body. Both she and the Card were careful to avoid actually striking him, even when there was an opening. Feiwang backed away as Sakura advanced.

Suddenly, with his back against the magical wall, Feiwang diverted Sakura's blade into the floor. With his index and middle finger outstretched, he summoned a gale that threw Sakura backward. He then twirled the sword, from which burst a torrent of fire. Sakura snuffed it with the Aqua Card.

Feiwang started to laugh. The barrier vanished, as did his sword, in a flash of light.

"You fight extremely well alongside the Cards," he said. "Xiaolang has trained you well." He shot his son a look of pride that made Xiaolang swell. He then clasped his hands and bowed before Sakura. "You have truly mastered these

Cards and made them your own."

Sakura deactivated her wand with a smile and returned the bow.

"Thanks for going easy on me," she said.

9 | Moon!

Before dinner, Sakura retreated to her room to clean up. She showered and washed off all the sweat from the flight and her spar with Feiwang. Then Meiling appeared with a pink hanfu for her to wear. The shy girl took a while to accept the gift, but not nearly as long to put it on. When she entered the opulent dining hall, Xiaolang rose from the table and almost fainted at the sight of her.

"Down, boy," joked Meiling.

The food was delicious, and Sakura ate her fill. Conversation drifted from Sakura's combat technique, to Xiaolang's teaching style, and then onto what she intended to do with the Cards. Sakura had little to say about that, given that she'd only focused on capturing them. She did mention that she liked using the Cards to make other people happy, such as influencing the shadow of a bully to teach its owner a lesson, or using the Lucis and Noctis Cards to alleviate a salaryman's depression. While Feiwang was receptive of such ideas, Yelan cautioned, "The Cards do have a far higher purpose than that, Lady Kinomoto."

"I know, Missus Lee," said Sakura. "Eriol told me that Clow Reed created the Cards to promote kindness in the world and defeat evildoers. But …" She thought for a moment. Frustrated that she couldn't articulate herself, she blurted, "I'm just a kid from Tokyo. I'm hardly qualified to fight bad guys, am I?"

"You may have to," murmured Yelan. Her eyes glimmered subtly, and Xiaolang exhaled slightly. Sakura heard his reaction, but she couldn't figure out his meaning.

Feiwang raised his hand and said, "Perhaps your small acts of kindness are precisely what Clow had in mind." His gaze fixed on Sakura, even though his words were targeted at Yelan. The woman only raised her eyebrows at her husband, but said nothing more.

The meal finished soon after. When the house staff cleared the table, they put a bowl of boiled rice in front of Sakura. Confused, but not wanting to be rude, she took her chopsticks to the bowl, only for Xiaolang to stop her. He shook his head silently, and motioned her to leave the bowl on the table[11].

Tea was served thereafter. Then Yelan and Feiwang took their leave. Meiling also left, explaining that she had some prior engagements. This finally gave Xiaolang and Sakura some alone time. They went to his bedroom and closed the door. Sakura followed Xiaolang to the sofa beside his desk and sat down with him. She noticed the small pink fimo shisa on his desk and stroked it gently.

"She can't wait to get back to Japan," said Xiaolang. Sakura shuffled over, nestled into his embrace, and rested her head on his shoulder. She sighed with contentment.

"Why didn't we do this sooner?" she mumbled.

"Didn't have time at the airport," replied Xiaolang.

"I was being rhetorical," said Sakura.

Absentmindedly, she threaded her fingers through his and kissed his knuckles. When she looked into his eyes, she remembered Meiling's jibes about nuptials earlier in the day. She blushed.

"What?" asked Xiaolang.

"I was just thinking about ... marriage," she

---

[11] This is a custom in Chinese culture. If she'd eaten the rice, she would have stated that the meal wasn't enough. By leaving the rice, she is stating she is full, and the meal was good.

stammered.

"You want to get married now?" Xiaolang choked.

"No!" snapped Sakura. "Not now, I mean. I still want to finish school. Plus, even with the Cards, I don't know if I want to be some master magician or something. I just …"

Xiaolang brushed a few hairs out of her face and cradled her cheek.

"Never mind about that," he said. "Why worry about stuff in the future? Just think about right now." He looked right into her eyes and smiled. She could see her own reflection in his amber irises, and decided she didn't like the perturbed expression she saw. She smiled instead.

"Can I sleep with you tonight?" she murmured.

Xiaolang's eyes widened. Sakura suddenly burst into a paroxysm of stammers and babble. Her face grew hotter than the sun as she blurted, "I didn't mean that! I meant just share a bed!"

Xiaolang laughed off his embarrassment. He calmed her down and said, "I'd love to share a bed with you tonight. But my parents won't allow it. Wei actually has instructions to escort you back to the guest bedroom after a certain time."

Sakura actually felt disappointed. It was as if she had a bedtime – something she'd not had since she was thirteen. She pouted, which made Xiaolang laugh even more.

They stayed in Xiaolang's room until long after dark. They discussed a few of the sights to see in Hong Kong during Sakura's trip. Eventually, Wei disturbed them and announced that Sakura needed to return to the guest quarters. She kissed Xiaolang goodnight, and moved to follow Wei.

The lights in the mansion suddenly went dark. Confusion fell over Sakura's mind as she glanced around in the sparse light from the Moon outside. She could see Xiaolang's silhouette move in front of the window. There was panic in his voice as he said, "Can you sense it?"

Be it fatigue or the lingering joy of being with her boyfriend, Sakura's senses were dulled. She shook her head and extended her awareness outward.

She sensed a horde of people at the edge of the Lee compound. They appeared as normal humans, but carried malicious intent. Among them, she sensed a presence, unwavering in shape and form, and yet crackling with bloodlust and an absolute absence of conscience. It hummed stridently, and yet the sound was dulled as if echoing through congealed blood.

"What is that thing?" she asked disgusted.

"A homunculus," said Xiaolang. "An immortal flesh-eater, and it's brought friends." He gave Wei commands in Cantonese.

Wei then took Sakura by the shoulder and led her out of the room. "Come with me, Lady Kinomoto."

Xiaolang left the room and went down the corridor. He heard Sakura call out to him, and he replied, "Stay with Wei, Sakura! Use your magic and protect the servants!" Then he clapped his hands and materialised his sword. He emerged into the entrance atrium, illuminated by a ball of energy held in Yelan's hand. The woman's stoic expression radiated only the slightest amount of disgust at the creatures that approached the mansion. Xiaolang joined her and Feiwang at the front door. His father had manifested a Chinese spear, which he held erect like a tribesman upon a mountain.

Five figures sauntered toward the entrance. The tallest wore baggy pants and a sleeveless shirt that barely concealed his muscular body. In the light of Yelan's orb, his face of Indian descent bore a sneer that upturned into a hungry grin. The second tallest was Chinese, whose long button-less jacket showed off his muscles. Two smaller gangly ones smiled sinisterly at the house and the people who stood to defend it.

Then there was the yellow-faced man in the single-breasted suit – the source of the homunculus signature.

His tiny eyes narrowed as his grin widened.

"Moon," he chirped. "Protracted period precluding perception, Clan of the utmost Lee-ness!"

"Not protracted enough, Nikolaev," replied Feiwang firmly. "I hear you prefer the name 'Moonface.'"

"Moon, that is correct," said Moonface as he craned his neck to soak the rays of moonlight. Then he said, "I vie for various valuables in your vault. Relinquish them and relax the remainder of your reverie."

"Or what?" snarled Xiaolang.

Feiwang's hand raised to silence him. The man tightened his grip on his spear, but spoke calmly and firmly.

"I am not in the mood for a fight today," he said. "Please leave."

Moonface inhaled manically and softly chimed, "Moon!" Then his underlings charged forward. The two gangly twins leapt into the air, and their bodies contorted. Their skin bled metallic entrails that formed the carapaces of two man-sized lobsters.

"They're homunculi too!" yelled Xiaolang, his heart racing with terror.

"A Witch's soul protect spell," said Yelan. "It hides their true nature!"

The creatures gurgled as they thrust their pincers at the trio. Yelan and Xiaolang withdrew into the atrium, while Feiwang somersaulted over them. The creatures scampered into the atrium to face Xiaolang and Yelan.

Moonface's henchmen cocked machine guns and unleashed them upon Feiwang. He held his fingers outstretched, erecting a magical barrier that harmlessly deflected the bullets. Then he diverted his mental energy into the shield, which burst with sound and light, and threw the attackers off balance. The Indian charged forward to bludgeon Feiwang, but the man was quicker. He swatted the gun aside and brought the blade of his spear down upon the man's shoulder. Then the Chinese man came at him with a sabre drawn from his belt. The duo working as one drove Feiwang back into the house, yet failed to land a successful blow.

Yelan meanwhile confounded the humanoid lobsters with waves of her hand, issuing ethereal flashes to disorient them, and forces of magic to bludgeon them. Xiaolang, unfortunately, couldn't find an opening for his sword. While one was dazed, the other was pressing the attack.

"They're twins, Xiaolang," said Yelan.

Xiaolang noted the identical striae upon their shells, and the synchronicity of their movements. He caught onto his mother's meaning. Together, they raised their hands and bellowed, "Soul Resonance!" The homunculi scampered backward in alarm as the mother-son duo began to shimmer green. The duo withdrew paper charms and held them high. "*Léidì zhāolái!*" they yelled. The paper charms crackled with electricity, disorienting the homunculi. Xiaolang then raced forward and decapitated them with his sword.

Yelan and Xiaolang raced through the cloud of decay wafting from the dead creatures. Feiwang and his wife handled the two henchman, while Xiaolang leapt over them to attack Moonface. The yellow-skinned beast dodged Xiaolang's downward swipe and backhanded the boy. Xiaolang recovered and slashed upward across Moonface's torso, tearing his suit in two.

Moonface snarled manically, and charged at the boy. He slashed and swiped at him, but missed each time. Xiaolang tripped up Moonface and brought his sword across the creature's face. Black blood burst from Moonface's yellow skin, but the pain only angered him further. He caught Xiaolang's sword-wielding arm and threw a punch into the boy's face. Then his jaw dislocated, baring a maw of large inhuman fangs.

"*Huǒ shén zhāolái!*" bellowed Feiwang. A fireball burst from his hand and hit Moonface squarely. The homunculus flew to the ground and writhed in pain. He rolled around to stop the fire. His cooked flesh stank of burnt rubber and rotten eggs. He pulled himself up, only to see the tip of Xiaolang's sword in his face.

"Gimme a reason not to," he said.

Feiwang and Yelan approached, having dispatched his remaining henchmen. Black blood dripped from Feiwang's spear. Moonface gazed up at them. And yet, despite his evident defeat and severe burns, he chortled.

"Delay my death to determine my design?" he asked.

"The Regiment will want to know how you used a soul protect spell," said Yelan.

"As do I," said Feiwang.

Moonface harrumphed. "Havin' a Witch helps." His response shocked them. He raised his finger. "*But!* You should have paid more attention to your surroundings." The trio exchanged mortified glances. Yelan reached out with her senses and detected trespassers approaching the vault deep within the mansion.

"He'd been the bait," said Yelan.

"Stay with Moonface, Xiaolang," barked Feiwang. Then he and Yelan pursued the creatures.

Xiaolang grabbed Moonface by his melted flesh and slammed him into a wall. He held his sword to the homunculus' throat and snarled, "Tell me what you're here for and I'll make your death quick."

"Ooooh, big boisterous boast blurted a billion times," retorted Moonface. "You, the Regiment, and even the Reaper … you're all sadistic slaughterers! I'm here to put a stop to that."

"How?" barked Xiaolang. "What do you need from our vault?"

"Moon! Something not even you could imagine," chirped Moonface. "But I'll do what I must to get our shorn shameless Shaula what she needs!"

"Shaula?" Xiaolang's eyes shifted as he scanned his history lessons. "You mean Shaula Gorgon? What does she need?"

"Not your giddy girlfriend, that's for sure," said Moonface. He snickered as he looked right into Xiaolang's horrified eyes. "Wouldn't mess up our plans if we kill her, would it?"

10 | Homunculus Assault

Trembling, Sakura stuck close to Wei as he led her into the lower levels of the Lee mansion's west wing. Her senses, heightened by anxiety, detected the incoming marauders.

"Lady Kinomoto, your magic," said Wei as he noted the ruffling of bushes outside the mansion.

"But these are ordinary people," said Sakura.

A glass window shattered around the corner, and Wei pulled Sakura against the wall near the intersection. He edged his gaze around the corner and saw two figures cloaked in black leap through the broken window. He turned to Sakura and said, "Did you not use your Cards against bullies? This is the same thing. If you'd please."

Sakura reluctantly withdrew the Star Key and transformed it into a wand. Then she activated the Veil Card. At her command, the shadows around the intruders came to life and ensnared them. The dark tendrils lifted them up and threw them against the wall. Then, with the Forest Card, Sakura enthralled the men in vines and bound them on the floor.

Satisfied, Wei scampered down the hall toward the intruders, and unmasked one of them.

"What are you doing here?" the butler demanded.

Instead of answering, the man opened his mouth wider than a normal human. Within were multiple rows of sharp teeth dripping green ooze. The man broke his bonds and launched himself at Wei, growling ferociously.

Sakura's mind went blank, and when she regained her senses, she saw the Star Wand held out in front of her. The Lucis Card returned to her pocket. The man fell backwards with a smoking hole through his head. Sakura backed away in horror.

"I just killed a man!" she cried.

"No, you didn't," said Wei. He showed her the creature on the floor. It had started to evaporate, throwing up puffs of black dust into the air. "It was another homunculus," Wei explained.

"But it felt like a normal human," exclaimed Sakura numbly.

"I'm not sure how, but they must have found a way to mask their signature," said Wei. He eyed the other man, who was still out cold, and took Sakura by the forearm. They ran down the corridor toward a door at the end, which they found locked. Wei knocked loudly and announced his presence. The door unlocked with a clack and opened a crack for the occupants gaze outward. Then it opened entirely and a barrage of hands pulled them into the servants' quarters.

Several of them Sakura recognised, but not all. Each of them wore expressions of horror and bewilderment. Sakura could certainly relate, having just killed what felt like a normal human.

The poor girl suddenly found herself enthralled in a bear hug. Meiling, tearful and scared, gripped her tightly.

"This is horrible, Sakura," exclaimed the fretful girl. "Our mansion is supposed to have protective barriers, but they all got through."

Sakura was completely befuddled. Having no frame of reference, all she could do was stand idly.

The servants shrieked at a pound against the entrance. A few windows broke inwards, and black-clad hands reached through the curtains. Sakura felt just as panicked as everyone else, until she heard Wei yell her name.

"Remember the young master's words," urged the terrified butler.

Somehow, within the depths of her flabbergasted consciousness, Sakura recalled Xiaolang's instructions. She drew a Card and proclaimed, "Expel these intruders, Guard!"

A translucent barrier burst outward from the Card. It enveloped everyone in the room, and pushed the attackers away. They snarled and grunted as they threw themselves in an effort to break in. As Sakura poured her energy into the shield, her senses heightened more. The intruders' hunger for flesh became clear. That only made her more determined to keep them out.

"Wei, why is this happening?" asked Meiling.

Frustrated, Sakura blurted, "Don't you have any magical powers, Meiling?"

"I'm a finance major! I never got into this!" replied Meiling. Several other servants nodded in agreement as they huddled together.

They're just normal people, Sakura thought. *I have to protect them.*

Sakura's shield held against the punches and blows of the homunculi outside. The monsters' growls intensified and grew more beastly, which only made the servants' wails more desperate.

There was a soft pop, followed by a hiss that within a second grew into a deafening shriek. Then Sakura felt as if a meteor had struck her. She fell to the ground. The air around her burned as rubble and dust coated her. She felt Meiling pull her out of the mess, and she looked around. Her vision was blurry and her ears rung. When her eyes cleared, she saw that one half of the servants' quarters had been blown off, exposing them to the encroaching monsters.

One of them brandished a spent rocket launcher, which he discarded. The ill-favoured man tore off his shirt and his skin exploded in a flurry of metal. To Sakura's amazement, he took the form of a robotic bear, and let out a high-pitched roar. A few of his comrades similarly discarded their human skin for the metal carapaces of various cybernetic animals. The rest unhinged their mouths and snarled hungrily.

They're not human, Sakura convinced herself. She shook her head and focused. Then she stepped out in front of the crowd of terrified people, and held the Star Wand before her.

"You will not touch these people," she growled weakly.

"Darlin', hush," said the bear with a Texan accent. Then it galloped forward. Sakura activated the Blade Card, and slashed through the monster's torso, cleaving it in two. The beast disintegrated, but Sakura hardly felt proud. Her body would not stop shaking, and her legs trembled.

One of the humanoid homunculi stepped forward and cracked her neck. She bared her sharp incisors and yelled, "Get her!"

Sakura's heart skipped beats as the creatures began to charge at once. Her eyes shifted and she panicked. Meiling couldn't help her, and neither could Wei. Kero and Yue weren't there. Eriol was gone. She was completely alone.

"Xiaolang!" she screamed.

The monsters stopped short of her, and there was a moment of silence. Sakura looked up from behind her raised arms, and saw two figures before her. And for some reason, these two made the homunculi awfully nervous.

To Sakura's left, the girl placed a hand to the talisman on her chest. She yelled, "Arms Alchemy! Valkyrie Skirt!"

To Sakura's right, the boy placed a hand to his chest and bellowed, "Arms Alchemy! Sunlight's Heart!"

Sakura fell on her backside, mesmerised by the flashes of blue and yellow energy that surrounded the pair. The blue light materialised into a set of four mechanical arms that terminated in sharp blades, attached to the girl's hips. The yellow light split in two, one half covering the boy's left arm in an intricate gold and silver gauntlet; the other half formed a short lance in his right hand.

"Astrid, you ready to be badass again?" said the boy with a clear Australian accent.

"You just control yourself, Nathan," returned the girl.

Then the pair raced forward, absent fear or hesitation. The homunculi started backward, but were too slow. Astrid leapt into the air and spun around, decapitating most of the monsters, and dismembering others. Nathan blocked blows from the attackers with his gauntlet before running them through with his lance. From the glimpses Sakura caught of their faces, they seemed to be having fun. That they were even there was more than Sakura could handle, but that they were enjoying themselves was just absurd.

Sakura stood and glanced around befuddled. She saw movement above her, and caught half a dozen more homunculi coming over the top of the wrecked wall. She quickly unleashed the Flare Card and incinerated them.

"Wei, where else is there we can be safe?" she asked. Wei shrugged absentmindedly. Sakura pursed her lips and pondered a moment. The ground beneath her feet, riddled with rocks and debris, gave her an idea. She drew a Card.

"Encase these people in a safe haven, Gaia!"

Suddenly, a wall of earth rose around the servants, with an arch to allow entry. Sakura stood guard before the bottleneck.

Nathan and Astrid seemed to hold their own just fine against the homunculi. Some went past them and charged at Sakura. She used the Maya Card to delude a few into attacking comrades, the Aqua Card to douse others, and the Spark Card to fry them. Then ,the biggest homunculus of all, in the form of a towering mechanical gorilla, lumbered toward her. By this point, she was tired, as were her Cards. Yet, she stood her ground and tried to gather enough strength to summon Flare one last time.

"*Léidì zhāolái!*" bellowed a voice that made Sakura jump

for joy. From the rooftop to her left came a devastating thunderbolt that tore through the creature. It didn't kill the homunculus entirely, but weakened it enough for Sakura to finish the job with a roaring fireball. She looked up in joyous relief at Xiaolang, who leapt off the roof and embraced her tightly.

"You're alright!" she cried.

"I should say the same," said Xiaolang. He glanced over at the battle on the hill, and the two mystery fighters engaging the remaining homunculi.

"Alchemic Warriors," he exclaimed. He saw the girl with the mechanical arms and chuckled, "Spartan!"

"You know them?" asked a bewildered Sakura.

"They're friendlies," said Xiaolang. "And I know that girl from a long time ago." Sakura shot him a suspicious look. "A *long* time ago, sweetheart," he added earnestly. He looked like he wanted to stay with her, but something drew his attention to the centre of the mansion. "Mother and Father are fighting the homunculi inside," he explained. "I'm going to go help them. Do you have everything handled here?"

Xiaolang's very presence had invigorated Sakura. Without a command, she held her wand up, activated the Veil Card, and felled a straggling homunculus with a barrage of shadowy spines. She didn't break eye contact with her Number One.

"I'll be fine," she said.

Xiaolang kissed her, and then raced into the mansion. Sakura remained a while longer, taking out any monsters that came near. The commotion eventually died down, and Nathan jogged toward her. He swiped his lance to kill the last surviving homunculus, and then looked around with a huff. The boy hadn't even broken a sweat, much to Sakura's amazement and curiosity.

The boy noticed her, and his expression went from surprise to unease. He gauchely approached her, eying her Star Wand, and the people inside the magically constructed stone bunker. He stammered as his eyes shifted and he fidgeted nervously. Sakura remained silent.

Finally, the boy pressed his gloved hand to his chest and said, "Nathan." Sakura pursed her lips shyly. The boy yelled louder, "Nay-thaaan!"

"I can speak English," she blurted.

Nathan stumbled backwards as if Sakura were a tiger lashing out. Then he laughed, "Sorry 'bout that. Wasn't expecting a Brit, since it's China and all."

"I'm Japanese," retorted Sakura. She smiled and held out her hand. "I'm Sakura Kinomoto."

Nathan hummed at her politeness and reached forward to shake her hand. At the last minute he withdrew and said, "Umm … Prob'ly not with this." His gauntlet and lance disintegrated into bolts of energy that flew back into his chest. Then he shook her hand. "Nice to meet ya," he said. He looked past her to the people inside the stone bunker. "Everyone okay?" he asked. "The homunculi are gone, so you'll be safe."

Wei was the first to emerge. He reverently bowed and expressed his gratitude to Nathan and Sakura. Meiling came out and threw her arms around the boy. She looked at him closely, as if he reminded her of a movie she'd seen many years ago. Then it clicked in her head.

"You're the Starlight Lancer!" she exclaimed.

Sakura frowned. "Who?"

Nathan and Meiling looked at her incredulously.

"Seriously?" they asked in unison.

11 | Scythemeister

The main atrium of the Lee mansion was a wreck. The servants, especially Wei, looked dejectedly at the state of the building they had worked so hard to maintain. Meiling did her best to console them, surprising Sakura and Nathan.

"She's not like other richies," intoned Nathan.

"She's way nicer than I imagined," said Sakura.

"Yeah, if it were my parents, they'd've fired the lot of 'em," said Nathan.

"Are you from a wealthy family too?" asked Sakura. "Are all rich families part of this world of magic?"

Nathan scoffed, "No! I kinda fell into this."

"More like *dove in*," blurted a voice from the front door. Sakura and Nathan turned to see Astrid. Sakura now had a good look at the woman who had saved her. The scar reaching across the bridge of her nose, along with the mechanical blades shimmering in the light, made her look really scary. Sakura edged behind Nathan as the woman approached.

Astrid dragged a smouldering creature with a familiar scent. She threw the thing to the floor in front of them and said, "Look what the cat dragged in and pissed all over."

Nathan looked at the giggling mass and recognised him. "Moonface!"

"Seems that this shithead has taken over after we killed Doctor Butterfly," said Astrid.

"No, Chouno took him out," said Nathan.

Astrid shot the boy a look that yelled, "Does that matter?" She noticed the girl hiding behind her friend and her tone changed. "This thing won't hurt you, Miss."

Sakura peaked out from behind Nathan, and eyed Astrid up and down. Astrid put on a softer expression, which lured the girl out of hiding.

"I'm Sakura," she mumbled. "It's nice to meet you."

"Oh, sorry," said Nathan. "Yeah, Sakura, this is Astrid Rachelle. She's my ..."

"Girlfriend?" asked Sakura.

"God! No!" bellowed Astrid with a jerk of the proverbial knee.

"Words can hurt, you know," said Nathan.

"Well, we don't want people getting the wrong idea, do we?" returned Astrid sarcastically.

Wei and Meiling approached and bowed reverently to the two Australian warriors.

"I must extend our gratitude for your assistance," said Wei.

"No probs," said Nathan.

"It's the Regiment's job to handle homunculi," said Astrid.

"Yes, handle haughty homunculi," chirped Moonface. Sakura withdrew from the creature, his horrid cannibalistic lust wafting from him like a disease. Astrid edged the points of her blades close to Moonface's every joint, and demanded his silence.

At that point, Xiaolang entered the atrium. He sighed with relief as he embraced Sakura. His gaze then fell on Nathan, and a twinge of suspicion hit him as he noticed the boy's gaze on his girlfriend. Nathan looked at him and grinned.

"G'day! I'm Nathan Grant," he said, offering a handshake.

"I know who you are, Starlight Lancer. I'm Xiaolang Lee," said the Chinese boy. He motioned to Sakura. "I'm her boyfriend."

Nathan facetiously threw his hands up and said, "Hey, don't feel threatened if women find me irresistible."

"Oh, Christ, Nathan," moaned Astrid as she face-palmed. Sakura just looked perplexed by the whole thing.

Xiaolang looked to Astrid and said, "Got your hands full with this one, don't you, Spartan?"

Astrid strutted over and shook Xiaolang's hand. She had an expression part way between a smile and a sneer, and she muttered, "He's got nothin' on you, Coyote!" Then the pair burst into laughter.

"How the heck've you been, Astrid!?" exclaimed Xiaolang. "What was it, four years since we last spoke?"

"Thereabouts," said Astrid. "California, right?"

Xiaolang pointed to Sakura, who was absolutely dumbstruck. "I see you've met my girlfriend."

"Yeah, I heard you'd had your heart stolen by a photo," jibed Astrid.

"And you had to give someone a heart, I hear," returned Xiaolang.

"Oh, you mean this idiot?" she asked, pointing at Nathan, who made an obscene gesture in response.

Sakura suddenly yelled, "What's going on here?" The toll of the night's events had finally appeared on her face. Her cheeks were flushed with her unfurling anxiety. She pointed at Nathan and Astrid and yelled, "Who are these people, Xiaolang?" She pointed at Moonface on the floor and bellowed, "And what is that thing?"

She clasped her arms around herself in a futile effort to stop shaking. Xiaolang placing his hands on her shoulders gently went a long way to calming her. He then explained Nathan and Astrid's identities as Alchemic Warriors, and the nature of their label. Astrid even deactivated her Arms Alchemy and showed Sakura the Kakugane. Xiaolang then explained the homunculi.

"Well, why are they here? Hunting?" asked Sakura, still shaken up.

"Moon!" gurgled Moonface. He eyed Sakura and made a hungry growling sound. Nathan stomped on his head to silence him.

"They're not hunting," said Yelan. All eyes turned to the Lee matriarch, who entered the atrium. She shot daggers at the Alchemic Warriors in her house, but focused her disgust on Moonface. The creature just grinned back at her, as if his life weren't in the surest peril.

Feiwang appeared behind her, a wooden box in his hand. The box confused everyone, except Moonface, who whistled with interest.

"The homunculi attacking our vault were after this," said Feiwang.

Nathan suddenly blurted, "That's the Silver Key, right?" He scrambled over to the man. "Can I have a look?"

"Nathan, stop," warned Astrid.

"Nah, I wanna have a look," Nathan insisted. "We came all this way to stop Moonface, so I wanna see what this thing is." He motioned for Feiwang to open the box, but the man refused, despite being taken aback by the Australian's forwardness.

"How do you know about the Silver Key?" asked Yelan.

"We received intelligence that the L.X.E. was after it," said Astrid, trying hard to silence Nathan with her glare.

The message evidently hadn't reached the boy. He went on, "Yeah, wasn't it like there were two of 'em, and Moonface and Shaula made off with one of them. That's why he's here now, to get the other one."

"Wait! The Regiment had the other Silver Key?" exclaimed Xiaolang.

"Yeah, they'd gotten some dude to research it," said Nathan. He looked straight at Astrid, whose rage blasted outward from her eyes. Once again, her meaning didn't reach him and he said, "What was the guy's name? Arthur or something?"

"Avalon," murmured Xiaolang.

Sakura jumped with shock. She looked at Xiaolang and gasped, "Dad?" She then looked at Astrid, who sighed with irritation. She disregarded Astrid's exasperated look and asked, "Franklin Avalon ... My father is working for you?" Astrid looked at her apologetically.

"*Was* working for them," chimed Moonface.

"What do you mean, *was?*" asked Sakura.

"He *was* working for the rancid Regiment," said Moonface. "Now, he's working for our wily, wanton Witch, Shaula ... for now, at least."

Sakura burst forward and grabbed the homunculus. Tears leaked from her eyes as she yelled, "Tell me where he is, now!"

Moonface champed his teeth menacingly, prompting Astrid to yank Sakura back. The poor girl was distraught, and demanded to know where her father had been taken. The malevolent creature smiled and murmured, "Not tellin'!"

"Sakura, look at me," said Astrid firmly. "We have ways of making homunculi talk. We'll take him back to our headquarters and find out where they took your father. Okay?"

Sakura sniffled back her tears and nodded. Meanwhile, Xiaolang walked across to Nathan, who was still trying to get a look at Feiwang's box. He yanked the boy away by the scruff of his neck and snarled, "Get away from him, Grant."

"Oi, just wanted to have a look," said Nathan indignantly.

"What does the Alchemic Regiment want with the Silver Key?" asked Yelan as she put herself between him and her husband.

"I dunno," replied Nathan. "I just busted outta there when I heard they'd lost it."

Yelan and Feiwang's eyes bugged out.

"The Regiment hasn't cleared you for active service," muttered Feiwang. "You still have the Black Kakugane within you."

"How do you know about that?" asked Nathan, rubbing his sternum nervously.

"I must ask you to leave now," said Yelan.

Nathan sighed, knowing full well their meaning. He cursed the talisman in his chest, which still hummed with the life-sucking fury of Victor Powers. He stepped away slowly and turned to Astrid.

"We'll leave with Moonface," he said as he hoisted the homunculus to his feet. He glanced at Sakura and said, "We'll make him tell us where your dad is, okay?"

Sakura sucked in a deep breath and said, "I'm coming too!" The whole room erupted into gasps and bellows. Xiaolang was particularly adamant about keeping his girlfriend away from the homunculi. But Sakura was determined. "I have to help find Dad." She clutched the Cards in her pocket and proclaimed, "I have this power. I need to use it to at least defend my family."

"I won't let you go alone," said Xiaolang. His parents tried to stop him, but he pulled away and stood by Sakura. "Mother, Father, I have to make sure that she is safe. She doesn't know their world, but I do." Nearby, Meiling cheered him on for being such a good boyfriend.

"We need you here," said Feiwang. "With the protective charms around our vault gone, the Silver Key is vulnerable."

Moonface chirped with excitement, and the stiff slaps Nathan and Astrid gave his head did nothing to dishearten him.

Xiaolang glanced between Sakura, Moonface, and his parents. He then walked to them and said, "I'll take it. I'll take the Silver Key with me. Sakura and I can protect it. Not to mention, the whole Alchemic Regiment."

Feiwang was about to refuse, but his wife rested her

hand on his shoulder to silence him. Her eyes were transfixed upon her son, and her irises glimmered subtly. Then she looked at Feiwang and said, "Let him take it."

* * *

About a half-hour later, Nathan and Astrid wove their way through the woods around Mount Cameron. They dragged Moonface along with them. Xiaolang and Sakura followed not far behind, having both changed into clean clothes. Sakura brought her travel pack, which included her essentials. Xiaolang had a backpack containing the Silver Key box and reams of paper charms.

"Thank you for coming with me," said Sakura.

"You're my Number One, and your father is in danger," said Xiaolang. "It's obvious I'd come along."

Sakura eyed Astrid up ahead and her eyes narrowed. "How do you know Astrid?"

Xiaolang sighed. "When I was in California — remember I told you about that? Astrid had been dispatched to clean up a homunculus infestation. My father asked me to give her a hand." Sakura pursed her lips and hummed suspiciously. Xiaolang held his hands up honestly. "We're just really old friends, I swear it."

"She called you Coyote," said Sakura. "Just like Alice Axilotl."

"That's just a code name, Sakura," replied Xiaolang. "It's actually what my name means in English."

"And why did you call her Spartan?" asked Sakura.

"Because my code name is Spartan Valkyrie, Cardcaptor," said Astrid over her shoulder.

Sakura raised an eyebrow, and glanced at Nathan. "And you're the Starlight Lancer." Nathan threw her a thumbs-up.

Between them, Moonface chortled, "Such silly pseudonyms."

"Shut up!" barked the quartet.

Not long after, they reached a clearing. Nestled

amongst the trees was the small aircraft Nathan and Astrid had stolen from the Regiment facility. They moved to board it, but were shocked by the sudden crunch of metal. The wings of the aircraft fell unceremoniously to the ground. The four looked around flabbergasted, as Moonface's grin widened.

"The brash blonde befalls," he murmured.

A pair of Converse shoes hit the fuselage of the wrecked aircraft, drawing everyone's attention. They looked up to see a girl in jeans and a yellow jumper. Her blonde pigtails wafted in the wind, beating gently against the handle of a black and red scythe resting on her shoulder.

"I'm afraid I can allow you to go no further," said the girl.

Astrid and Xiaolang exchanged glances, knowing full well the girl's identity. They stepped forward, motioning for Nathan and Sakura to guard Moonface.

"Since when does the Reaper interfere in Regiment affairs, Maka Albarn?" asked Astrid.

Maka's dark green eyes gleamed in the moonlight.

"When the fate of the planet hangs in the balance," she retorted.

The face of an albino boy appeared in the blade of Maka's scythe. He slurped up a line of drool and bellowed, "Hand over Moonface and the Silver Key, or ..."

"I'll take your soul!" roared Maka.

She charged Astrid and Xiaolang, who summoned their weapons. Maka swiped first at Astrid, who leapt back and retaliated with her four mechanical blades. Xiaolang attacked with an intentionally blunted sword, but Maka blocked it with the butt of her scythe. The girl single-handedly defended against the attacks of both masters, wielding the scythe as if it were weightless.

Xiaolang pulled out a paper charm.

"*Fēnghuá zhāolái!*" he bellowed. A vicious gust of wind burst from his sword and blasted Maka into the trees. He and Astrid raced toward the tree on which their opponent had found her footing. With a boost from Xiaolang's wind magic, they shot into the air toward Maka.

The battle took to the skies as Maka twirled in mid-air to parry and block their every attack. She winded Xiaolang with the head of her scythe before bringing it around to strike Astrid. The mechanical arms of the Valkyrie Skirt only just managed to keep Maka's attacks at bay. Astrid flipped in mid-air and the resultant spinning of her blades threw off Maka's defences. Astrid then twirled, bringing the blunt edges of her blades across Maka's face. This only gave Maka a bit more momentum to spin and knock Astrid's head with the butt of her scythe. She then kicked Astrid away, which pushed her back toward another tree.

As she fell back to the ground, Maka heard Xiaolang roar, "*Huǒ shén zhāolái!*" A barrage of fireballs flew from the Chinese boy on the ground. Maka spun her scythe as fast as she could, making a shield of it to deflect the blasts. She hit the tree and rebounded toward Moonface.

Sakura stood in front of the homunculus, spurred by the mental image of her imperilled father. She held her arms wide and screamed, "Stop!" But Maka couldn't stop.

There was a deafening clang of metal on metal. Nathan stood between Maka and Sakura, his gauntlet raised to block Maka's blow. The scythe's blade rung with a painfully strident tone. Nathan flicked his arm and sent Maka flying. She hit the ground, and her scythe fell beside her.

Nathan slowly advanced, his fingertips slightly crimson and his hair roots shimmering fluorescently. Maka sat up and felt her energy slowly leave her. She scrambled away from Nathan, but could not find her feet. The Starlight Lancer stood over her and glared down at her. The scythe suddenly transformed into the albino boy, who covered her body with his own.

"Stay the Hell away from my meister!" he snarled.

"You gonna behave yourselves?" asked Nathan, his

voice a deep growl. Maka exchanged glances with the boy, and then nodded. Her eyes radiated hostility, but they were honest too.

Nathan deactivated his Arms Alchemy, and willed his body back to normal. He reached down and offered the pair his hands. They took them hesitantly and he pulled them up.

"I'm Nathan Grant," he said with a smile. He pointed out Sakura. "That chick's Sakura. That's her boyfriend, Xiaolang. And that's my friend, Astrid."

"I know who *they* are," snapped Maka. She shot an especially dark look at Sakura. Then she looked at Nathan. "I'm Maka Albarn of the Demon Weapon Meister Academy. This is my weapon partner, Soul."

"I take it you're that Starlight Lancer what's been screwin' everythin' up," said Soul.

"You're right about that," said Astrid. She eyed the wrecked aircraft and sighed. "Why did the Reaper send you here?"

"We were ordered to recover the Silver Key before the Regiment started screwing around with it," said Maka. "We also have to neutralise Moonface."

"You can't!" snapped Sakura. "Moonface kidnapped my father, and I need the Regiment to find out where he is."

Maka looked almost sickened by the mention of the word 'father.'

"It's too dangerous. He must be taken out," she snarled.

Astrid and Xiaolang advanced, their weapons at the ready.

"The Alchemic Regiment will take jurisdiction here, Albarn," said Astrid. "We also need to know where Moonface is keeping Doctor Avalon. That's where the other half of the Silver Key is."

"Also Shaula," put in Xiaolang. "I hear you two have a bone to pick with her."

The hairs on Maka's neck stood on end, while Soul clenched his teeth. They exchanged glances as they considered their options. They couldn't well let their target out of their sight.

Soul finally spoke up, "We'll need to report to Lord Reaper."

"Lord Reaper?" asked Nathan.

"The head of their organisation," Astrid explained.

"If he agrees to let you have Moonface, we'll take you back to the Regiment," said Maka begrudgingly. There was a twinge of hope in her voice that the Reaper would side with her.

Nathan, Astrid, and Xiaolang exchanged glances and silently agreed. Sakura looked at the wrecked aircraft and raised a hand.

"How do we get there?" she asked.

12 | The Reaper

Maka and Soul emerged from the mirror with four companions and one prisoner in tow. Maka would have preferred they'd all been prisoners, but reality rarely went her way. When everyone was through, the newcomers took a moment to get their bearings.

Astrid and Xiaolang were quite excited to finally see the inside of the fabled DWMA. They'd heard about it many times, and had even met some of its graduates. But to stand in the legendary fortress was something else entirely.

"It's like something out of Cartoon Network," said Nathan as he gazed at the skull emblem on the floor.

Sakura pointed out all the colourful tapestries and choices of paint.

"It looks really cool," she said.

Soul offered the girl a fist-bump.

Maka noticed it and growled irately, "Let's get going! The Reaper will want to know why a homunculus is in his house."

She power-walked down the hall, beckoning the others to follow. Nathan thrust Moonface into Astrid's hands, and jogged to catch up to Maka. He began assaulting her with questions about the DWMA. Maka answered them curtly, but soon stopped listening. As far as she was concerned, this boy was responsible for their mess.

Soul was far more forthcoming, and happily answered Nathan's questions. He explained that DWMA taught people with Demon Weapon abilities to control their powers.

"It's like the school in X-Men, right?" laughed Nathan.

"That movie ripped us off!" snapped Maka.

"Okay, no need to get snarky," replied Nathan defensively. He then turned to Xiaolang and Sakura. "We got magic and Witches too. Maybe the religious nut-jobs were right."

"What's that supposed to mean?" asked Xiaolang suspiciously.

"Well, maybe J. K. Rowling really is a Witch!" exclaimed Nathan. He was clearly joking, and Astrid and Sakura couldn't help but laugh.

Maka, however, stopped in her tracks, swivelled and pointed at Nathan.

"J. K. Rowling is not a Witch," she barked.

"She's a Demon Weapon," said Soul.

Every eyebrow went sky-high. Even Moonface was surprised. Maka and Soul led them to a nearby wall. Maka pointed to a photo on the wall, with a plaque reading, 'N.O.T. Class of 1979.' A young girl who clearly looked like the famous author stood to the right most of the middle row of children.

"She's one of the school's most celebrated N.O.T. students," said Maka proudly. "What? You think she got the idea on a train or something?"

Sakura frowned. "Wait, I thought you said she *was* a student."

"Yeah, a N.O.T. student," said Maka.

"Why're you saying she wasn't a student then?" asked Nathan.

"A *N.O.T.* student!" barked Maka.

"What the fuck're you talking about?" exclaimed Nathan.

"It ain't N.O.T. as in 'no,'" Soul explained. "It's N-O-

T. It means Normally Overcome Target."

"Oh, so it's an acrobat," said Nathan.

"Acronym!" snapped Astrid.

Maka looked at the group, very annoyed, and snapped, "It's a basic qualification at DWMA. N.O.T. students learn to control their powers." She shot daggers at Sakura and Nathan. "Not exploit them," she added.

Sakura looked hurt, while Nathan just shrugged. He looked at Soul and said, "So J. K.'s like you, huh? She turn into a scythe too?"

"Nope," said Soul as he rubbed his head. He led them a bit further down the hall to a row of alumni pictures. There was Rowling as a student. Next to the photo was a picture of her weapon form. They all studied the picture closely and exclaimed, "Ooooh!"

"Moon!" chirped Moonface. "Such majesty!"

"Okay! Enough with the tour," snapped Maka. "We need to get to Lord Reaper's chambers."

"Yes, please," said Sakura, thinking of her father.

The group passed by a few faces, most of which belonged to children heading for classes. The kids recognised both Nathan and Sakura, and excitedly cried out the names by which the Internet knew them. Sakura blushed a little, while Nathan grinned cockily.

Maka fumed.

Finally, they stood before the doors to the Reaper's office. Sakura took a bit of convincing to go through the doorway, the carvings of which frightened her. With Xiaolang clutching her hand, she managed to move through into the white room. All the newcomers frowned at the sight of the black crucifixes littered around the dais, upon which sat a large full-length mirror. The Reaper stood in front of the mirror, his misty black cloak wafting around him. His son, Death the Kid, stood beside him.

"Welcome to my castle," said the Reaper. He turned to reveal his cartoonish skull mask and large white cuboid hands. "And it is so nice to meet you all!" he exclaimed.

"Are you supposed to be this Reaper guy?" asked Nathan.

"Oh, but of course, Mister Grant," said the Reaper.

"You look like the guy from *Grim Adventures of Mork and Mindy*," retorted Nathan.

Billy and Mandy, you idiot, Astrid moaned internally.

"Don't be silly," exclaimed the Reaper. "I'm way nicer than that guy."

"Father, could you be serious?" muttered Kiddo.

The Reaper seemed not to have heard him, as he turned to Maka and chirped, "Maka, m'lady, where's your gorgeous black jacket and blouse combo?"

Maka glared at Soul and said, "I got minestrone on it when we were in Italy. It's soaking at home."

The Reaper shrugged and then looked at the newcomers. He hummed with disappointment.

"Where's the sixth one?" he asked.

Xiaolang coaxed Sakura out from behind his back. The girl stammered nervously under the eyeless gaze of the Reaper. She forced herself to be polite and introduce herself, but could not stop edging away from the dark figure. She shrieked and froze as the Reaper hooked a cuboid finger under her chin to look into his face.

"What a cute girl!" chirped the Reaper. "It doesn't really suit you to have such a scaredy-cat look, does it?" Sakura looked into the cartoonish mask, which craned left and right. The Reaper made a sound like a cat, which made Sakura burst into laughter. "That's better, isn't it?" said the Reaper, patting Sakura on the head.

"You seem like a nice person," said Sakura. "Not what I expected from the Angel of Death."

"I ain't no angel, sister," retorted the Reaper sassily. That made Sakura laugh even more.

Maka groaned impatiently, but the Reaper ignored her as well. He turned to Astrid and offered a handshake.

"Wonderful to finally meet the Spartan Valkyrie," he said reverently. "You've got my utmost respect in handling

Grant here."

"Oh, well, it's nice to see someone's noticing," said Astrid, ignoring the rolling of Nathan's eyes.

The Reaper turned to Xiaolang and said, "I don't usually entertain the child of a Witch, but for someone as kind-hearted as yourself, I'll make an exception."

"I appreciate it, Lord Reaper," said Xiaolang. Sakura beamed proudly as she clutched his arm.

"Father! Could we proceed with our business?" snapped Kiddo.

"Who're you supposed to be then? Li'l Grim or something?" asked Nathan.

"I am Death the Kid," said Kiddo proudly. He sneered at Nathan's dishevelled appearance. "I'll ask someone so asymmetrical to not speak in my presence."

"Asymmetrical?" asked Nathan. Soul quickly cut him off with a non-verbal warning.

The Reaper turned his attention to Moonface, whom Nathan hurled onto the floor. A hostile glare burst from the cartoon mask. The homunculus hardly seemed to care, or even notice, as he glanced around as if on safari.

"So, why've you six brought this thing into my house?" asked the Reaper.

Maka stepped forward. "You dispatched us to reclaim the Silver Key and eliminate Moonface."

"Like how you didn't say *kill*," muttered Moonface. He giggled when Astrid kicked him.

"We didn't let her," said Astrid. "We need to interrogate Moonface regarding the location of his L.X.E. stronghold. That's where we'll find Shaula."

Sakura stepped forward and looked up into the Reaper's face. "They kidnapped my Dad, Mister Reaper. They're probably torturing him. I need to know where they took him so I can save him."

Kiddo cocked his head, intrigued by the wounded homunculus.

"Where did you catch him?" he muttered.

"He and his forces attacked my house," said Xiaolang. "Were it not for Astrid, Nathan, and Sakura, they'd likely have succeeded in raiding our vault."

"And obtaining the other half of the Silver Key," intoned Kiddo.

Xiaolang's jaw dropped. "How did you know about that?"

"The Scotsman told us," said Astrid, intercepting Kiddo's retort.

"You mean Eriol?" asked Sakura. "He's working for you?"

"He works for no one, that one," said the Reaper. He eyed Xiaolang's bag. "You have the other half with you, don't you?"

Xiaolang's eyes shifted nervously. He tried to meet the Reaper's piercing gaze, but couldn't hold his ground. He quickly unzipped his backpack, procured the box, and opened it to reveal the artefact inside. Its lustrous metal shell glimmered with engraved glyphs and tracks. Nathan whistled while Sakura hummed with interest.

"Why did you bring it with you?" exclaimed Maka. She eyed Moonface, who looked around nonchalantly. "Don't you realise he might be leading you into a trap?"

"How? He's not leading us anywhere," snapped Nathan.

"Dude, ya shoulda told us ya had it on ya," said Soul irately. Kiddo agreed vociferously. Xiaolang held the box close to his chest and retorted. Sakura butted in to defend her boyfriend from the verbal onslaught. Astrid backed away with her face in her hand, while Nathan just chuckled at the chaos.

A force, like that of a meteorite hitting the Earth, floored everyone. They stood up, rubbing very sore heads, to see the Reaper, ready to karate-chop anyone else who wanted to argue.

"No more bickering, or you'll get the Reaper-Chop!" snapped the Reaper. He looked at Xiaolang. "Why'd ya bring the Silver Key?"

"Safekeeping," grunted Xiaolang. "Our family vault was damaged by this a-hole. I'm holding onto it."

The Reaper gazed a moment at him. Then the cloaked entity looked at Sakura, then Nathan, and then Astrid. He made a sound that resembled a sigh and shrugged, "Good enough."

"Father!" snapped Kiddo. Maka was also adamant that it was a bad idea, but the Reaper overruled them.

"Look, like it or not, the Regiment is the best one to interrogate Moonface," said the Reaper to the two protesters. He turned to Astrid. "I'm going to let you go to the Regiment headquarters in Australia. You'll take Moonface, and interrogate him. Understand?" Astrid nodded resolutely.

"I'll go to supervise the interrogation," said Kiddo.

"Not a chance," said the Reaper. "Not after you ran out on the last meeting. Instead, I'm sending my Death Scythe along."

Maka cried with dismay. She clambered at the Reaper's cloak, begging for someone else. Before Nathan or Sakura could ask what her problem was, the doors of the chamber flew open, and in walked a man who looked like something out of a Quentin Tarantino movie. His long red hair waved about as he strode to the dais and said, "Your Death Scythe is ready to embark, Lord Reaper." He winked at Maka, who wailed.

"I'm not going anywhere with you, Papa!" snapped Maka.

Spirit Albarn tried not to look hurt as he eyed the rest of the group. "You gonna introduce me to your new friends, darlin'?"

"Not even if they *were* my friends!" roared Maka.

"Well, *I'll* introduce them," said the Reaper. He gave the names of each newcomer. Spirit gave an especially forward greeting to Astrid and Sakura, which made Maka's blood boil. She turned to the Reaper, who interjected, "My decision has been made, Maka. End of discussion."

Maka continued to fume, and Soul laid a hand on her shoulder to calm her. Xiaolang tried to put himself between Sakura and Spirit, while Astrid tried to ward the man off with a glare that crinkled her nose scar. Nathan leaned over to Kiddo to ask what the man's problem was, but the Reaper's son just shook his head.

"Now that everyone's introduced, it's time you all popped off," exclaimed the Reaper. He waved his cuboid finger over his mirror, and it flashed to life. "This portal will take you to the Regiment headquarters." He pointed at Moonface. "Kindly get that piece of shit out of my house," he added politely.

"Moon!" snarled Moonface.

13 | A Much-Appreciated Call

The sterile white room hummed with an odd noise. A single chair composed of titanium composites sat right in the middle of the chamber. From the observation window, Sakura, Maka, and Soul watched as four men dragged Moonface toward the chair and strapped him in violently. As soon as the yellow-skinned homunculus entered the room, he grit his teeth with discomfort, and tried in vain to block his ears with his shoulders.

Bravo entered the observation booth with Spirit in tow. They approached the window and gazed down at the homunculus. Bravo smirked at the sight of the uncomfortable creature.

"We'll leave him to stew in there for a while, then take a crack at him," said Bravo.

"Is this how you usually interrogate prisoners?" asked Spirit.

"Just homunculi," said Bravo. "The room is vibrating with a dull noise just outside the human aural range, so we won't hear it. But him," He grinned at the shuffling creature. "He won't be able to stand it."

"You're torturing him?" asked Sakura meekly.

"So we can get your father back, yes," said Bravo. He placed a hand on her shoulder and said, "Don't feel bad for that thing. He's murdered countless innocent people.

It's a gift as opposed to what he deserves."

Though Sakura could see the logic, she couldn't shake the feeling of empathy as she watched Moonface cringe. Bravo left the room, but Spirit lingered a little longer. He stepped up to her and patted her head.

"Don't you worry, little one," said the red-haired man. "We'll figure this whole thing out." Sakura smiled a little. "Yeah, that's much better. You're just as cute as my little Maka, you know?" He took Sakura's hands and his smile widened. "Perhaps, later, you and I could grab a coffee?"

Spirit hit the ground. He clutched his groin and curled into a foetal position. Maka stood over him, murderous rage in her eyes.

"Make yourself scarce, Papa!" snarled the pig-tailed girl. Spirit fled from the room, wailing and decrying his daughter's terrible treatment.

Sakura backed away flabbergasted. Soul leaned over and said, "Don't worry about it. Spirit Albarn is a notorious womaniser."

"He's a pig!" snarled Maka. "Forget that, he's just a *man*."

Sakura gasped and stammered a retort. Soul quickly silenced her and, with a shake of his head, told her not to worry. Despite his uncouthness, Spirit's presence reminded her of her own father. That then made her think of her family.

"I just realised," she thought aloud. "Big Brother doesn't know what's going on. I should call him." She raced out of the booth and chased after Bravo.

Soul remained a moment, and turned to Maka.

"You should keep the Tumblr shit to a low around that one," he said.

"Why? She'll learn sooner or later," spat Maka as she glared absentmindedly out the window.

"Prob'ly not," said Soul. "This dad of hers might be great. Plus, she's got a good boyfriend." The albino leaned in closer. "You got at least one of those too," he added, trying to encode his frustration into his glare. He didn't remain to see if it got through, and left Maka alone to admire the torture tactics of the Alchemic Regiment. He caught up to Sakura, who was entreating Bravo to be allowed to call her family. The man sighed and directed her to the communications secretary of Regiment headquarters. From there, they had to go to some security officer, who sent her straight back to Bravo. They went around like that twice, winding up at the communications secretary again.

Soul could clearly see Sakura's mounting distress, and finally snapped. His hand turned into a scythe blade, which he held to the secretary's throat, and he snarled, "Give her a goddamn phone, or heads'll roll. Got it?"

The horrified officer almost wet his pants. A man of Indian descent appeared and said, "No need for that, Soul Eater." He motioned for Soul to release the man, and then turned to Sakura. "Miss Kinomoto, I am General Vasuman. I understand you wish to contact your family and appraise them of your father's condition." Sakura nodded, tears near her eyes. Vasuman's expression softened. "Allow me to arrange a communiqué."

Vasuman took them to speak with General Rodrigo, who was far too preoccupied with the impending interrogation of Moonface. He haphazardly gave permission, with a warning to consider security. Then Vasuman procured a laptop for the girl.

"Might I suggest you take the call somewhere private?" said the general. He led Sakura down through the Regiment headquarters to a containment room, not unlike that which held Moonface. Inside was Nathan, seated unrestrained on a sofa. He had an annoyed look on his face, as did Astrid who sat with him. Vasuman took his leave just as Xiaolang walked in. The Chinese boy wrung his hands with frustration.

"What's the matter, Xiaolang?" asked Sakura in a monotone.

"Nothing, I'm just irritated," said the boy. "It's annoying sitting here and waiting."

"Try doing it for six months," said Nathan.

Xiaolang approached Nathan and growled, "You trying to one up me?"

"No, I was feeling for you," retorted Nathan.

Xiaolang sighed and backed away with an apology. The atmosphere was tense following their arrival at Regiment headquarters. They'd gone through so many security checks, including searches of their bags. Xiaolang found it especially irritating when they tried to take the Silver Key fragment from him. It reminded him of why he'd not worked with the Regiment since meeting Astrid.

When Xiaolang looked at Sakura, much of his irritability went away. He hugged her as if she were a salve to a burn. Then he noticed the laptop in her hands.

"That general gave me this so I could call Big Brother," said Sakura.

Nathan shot to his feet, as if he were starving and the laptop was an all-you-can-eat buffet. Astrid managed to restrain him and insisted that Sakura use the computer first. They booted up the device and opened the video chat app. Luckily, Touya was online, and he answered the call.

"Oi, Kaiju!" he said snidely. Sakura didn't respond with her typical retort. The look on her face told him something was wrong. "What's the matter?" he asked.

"Dad's missing," she said solemnly. "And ... it's ... it's partly because of me and my ... you know."

Touya stared blankly for a moment, and then chewed his lip thoughtfully. He grabbed his phone and typed a message.

"I'll get Yuki over here," he said. "You want Daidouji too?"

Sakura nodded. "Bring Kero too," she said.

It was all in Japanese, so no one but Xiaolang could understand her. Everyone else just sat quietly while they spoke. Touya brought his laptop into the living room.

Yukito and Tomoyo sat on the sofa beside him, with Kero on Tomoyo's lap. Sakura explained everything calmly, doing her best to keep herself from breaking down.

The people on the other end took a moment to process everything. Yukito was the first to speak up.

"Where are you now?" he asked.

"Australia," said Sakura. "I don't know where. I'm with a group called the Alchemic Regiment."

"What!?" growled Kero, sticking his head right into the camera. "You're hanging out with that bunch?" He switched to English. "That must be a cell, eh? You got my Master locked in a cage, do ya?"

Astrid, Nathan, and Soul looked up in confusion. When Kero demanded they show themselves, they moved into the view of Sakura's camera. Xiaolang joined them.

"Brat!" exclaimed Kero upon seeing Xiaolang's face. "You led my Sakura into the hands of these nincompoops?"

"Nincompoops?" replied Astrid. She shook her head. "What is this? Why am I talking to a teddy bear?"

"That's a teddy bear?" mumbled Nathan.

Kero fumed, "I ain't no teddy bear!"

"And he sounds like he's from Queens," chortled Soul.

"Say that again, you albino creampuff," snarled Kero. "I'll obliterate you, if my name isn't Kerberus!"

Sakura winced and rubbed the bridge of her nose. "Kero, could you please stop?"

"Kero?" chuckled Nathan. "As in kerosene?"

"Nathan, don't antagonise him," muttered Sakura.

Astrid pursed her lips and thought a moment. Then she said, "Speaking of which, Kerberus is the name of the dog that guards the Gates of Hell. The Greeks called it the hellhound."

"And this hellhound'll knock you on your butt with a rocket launcher!" proclaimed Kero.

The mention of a rocket launcher elicited a recollection in both Nathan and Soul's mind. They exchanged glances and read each other's thoughts. Then they turned to the screen, utterly mortified at the image of the flying plush toy, and exclaimed, "You're *Hellhound99?*"

Kero grinned ecstatically. He posed like a rock-star and yelled, "My reputation precedes me! I guess you're the third-rates I've been butt-kicking up and down the Internet!" The plush toy proceeded to wave his backside in front of the camera.

Sakura buried her face in her hands and moaned, "He does this whenever he wins a game."

Nathan glanced at the stressed girl and folded his arms. He glared at the screen and said, "Kero, has anyone ever told you you're a total douchebag?"

"Yes!" bellowed Xiaolang and Touya simultaneously.

Suddenly, Kero flew straight into Tomoyo's arms and sobbed on her shoulder. He wailed in Japanese, which was a welcome change for Tomoyo who didn't speak English.

While Kero threw a tantrum, Yukito leaned forward and asked, "Sakura, do you need us to come?" He gave her an earnest gaze that told her there were people who cared for her. But even if Sakura knew where exactly they were, she didn't want her friends involved in a fight with flesh-eating monsters.

She didn't even want herself involved.

"No, it's best that you stay where you are," she stammered. "I want you, Yue, and Kero to look after Tomoyo and Big Brother. Okay?"

"Will do," said Kero, quickly recovering from his sulking.

"Sakura," Tomoyo began. "You have the bag I gave you?" Though it was pixelated, Sakura could see the characteristic gleam in her best friend's eyes. But she'd left the bag in Hong Kong! She decided to lie, and nodded with a smile. Tomoyo grinned excitedly. "Oh, if only I were there to record it all," the dark-haired girl exclaimed.

"Record what?" asked Sakura.

"Your battle alongside your new allies, of course!" said

Tomoyo. Sakura almost fell off her chair with dismay.

They finished their call soon after. It had lifted Sakura's spirits enough that she was able to smile again. She stood up from the laptop and embraced Xiaolang. Meanwhile, Nathan swooped in front of the laptop and entered someone else's username.

"Who're you lookin' for?" asked Soul.

"My sister," said Nathan. He found the username, but the girl wasn't online. He sighed with disappointment and looked for another name. This one was online, and he made a call. On the display, a shirtless boy about Nathan's age scratched his ruffled hair and rubbed his tired eyes. He looked closely at the image feed, and his eyes widened in amazement.

"Jesus!" he screeched. Then he raced out of the room, leaving Nathan shocked. Through the feed, he could hear yelling and confused shrieks. Then the boy pulled two more people into the camera view.

"Holy shit!" screamed the shorter blonde with glasses. "Nathan!"

"Where are you?" exclaimed the taller boy.

"Can't really tell ya," said Nathan. "How've you guys been?"

"Forget us!" snapped the first boy. "What're you doing? Fightin' homers, I hope."

"Nup," said Nathan. "Mostly, I've been eating Astrid's Anzac biscuits."

Astrid poked her head into the view and waved.

"Hey guys," she said warmly.

The first boy glared at her and said, "You've been lookin' after him, like I told ya?"

"Yes, Klein," said Astrid. "You really should confess your love for him."

Klein rolled his eyes and gave her the finger.

Nathan grinned and glanced at the others in the room. He beckoned them into view of the camera and introduced them. He pointed to Klein and said, "This is Klein

Stevens, my oldest mate." He pointed at the shorter boy with the glasses and said, "This is Paul Cuyper, and that taller dude is Jessie Nelson. These're friends of mine from school."

"And they know about you?" asked Soul. Nathan nodded.

"Oi, who's the red-eyed dude?" asked Klein.

"Call me Soul Eater," said Soul.

"You a warrior like Astrid and Nathan?" asked Jessie.

"Something like that," said Soul, but divulged nothing more.

Nathan pointed out Sakura and Xiaolang, and introduced them. Jessie recognised them as the kids from the Cardcaptor videos, and all the boys were equally shocked to realise said videos were more like documentaries.

"We've sorta gotten together to track down one of the homunculi who attacked the school a few months back, remember?" said Nathan. The boys nodded stoically at the recollection. "The Regiment's also been trying to get the Kakugane out of my chest," Nathan went on. "So far nothing."

"Who cares?" exclaimed Klein. "You should be using that power to kick arse."

Astrid glared at Nathan. "Now I know where you get it from."

"And you too, Astrid," said Klein.

Paul interjected, "And since you've got allies there with you, it's like you're forming a bit of a team there. You should go all out."

Soul chortled, "I think you're goin' a bit off the rails, *mate*." The boys on the screen laughed.

"Remember what I said, Nathan," said Klein. "The world should see you for what you are. You guys should make something of this, ya know."

Astrid waved him off. "That's a bit too far, Klein. Soul and Xiaolang's organisations don't really mix well."

"But we are," muttered Soul, his eyes fixed on the battle-scarred girl.

Nathan quickly changed the subject. "Klein, is Ariadne there?"

"I'd've brought her in if she was," said Klein. "She hasn't been back to school since the L.X.E. attacked. I figured your parents took her."

"And she hasn't called?" asked Nathan hopefully. Klein shook his head. Nathan sighed. "She's not online either. If you get in touch, let her know I'm thinking about her. Okay?"

"Got it, mate," said Klein.

"You just figure out your stuff, alright?" said Jessie.

"And forget about the cricket ball too," urged Paul.

Nathan harrumphed, "Will do."

The call ended. Nathan leaned back in the chair and sighed contently. He felt Astrid grip his hand warmly, and he squeezed it in reply.

"What's this about a cricket ball?" asked Sakura. Nathan just waved her off.

Soul couldn't stop grinning. A line of drool leaked between his sharp teeth, and he chuckled, "Sounds pretty cool though ... a team." The other four smiled at the thought, though Astrid and Xiaolang were less enthused than Sakura and Nathan.

Sakura yawned and plonked down on the sofa next to Nathan. Soul sat on the arm of the sofa and leaned back against the cushions. Astrid and Xiaolang exchanged glances, and then said, "Who wants a drink?"

The other three gave their requests, and Astrid led Xiaolang to the vending machines. They exchanged coins for the desired products, and then made their way back to Nathan's holding cell.

"She must've really got you," said Astrid, a cheeky smile riding on her lips.

"Like a wrecking ball," replied Xiaolang. Then he shot a sly glance at his old friend. "But *you!* I never saw you smile so easily before. And what's this about you baking cookies? You once said you'd never go into a kitchen! What did Nathan do to you?"

"What do you mean, do to me?" cried Astrid, her hand clasped over her chest.

"You know I didn't mean *that*," said Xiaolang, blushing slightly.

Astrid sighed and thought about her experiences over the last two years. Despite all the insanity, she couldn't help but smile at every single shenanigan, each catastrophe, and every pain Nathan caused her. Because, she had to admit, it had been the most fun she'd ever had.

"It wasn't what he did to me," she said pensively. "It's what *I* did to *him*. I gave him a new life with that Kakugane, and he gave me a new life in return."

She raised her eyes to meet Xiaolang's gaze, and saw her friend grinning.

"Sounds like you found your Number One," he said. Astrid turned away, fuming and blushing, which only invited more teasing. "Astrid and Nathan, sittin' in a tree ..."

"Shut up!" grumbled Astrid.

They made it back to Nathan's holding cell just as Maka came storming in. The irate blonde blew her bangs out of her face and exclaimed, "What are all you doing, just lounging about? And drinking soda while you're at it?"

"We're waitin', Maka," said Soul. "Not much we can do until they get Moonface to talk."

"Well, Bravo and Papa are interrogating him now," said Maka prissily.

"Let me know how it goes then," said Nathan. "I'm stuck in here."

Sakura recalled the image of Moonface in the interrogation chamber, and shuddered at the thought. She declined to go. Xiaolang opted to stay with his girlfriend. Astrid preferred to keep an eye on Nathan after his earlier stunt. Soul simply moaned, "Interrogations ain't cool."

Maka groaned, "Are you being serious? The fate of the world could be at stake. And you just want to wait around?"

"Hey, when Bravo gets the location of Moonface's base, then we'll go," said Soul. He tossed her a can of soda. "In the meantime, chill, girl."

Maka rolled her eyes, but fatigue weighied her down. She finally sat down on the sofa with the rest of the group, and sipped her drink.

14 | Interrogation

Spirit and Bravo gazed through the annular window, straight at Moonface. The homunculus writhed with discomfort, but still kept a wide grin. Bravo silently wondered if that was Nikolaev's only expression, regardless of whether he was happy or in white-hot agony.

"I don't like this," said Spirit, crossing his arms. "He looks like he's having the time of his life. He's worse than my first meister." The man shuddered at the recollection.

"All that means is he's a masochist," said Bravo.

"No, it's more than that," said Spirit. "I just think he's leading you on. I mean, you had a tough time taking him on at that school. And then the son of the Lee Clan, who's magic isn't even at full power, manages to take him out?"

"Mind you, Moonface had a Kakugane when he fought me," said Bravo. "So far, our intelligence suggests the L.X.E. remnants have only conventional weapons. No match for a magician even as novice as Kinomoto."

Spirit shrugged, "Good point." He huffed. "Well, I'm a little inexperienced with homunculi, so I'll let you take first swing."

"That was the plan," said Bravo, shooting the Demon Weapon a glance that yelled, "Stay off my turf!" He entered a code into the panel beside the door, which slid open with a hiss. The gnashing of Moonface's teeth reverberated through the cell, but that only excited Bravo even more.

"Moon! Fancy that! A Demon Weapon working with an Alchemic Warrior," rasped the homunculus. He leaned as far forward as he could and sniffed at Spirit. "Oooh, and a Death Scythe no less."

Bravo procured his Kakugane from his pocket and activated it. A metal jacket formed over his body. Then he threw a meteoric punch across Moonface's cheek. The creature gurgled black blood and spat out a tooth.

"I see your interrogation methods haven't changed," groaned the homunculus. "Last time I was caught, I escaped because one of those delectable ... dumb-faces got too close." The noise had evidently reached a new level of pain for him, and he found it difficult to concentrate. "Got my hands on a Kakugane and *kaboom!* Bye-bye, Restigouche!"

"Where's Shaula Gorgon?" snarled Bravo.

"In my pants!" retorted Moonface.

Bravo threw another swipe, knocking more teeth from the homunculus' mouth. They quickly regenerated, completing his immovable grin.

"Where is Shaula Gorgon?" Bravo repeated. Moonface shrugged, and Bravo hit him again.

The homunculus continued to giggle as Bravo hit him harder and harder, black blood dribbling from between his teeth. His chuckles mixed in with agonised gasps and wails, yet they persisted. Moonface eyed Spirit, whose lips were pursed with concern.

"You don't like this anymore than I do," grumbled Moonface.

Spirit sneered, and his hand transformed into a black scythe blade. "Trust me, I'd gladly end your ass. Don't think I feel for your kind."

"Yes," chortled Moonface. "I am the Asura Egg to your Demon Weapon." The homunculus glared up at Bravo and snarled, "But the Reaper didn't create the Asura, did he?"

Spirit glanced at Bravo with a twinge of confusion. He knew that the antecedents of the Regiment had created the homunculi centuries ago, but the tone of Moonface's voice told him that there was something personal at work.

"You made the choice to become a monster, Nikolaev," spat Bravo as he massaged his hand. "Don't play the victim now."

The homunculus started to laugh in long languid cackles. He spat out another mouthful of black blood and glanced at Spirit. "Like smokers and lung cancer ... they brought it on themselves, so they don't deserve our care, eh?

"And what of the single mother who lost a child to cancer, and could never get past it? What about the awkward boy with a fondness for pink, lynched by bigots and forever traumatised? What about the child who watched from afar the fall of those towers, but couldn't see his father leaping from the roof? What of the father whose daughter was groomed?

"*They* didn't bring it on themselves to become Asura Eggs ... no! It was the big bad world! So they get quick deaths ... because it's not *their* fault."

Spirit had been so transfixed by Moonface's words, he hadn't noticed Bravo's breathing quicken. He fell back in shock as Bravo proceeded to savagely beat the homunculus in the chair. He reached forward and pulled the manic Bravo away from the prisoner.

"Commander, calm down!" yelled Spirit.

Moonface's visage was almost a black liquid, like bubbling tar. He struggled to breathe through the swelling. Yet he somehow stayed alive. The wounds healed, but slowly, owing to his advancing hunger.

"That's how we do things," panted Bravo as he came down from his rage high. "We put these things under discomfort, and then injure them until the hunger gets to them. Then they'll tell us whatever we want." He turned to Spirit. "It's the advantage of dealing with creatures that still have some semblance of humanity, even if it is twisted."

Spirit pursed his lips. He almost wanted to bring his daughter in to check the status of Bravo's soul – just in case there wasn't any risk of a future Asura Egg. He turned to Moonface, who was motionless save for the slow rising and fall of his chest.

"What's your plan?" asked Spirit.

"Status quo," muttered Moonface. He forced his head up to look at the men. "You have fought wars against Asuras, Witches, and Homunculi, for centuries. All for what? To stem the world's tendency to chaos? All you've done is cause more chaos … more *madness.*"

"We protect order in the world," said Bravo proudly.

"And who are you to declare what order the world should be in?" spat Moonface. "Who is the Reaper to decide that?"

"One who is wiser and more powerful than you," proclaimed Spirit.

"Not for long," chuckled Moonface, though it came out in a fit of coughs and splutters. "The Silver Key will open the Ultimate Gate – the doorway to a new order!" Bravo choked, overcome with a horrified realisation. "Moon! You know what the Silver Key does, don't you?" mumbled Moonface.

Bravo wasted no time. He punched Moonface up and down the torso. He then gripped the homunculus' arms and glanced at Spirit.

"His fingers!" he yelled.

Spirit drew a deep breath and, with his hand as a scythe blade, lopped off the homunculus' fingers. Black blood pooled on the floor as the digits disintegrated into smoke. Moonface wailed, finding it more difficult to speak. The fingers regrew, and Spirit cut them off again. They repeated the process meticulously, Bravo growing more furious and Spirit becoming more reluctant.

"Fine!" bellowed Moonface. He panted and sobbed, anxious to be done with the whole interrogation.

"Somerset Dam," he moaned. "That's where she is. She's holding Doctor Avalon there too."

"How many?" asked Bravo.

"The remains of my forces … eleven humanoid and thirty-nine animal and plant types," said Moonface with a resigned tone.

Bravo and Spirit stepped away. Bravo deactivated his Silver Skin, and Spirit stowed his scythe form beneath his skin. The exchanged glances and then left the room.

* * *

The hangar of the Regiment headquarters was a flurry of activity as Bravo's strike force prepared to embark. Ten men and women lined up beside an aircraft, with Kakugane strapped to their chests, ready for action. Bravo laid out the plans for the assault, based on the intelligence from Moonface. He pointed to Spirit, Maka, Soul, and Xiaolang, who also stood ready.

"This will be a joint operation with DWMA and the Lee Clan," said Bravo. "Our objectives are to neutralise the enemy force, apprehend Witch Shaula Gorgon, recover the Silver Key, and rescue at least one hostage, Doctor Avalon. All homunculus targets are to be eradicated. Understood?"

"Yes, Captain Bravo!" bellowed the strike force.

"Bravo! Get on board and prepare for take-off," yelled Bravo. He approached Maka and Soul, the former of whom wanted to be as far from her father as possible.

"I'd happily come along, if *he* weren't," snarled the blonde.

"We'll need an extra pair of hands," said Bravo.

Maka pointed at Sakura, who stood behind Xiaolang like a bride seeing off her soldier husband. The blonde complained, "Why isn't *she* coming then? She can fight homunculi."

"I want her here looking after the Silver Key," said Xiaolang.

"What about Nathan and Astrid?" exclaimed Maka.

"They're grounded," snapped Bravo. "I can't trust two loose cannons in the field. And," he glanced at Sakura, "no offence, Miss Kinomoto, but I don't think it'll be best for you to be there. I'm afraid you'll get distracted, since your father's involved."

Sakura pursed her lips to hide her relief. She chastised herself for her cowardice as she said, "Just bring him home." Her words were more directed at Xiaolang, who turned and kissed her forehead.

"I'll definitely bring him home," he said confidently. He tapped the box in Sakura's arms. "You just keep this close, okay?"

Sakura nodded with determination. She trembled with fear as Xiaolang's touch left her. The ground crew guided her away as the aircraft lifted off and soared through the hangar door. She skulked back to Nathan's holding cell.

"They've deployed?" asked Astrid upon Sakura's entry. Sakura nodded, but said nothing more.

"And left us with our thumbs up our bums," grumbled Nathan as he stretched out on one of the chairs.

"We *did* disobey orders," said Astrid. "I'll be lucky to get a desk job after that."

She huffed with irritation. Her hands had been shaking with idleness ever since she'd handed over the Kakugane. As she gritted her teeth, she noticed Sakura plonk down on the chair opposite her. The girl had a troubled expression.

"I wish I was home," said Sakura when Astrid asked. "I'm only here because I won a trip to Hong Kong in a lottery. I only wanted to see Xiaolang." She gripped the box in her hand tightly. "Now I'm in a foreign country, on my own, in a strange place, where there's cannibal monsters that kidnapped my Dad and …"

She broke down.

Astrid's expression softened and she strode across the cell to sit beside the distraught girl. She hesitantly reached out and patted the girl's head in an effort to comfort her. She felt clumsy doing it, but it diminished Sakura's sobs. The girl shifted toward Astrid and placed her head on her shoulder, surprising the older woman.

Sakura looked up at Astrid and said, "Thank you, Miss Rachelle. You're a nice person."

"You're welcome," said Astrid. She eyed Nathan, who lounged on the sofa nearby, and silently thanked him and his younger sister.

Were it not for you, I wouldn't be able to do this, she thought.

Sakura sniffed back her tears and sighed, "You're way nicer than that girl, Maka."

"I reckon," chuckled Nathan. "What's up her butt, anyway?"

Astrid shook her head incredulously, as did Nathan. Sakura wiped away the last of her tears and mumbled, "If she smiled, she'd probably look really cute."

"Who would?" chimed a voice that made Astrid gasp with dismay.

Sakura shot up in surprise and exclaimed, "Eriol! What're you doing here?"

"Just consulting," said Eriol. He brushed off the guard who tried to dissuade him from entering the cell. Then he glanced at Astrid and said, "Triddy! How's it going?"

Astrid wished her glare could kill.

"Do not call me Triddy," she growled.

"Oooh, so scary," retorted Eriol.

"Wait, Astrid, you know Eriol?" asked Sakura.

"From a long time ago," muttered Astrid. "We worked on a mission together, and he was just unbearable! No sense of respect for privacy or even human decency." Eriol let out a pshaw, but said nothing more. Astrid glared at Sakura. "I assume he trained you in magic?"

"In a sense," said Sakura, smiling warmly at the man. "He disguised himself as an English teacher at my school and secretly helped me transform the Clow Cards into my own."

"Well, if you know him, how can you put up with him?" exclaimed Astrid. "He's so obnoxious."

"He's quirky," said Sakura, looking affectionately at Eriol. "And I like quirky people."

Eriol smiled warmly in gratitude. But Astrid wouldn't have it.

"Coyote's perfectly normal, and you like him," she said.

"He attacked me when we first met," retorted Sakura.

"He's what!?" exclaimed Astrid.

Eriol left the girls to talk about Xiaolang, and skirted around them toward Nathan. He looked down at the boy, still lounging on the couch. He smiled softly, and his gaze pierced into the boy.

"I'm honoured to finally meet you, Starlight Lancer," he said.

"I take it you're another wizard or something?" said Nathan. He stood and looked the Scotsman in the eye.

"I am Eriol Lamperouge," he said, holding his hand out.

Nathan gave a one-sided smile and said, "Nathan Grant." He took the man's hand and shook it.

In the blink of an eye, the room around Nathan vanished. He found himself standing amid a sea of stars. Around him stood five silhouettes, each of them holding some kind of weapon or staff. Despite the brightness of the stars around him, he could not make out their faces. Then he looked outward. A forest of spiralling galaxies surrounded him. In the distance, he saw one of them disappear. Then another suddenly vanished, then another, and then another. Some shadowy entity grew closer and, as it did, Nathan realised the galaxies were being consumed in its wake.

The entity besieged him and the ghostly figures around him.

Then he held up his lance, and the others around him held up their own weapons. Terrific luminance burst from them, blasting outward toward the entity. Bars of light cleaved the entity, shredding it until it was gone, leaving the stars around them to shine in ever-increasing brightness.

Nathan found himself back in his cell. He was still holding Eriol's hand, and the girls were still gossiping. Not a second of time had passed.

Eriol noticed the boy's perturbed expression and he inquired, "Something the matter?"

Nathan's brow furrowed with confusion. He couldn't work out whether the vision had been a memory, a fantasy, or something else entirely. But he elected not to discuss it. He shrugged Eriol off, and sat back down.

Eriol regarded the boy with a wide smile. He sat down beside Nathan, and glanced over at Astrid and Sakura. He said, "Thanks for keeping Sakura company. It'll help keep her mind off her father's rescue mission."

"No problem," said Nathan. "To be honest, it's nice to have visitors."

15 | Skirmish in the Dam

The Alchemic Regiment's stealth craft cleaved the high skies. Its crew was restless. Most of them stood eager to cleanse the Earth of more homunculi. Others were determined finish the job so they could go home. One in particular just wanted to save his future father-in-law.

Of course, should you be thinking about that? Xiaolang asked himself. *Oh, come on. You knew it the moment you saw her.*

Xiaolang's hand clenched with determination, earning a few glances from the Alchemic Warriors lining the plane's cabin. Some turned their noses up at his age and stature, while others regarded his magical nature with awe.

Soul glanced his way, and found himself curious about something else entirely. He unbuckled his harness and stood, much to the chagrin of his meister.

"Soul! Where are you going?" snapped Maka.

"I ain't your daddy-shield," retorted Soul as he walked down the cabin to Xiaolang. Spirit took the moment to shift one seat over to chat with his unwilling daughter.

Soul sat down next to Xiaolang with a sigh.

"*Shao-lan* is the right pronunciation?" he asked. Xiaolang corrected him, but Soul still got it wrong. "Sounds like Bruce Lee's real name. No relation?"

"That's Xiao*long*," said Xiaolang. "And no, I'm not related."

"Well, screw it, I'm just gonna call you 'Bruce,'" said Soul. "Listen, I wanted to ask you something."

He directed Xiaolang's gaze to Maka, who leaned away from her jabbering father with a scowl. Spirit paused to wink at one of the female Alchemic Warriors, earning a disgusted scoff from his daughter. Xiaolang pursed his lips and glanced at Soul with a questioning glance.

"You and your girlfriend are so tight," said Soul. "I mean, you're happy together. How did you get her to, ya know, not be like Maka?"

Xiaolang looked hurt by the question, and he quickly replied, "She was *never* like that. Sakura has always been a wonderful person. She does sometimes lose her temper, but only if someone's threatening her or her family. But I didn't have to do anything to make her nice person." He glanced at Maka, who was now plugging her ears. The altercation had become uncomfortable for the other passengers. "Albarn sounds like she has issues you can't fix," he added.

"Yeah," said Soul with a resigned tone. "And you can guess it's the parents."

"Her father looks like he has mental issues," intoned Xiaolang.

"And her mom's dead," said Soul. "Cancer, she told me."

Xiaolang raised an eyebrow. "Sakura too. But her father is a wonderful man. That might have been the difference." He patted Soul on the shoulder. "Sorry, dude, but that's one thing I can't fix."

Soul smirked and shook his head. As Xiaolang withdrew his hand, Soul noticed a stain on his forearm, only slightly hidden by his sleeve.

"Hey, what's this?" he asked inquisitively. Xiaolang held his forearm defensively. "C'mon, man, you got a gang tattoo or somethin'?"

Xiaolang sighed, and rolled back his sleeve to reveal the Rainbow Dash tattoo on his forearm.

"Got a problem?" he muttered.

The corner of Soul's mouth upturned and he glanced around the rest of the cabin. Then he removed his beanie to reveal an embroidered picture of Applejack. Xiaolang chuckled and said, "Respect!" He then fist-bumped Soul.

Soon after, the pilot announced they were nearing Somerset Dam. It was dark out, with sparse light from the township to the southwest. The pilot landed the craft silently behind the hill on the opposite side of the lake. The troops flooded from the craft's rear hatch and took up positions looking out over the dam. Bravo left two soldiers with the craft as defence, and then moved to the lookout.

"Commander Costable, I make two guarded entrances on either side of the river," said one of the Alchemic Warriors as he glanced through a set of binoculars.

"Warrior Sati," said Bravo. "You have a rifle form to your Arms Alchemy, correct? Take up a sniper position and radio when you have a shot." The Indian woman to his left nodded and skulked through the trees, down the hill toward an outcropping of rocks. She concealed the flash of her weapon's activation, and laid it on the rock.

"I have a shot on both entrances, Commander," said the woman.

Spirit whispered to Maka, who closed her eyes and reached out with her soul. She sensed the horde of homunculi within the dam. Among them, she could smell the familiar wretched stink of Shaula Gorgon. A single, distraught human soul sat near her.

"That's likely Sakura's father," said Xiaolang.

"They're on the west side, lower floor," said Maka. "But there's something else. There's a soul I can't identify on the east side. It's alone in a square chamber on the upper floor."

"They've got another hostage, maybe," said Soul.

Bravo interjected, "Alright! Alpha team takes the east side. Kill everything with black blood, and check if they've got another hostage. Spirit, Coyote, Maka, Soul, you're with them. Beta team is with me. We'll take the west and rescue Doctor Avalon and secure the Silver Key."

"I'm going to get Mister Kinomoto," Xiaolang snapped.

"And you'll need me against Shaula," said Maka.

"You should take them, Costable," said Spirit.

Bravo huffed, annoyed at being disobeyed. He acquiesced and said, "Ten minutes, in and out. Understood?"

"Yes sir," said the battalion.

Bravo leaned into his radio. "Sati, wait for my signal then take out the guards." The woman replied obediently.

The battalion, Bravo included, placed their hands to the Kakugane on their chests and proclaimed, "Arms Alchemy." Their weapons materialised in technicoloured flashes. Xiaolang clapped his hands to summon his sword, and Soul took his scythe form in Maka's hands.

"Mission start," said Bravo.

Alpha and beta team started down the hill. They moved with all speed, making every effort to not disturb the foliage as they descended. They reached the river, at which point they halted just short of the woodland's edge. Bravo issued the order, and a second later, the sentries at the east entrance collapsed and disintegrated. The sentries at the west entrance, spooked by the final grunts of their comrades, darted out of the way of the sniper fire.

"Shit!" growled Bravo. Panic filled him as the sentry reached for the alarm button.

Useless frigging tools, Maka internally growled. She lunged forward, out of the clearing, toward the west entrance. Soul didn't get a chance to protest before Maka leapt through the air, twirling his scythe form, and decapitating one of the sentries. The other tried to fight back, but Maka hooked her blade between his legs and cleaved him in half. She blew her dishevelled fringe out of the way and slashed the door open.

"Albarn, wait," pleaded Bravo, but she was already

inside wreaking havoc. "Damn it!" Bravo snapped. "Move in! Move in now!"

Inside the dam, Maka met with three homunculi. Two of them woke with a start to see the third being vivisected by the scythe-meister. Maka twirled her weapon to deflect the bullets from their guns, before depriving them of their arms, legs, and finally heads.

"Maka, wait for the others," Soul growled.

"They'll just slow us down," retorted Maka as she embedded Soul's blade in a gecko-type homunculus' head. She marched down the sparsely lit corridor. She took out another homunculus in the middle of a transformation into a mechanical moth, but didn't notice the incoming humanoid enemies wielding sub-machine guns. Soul heard them, reverted to his human form, and dragged Maka into an open storage closet.

"You almost got yourself killed, Maka," snarled Soul. "Wait for the others."

"This is Shaula we're talking about, Soul," retorted Maka over the sounds of gunfire and clashing of Arms Alchemies. "We have to get her for Abhilasha and Tamika! Or have you forgotten that?"

Soul rubbed the bridge of his nose. "Jesus Christ, Maka! You know how I feel about that, so don't be unfair."

Maka fumed. "Then help me get her! We don't need these Regiment hacks!"

"And how do you know that Shaula isn't killing Sakura's dad right now?" asked Soul. Maka made an expression loaded with surprise, disgust, and fury. Soul stepped back as much as the closet would allow and said, "Ah, so *that's* what this is about."

"I don't know what you mean," grumbled Maka, diverting her eyes.

At that, the door burst open, a Silver Skin-clad Bravo wresting it from its hinges.

"What's this? Make out time?" he barked. "Get your

arses out of there and do your job!" Then he went back to beating the homunculi with his fist.

Soul and Maka exchanged glances. She let out a sigh and held out her hand. He took it, and transformed into a scythe. Maka leapt out from the closet and filleted a piscine homunculus.

"She's on the lower floor," she said after checking with her soul perception.

Bravo turned to his warriors. "You handle all the homunculi on this level and the ones above." To Maka and Xiaolang, he yelled, "You're with me." He darted down the corridor and turned left. He held his arms out and made a shield of his Silver Skin, which blocked the barrage of bullets the homunculi sent his way. He heard their guns click, at which point he lowered his shield.

Maka raced forward, again without permission. The lead homunculus had already started to contort and shed her skin. Maka brought Soul's blade down on the creature's head, but it passed through it as if it were made of gel. The homunculus assumed its true jellyfish form. Maka darted backward as a scorpion homunculus beared its pincers and swiped at her. She tried to deflect its blows with the handle of Soul's scythe form, but the space was cramped.

"*Huŏ shén zhāolái!*" bellowed Xiaolang. A stream of fire burst down the corridor, darting harmlessly around Maka, and enveloping the homunculi. The jellyfish evaporated while the scorpion shrieked and thrashed before her. Then Bravo dashed past her like a streak of silver, and embedded his fist in the creature's thorax, ending it.

Bravo glared at her from beneath his encompassing coat, and then raced down the corridor. Maka cursed him for making her feel foolish.

Watch yourself, Albarn, thought Soul.

Xiaolang passed her as well and brandished a paper charm.

"If Sakura's father is dead, I'll blame you," he said with

a menacing tone.

Soul's face appeared in the sheen of his blade and said, "Don't threaten my meister." He had to admit, though, Maka had it coming.

Maka watched Xiaolang and Bravo head down the stairs to the lower level. She drew a deep breath and steeled herself.

I must get Shaula, she thought.

She followed the pair down the stairs, and took out the homunculi Xiaolang and Bravo had missed. Bravo kicked down the door that was no longer guarded, revealing a brightly lit laboratory. A stack of networked computers lay in the corner, their number crunching having turned the room into an oven. Along one wall was a bench covered in papers, drawings, photos, and notebooks. A rectangular outline marred the concrete floor, indicating that something had been moved recently.

"Doctor Avalon!" yelled Bravo. Maka looked over and saw Bravo and Xiaolang frantically release a man tied to a chair in the corner. Xiaolang delicately tore away the duct tape over the man's lips, allowing the man to unleash his horrified shrieks.

"Mister Kinomoto, are you alright?" asked Xiaolang.

"Mister Lee?" panted Franklin. He seemed delirious.

"We need to get out of here now, Doctor Avalon," said Bravo.

"Wait! Where's Shaula?" yelled Maka.

Franklin hardly took notice of her as he faltered and gasped for breath. His eyes unfocused a moment, and then widened in horror. He looked at the large circular hatch on the wall beside him. He stammered incoherently, pointing at the hatch. Maka tried to slash it open, but Soul's blade couldn't even dent it. Xiaolang stepped forward and cast out a paper charm.

"*Léidì zhàolái!*" he proclaimed. The seams of the hatch crackled with electricity, and the locks broke. Bravo then grabbed the edges of the hatch and wrested it open.

Beyond was a makeshift hangar, as if someone had haphazardly scraped away the bedrock. A saucer-shaped craft stood in the hangar. The design reminded Bravo of Doctor Butterfly's rejuvenation tank. From the cockpit window, Shaula Gorgon waved. Her red-cyan eyes glimmered mischievously, as if not even her mangled hair could dampen her spirits.

It made Maka's blood boil. She raced forward.

"Maka, stop!" snapped Soul.

Maka's face hit the ground as Franklin tackled her. He wrested her up and dragged her out of the chamber. Ignoring her protests, the terrified man looked at Bravo and Xiaolang.

"We have to get out of here!" he cried. "This hangar is going to flood!"

Just as he finished yelling, the saucer's underside flashed blue. The craft then blasted through the ceiling of the hangar. Seconds later, water started to crash into the chamber.

"*Bīng shén zhāolái!*" yelled Xiaolang. A floe burst from his sword and sealed the hatch with a wall of ice. Sweat quickly beaded on his brow as he threw as much energy into the floe as he could. He released his breath in a low sigh and leaned against his sword. "That won't hold for long," he said.

Bravo tapped his radio and exclaimed, "All units, fall back. Fall back now!" He and Xiaolang hooked their arms under Franklin's shoulders and fled the room. Maka lingered a moment longer, much to Soul's worry, and scanned the notes on the table.

"Oh, my God," she whispered.

The ice barrier started to crack, drawing her attention from the unsettling documents.

"Maka, let's go!" snapped Soul. Maka finally obeyed, and sprinted through the door. She caught up with Bravo, Xiaolang, and Franklin at the top of the staircase. They then made for the exit.

Bravo touched his radio a second time. "All units, pull out. The dam is about to flood."

"Bravo, we've got a situation here," replied Spirit's voice.

"Did you secure the other hostage?" asked Bravo.

"Negative," said Spirit, his tone nervous.

"Never mind then, fall back!" repeated Bravo. He and Xiaolang carried Franklin out of the exit, followed by Maka, just as the dam started to shudder. Far behind them, the ice barrier broke, and water rushed into the dam, like a tornado through a sleepy town.

On the east side, alpha team scurried from the exit. A few were injured, being shouldered by their comrades. They sprinted across the small bridge connecting the two banks, just as water blasted out the east and west entrances. The river started to rise over the bridge, knocking over several Alchemic Warriors. Xiaolang drew a paper charm and used his magic to hold back the incoming tide. It gave alpha team just enough time to make it across the bridge.

Bravo diverted them all into the woods as quickly as possible, and ordered them up the hill toward the stealth craft. Spirit raced up the hill ahead of his team, almost knocking over Maka in the process. He finally caught up to Bravo, who was commanding the stealth craft pilot to track Shaula's ship.

"Costable!" he yelled for the third time. "We have a problem!"

"What?" snarled a stressed Bravo.

"That other hostage wasn't a hostage," said Spirit.

"What do you mean, Papa?" exclaimed Maka.

"It was Moonface," blurted Spirit.

"Spirit, are you high?" exclaimed Soul. "Moonface is back at Regiment HQ!"

"He's not lying," said a wounded member of the alpha team. "It was Moonface in that chamber."

"But that couldn't be," replied Bravo. He thought for a

moment, until a horrible idea dawned on him. "Unless …"

At the foot of the hill, the Somerset Dam started to buckle. The residents of Lake Wivenhoe were about to have a really bad night. But it wouldn't be nearly as bad as what the Regiment Headquarters were soon to experience.

16 | The Trojan

It took longer than Moonface had expected for his wounds to heal. Though it wasn't surprising, given the strength of the mad man who made them. The languid pace of his recovery was fortunate, however, as it concealed the nature of what he hid in his stomach.

Moonface stretched out his yellow face and clenched his teeth to loosen up his skin. Then he eyed the watch, still intact on his wrist.

Just in time, he thought malevolently.

He reached deep within, tightening his stomach and chest muscles. He pushed upward with his gut, slowly edging an object up his oesophagus. A heavy metal pellet slid upward into his mouth, which he held within his teeth. He took aim at the glass window, drew a deep breath, and spat the ball. It dinged against the glass, but didn't break it.

That wasn't the point.

The warrior guarding the cell shot up with a start. He looked into the cell and saw Moonface grinning and chortling. The homunculus started to convulse and gag. Curiosity overcame the man. He placed his hand on the Kakugane on his chest.

If it moves, I can kill it in a heartbeat, he thought confidently. Then he opened the cell and stood with his toes just beyond the threshold.

"What is it, you piece of garbage?" muttered the

warrior.

Moonface grinned, and then spat out another object. This one was larger. It cracked open in mid-air, revealing the writhing, voracious creature that had waited within. The veiny, bio-mechanical thing pawed and slashed at the air between it and the man, whose blood ran cold. He didn't get a chance to activate his Arms Alchemy, before the creature landed on his eye and savagely clawed its way into his head. He shrieked with panic, before falling to the ground, gripping his head and wailing.

He soon stopped thrashing and fell limp, only to awake a split-second later with a strident gasp. The man rose to his feet and gazed absentmindedly at Moonface.

"Release me, you neonate knob-head," exclaimed Moonface. The newborn homunculus summoned its host's memory, and moved forward to release the restraints. Moonface pivoted onto his feet with a long, relieved sigh. He then regurgitated a broach in the shape of a crescent moon, which he set to his shirt. Instantly, his flesh and clothing renewed themselves, much to his delight.

"Moon!" he giggled. He checked his watch. "Shaula should show shortly. Let's steal that Silver Key, eh?" His new slave grunted obediently.

Moonface strode out of the cell. He regurgitated another capsule and smashed it onto the head of an approaching warrior. The embryo therein happily dove through the woman's skull and possessed her. Moonface regurgitated ten more capsules and handed them to his new subordinates.

"Courier some chaos, kiddies!" he chirped. The homunculi grinned most maliciously, and then started down the hall in opposite directions. Meanwhile, Moonface shuddered, and split off a clone of himself, the head in a gibbous shape. He did this repeatedly, until thirty of him lined the hall. Each of them complemented each other on their handsomeness, before darting down the corridor, in search of the Silver Key.

* * *

Alarm bells blared throughout the compound. Nathan and Astrid shot up, while Sakura whimpered with worry and confusion. Eriol frowned in alarm. Astrid marched across the cell and banged on the doors.

"Report!" she bellowed.

The door slid open and the guard poked his head in. "Moonface has escaped custody. There are homunculi in the facility."

"What?" yelled Astrid.

"How the Hell is that possible?" exclaimed Nathan.

"General Rodrigo has dispatched security," said the guard. "You are all to remain here."

"Rubbish!" snarled Nathan. "Your warriors are all out at Somerset Dam! If Moonface got out, we're the best ones to take him."

"He's got a point," said Eriol.

The guard pointed at Eriol and barked, "You're not an authority here, Scotsman! Stay put!" Something grabbed the guard's leg. He grunted in surprise, and then shrieked in horror as a long tentacle dragged him out of the cellblock. His cries abruptly ended, followed by a slurping sound. A series of heavy, wet footfalls echoed from around the corner, and a giant mechanical mole appeared in the corridor.

Astrid backed away, her arm around a trembling Sakura.

"Nathan, I don't have a Kakugane," she yelled.

Nathan, meanwhile, was breathing slowly in an attempt to settle his mind. He muttered, "Give me a second, or I'll go Victor."

"Eriol, use your magic," pleaded Sakura as she gripped the Silver Key box.

The Scotsman was already in action. He procured his sun-shaped key from his breast pocket, and hastily activated it. The mole lunged at the sight of his wand, which issued a fire blast. The creature flailed about, smashing the walls of the cell, setting the flammable parts of the room ablaze.

"Nathan!" yelled Astrid in alarm.

Nathan saw the mole, its carapace smouldering. The homunculus glared at Astrid, and the tentacles on its nose flagellated with hunger. Suddenly, Nathan's chest exploded with dark and purple discharges. In the next instant, he had buried his lance in the mole's body, and the thing disintegrated. The death of the creature stirred within him an unbelievable sense of satisfaction, and he relished the sight of the black blood that oozed from its wrecked metal carapace.

Nathan felt a tiny sting on his shoulder, as if someone had thrown a small pebble at it. He glanced over and saw Eriol, panting and sweating as if he'd run a marathon. Wisps of energy wafted from him, Astrid, and Sakura, toward Nathan's feet. Nathan looked down in terror to see his skin had turned crimson.

I went Victor!

He fell to his knees in a panic, and gripped his chest to find some semblance of a centre. The sight of his friends slowly losing their energy horrified him, and made his point of control a moving target. He grit his teeth and punched the floor in an effort to control the monster within, but the fight was not going his way. He looked at Astrid, who stared straight back at him. Her eyes, weighed down by fatigue, pierced into him, and reminded him of the day he'd come back to life for the second time.

Only your body has become a monster like him! Don't let your mind go too.

Those words had been the spell that brought him back. He gripped his lance tightly, and pressed his other hand to his chest.

My mind has not changed … My mind has not changed …

He repeated the mantra over and over, until he found that steady rock amid the maelstrom of power and hunger. He grabbed onto that place in his mind and, with a roar, deactivated his Arms Alchemy. His crimson skin broke off from his body like a glass coating, revealing his human form underneath. He felt dizzy. He glanced over, and saw Eriol barely able to stand. Astrid nursed Sakura, who was delirious.

Nathan scrambled over and hoisted Eriol to his feet.

"I hit you with everything I had," exclaimed the Scotsman weakly.

"You're getting stronger," grumbled Astrid.

Nathan didn't like the sound of that at all. He glanced around the wrecked cell and sighed.

"We need to get out of here," he said.

Eriol shook his head and slapped his knees to get feeling back into them. Then he edged out of the cell, using his wand as a walking stick. Astrid pulled herself up with sheer willpower, and tried to rouse Sakura. The girl was definitely breathing, but was sound asleep. Nathan lifted her onto his shoulders and Astrid grabbed the box containing the Silver Key. They followed Eriol down the hall. The corridors of the building echoed with screaming and booms, evidence of Moonface's mayhem.

"What should we do?" asked Eriol.

"Obviously, we need to get out of headquarters," said Astrid. "We can get to the hangar this way." She led them down an adjacent corridor. She stopped a moment to pick up the Kakugane left by the mole's last meal. She activated it, and her Valkyrie Skirt's blades stood at the ready. She led the way, Eriol bringing up the rear.

They passed through a number of passageways, before reaching the hangar bay. It was chaos. At least two homunculi were wreaking havoc against teams of technicians and engineers armed only with handguns.

"Don't they know those won't kill homunculi?" exclaimed Eriol.

"There aren't any more Kakugane available!" replied Astrid. She thrust the Silver Key box into Eriol's arms and raced forward. The surviving officers saw her advance and cheered desperately, alerting the homunculi to her presence. The one nearest the cowering group, having taken the shape of a wolf, snarled and galloped to meet her. It lunged, and tilted its head to ensnare her in its open jaws. Astrid slipped onto her backside, and slid under the beast. With her blades outstretched either side, she sliced through the homunculus' legs, leaving the creature to hobble on four stumps. It leaked black blood from its stump legs as Astrid skidded to a halt, and then leapt back over the monster and stabbed it through the head.

Amid the battle, Eriol leaned toward Nathan and muttered, "God, I miss watching this."

"Too right," replied Nathan.

Astrid turned and charged the other homunculus. The hulking mass of vines resembled a metal Venus flytrap, whose wide jaws clapped together as it snared one of the unarmed officers. The vines constricted the man, constraining his flailing arms as they brought him near the creature's gaping mouth. Astrid sliced through the vines, and then launched herself onto the creature. She hacked and slashed until the wailing being was no more.

Eriol and Nathan moved into the hangar toward Astrid and the other technicians. It was then that Sakura started to stir, and realised she was clinging to Nathan's back.

"You can put me down," she mumbled. Nathan released her, and Eriol handed her the Silver Key box after checking her condition. She yawned, "Was just tired. It felt almost like changing a Clow Card."

Eriol eyed Nathan and said, "It's a lot worse than that. Keep the Silver Key close, and get ready to use your magic."

Sakura's eyes darted around the hangar, and noticed the decaying homunculus nearby. Everyone else was still on high alert. Sakura activated her Star Wand reluctantly, and resonated with the Cards in her pocket. They stood at the ready, and she gazed toward the entrances.

"How many more hostiles?" Astrid asked a nearby

officer.

"Two came into the hangar," said the officer. "We're getting word of more from else where in HQ. They have micro incubators for homunculi embryos."

"Moonface must've swallowed them before getting captured," Eriol concluded.

"The bastard planned this," snarled Astrid. She glanced at Nathan. "You able to fight."

"I doubt it," said Nathan. "I don't think I'm centred enough to activate my Arms Alchemy without going Victor."

"Going what?" asked Sakura.

"I'll explain later," said Nathan.

Astrid turned to the officer. "Any transports able to fly?"

"Them beasts smashed the engines of every plane we got," said the officer.

"Shit!" bellowed Astrid.

Suddenly, the wall of the hangar exploded. Debris and rubble rained down upon the small group. Sakura quickly cast out the Guard Card, and the shrapnel harmlessly dinged against her shield. She then cast out Gale to clear away the smoke, which earned her a round of applause from the smartly-dressed figure standing in the middle of the destruction.

"Moon! Such marvellous magic, Madame!" exclaimed Moonface. He held out his hand and beckoned. "Relinquish the riches!" Sakura gripped the Silver Key box tightly. She raised her wand with a hostile expression. Moonface sighed with disappointment. "Oh well, I'll come and coerce you then."

Eriol held up his wand and shot a beam of energy straight through the homunculus. The smiling creature promptly vanished in a puff of smoke. Before anyone could relax, another Moonface emerged from the hole in the wall. This one had a different shaped head.

"Moonface has an Arms Alchemy!" yelled Astrid.

"Everyone, fall back."

The group started to move away, as Moonface advanced. More emerged from the hole, some of them splitting into more Moonface copies. The different phases on the copies' heads grinned wider and wider, as they drew nearer to the group.

"Can you kill us all in one go, Scotsman?" chuckled the Moonfaces in unison.

Eriol's eyes darted between the encroaching army of clones. Sakura's wand shuddered in her hands, while Astrid growled with frustration and mounting fear. Nathan rubbed his chest, making the unarmed technicians nearby even more nervous.

The group heard footfalls to the left, and glanced over. They saw a female Regiment officer charging from one of the hangar entrances. She was alone.

Warrior Peterson, thought Astrid, recognising the woman as the sole survivor of Moonface and Shaula's first attack. But the woman seemed almost delighted.

Astrid glanced at the Moonface army, who giggled. A horrific realisation set in.

"Everybody watch out!" Astrid yelled.

It was too late. Warrior Peterson leapt into the air, and her body contorted and split at the seams. A mass of metal and entrails burst from her unhinged mouth and folded in on itself, forming a mechanical cephalopod. The ballistic creature lashed out with its tentacles, knocking the group over as its beak vectored for Sakura.

"Launch!" Sakura screeched at the last minute. Her shoes sprouted wings and she soared out of the squid's grasp. She landed on the wing of a suspended plane, the Silver Key box held tightly in her white-knuckled hands.

One of the Moonface clones leapt onto the wing and sauntered toward her.

"Stay away!" cried Sakura, unleashing the Lucis Card. A searing laser beam blew Moonface away. But another just appeared, grinning even more maliciously.

"Now, now, munchkin," said Moonface with a wave of his finger. "It's time for you to be a good little girl."

"You're not getting this key!" snapped Sakura.

"Do you even know why you're guarding it?" chuckled another Moonface who appeared from the other direction.

Sakura was being boxed in. She quickly cast out Flight, and flew away from the aircraft. Suddenly, one of the Moonface clones leapt from the floor below, grabbed her, and threw her against a wall. The horrific creature held her there.

"You cannot escape, little cherry blossom," giggled Moonface. His jaw started to widen, and Sakura's body thrashed with panic.

Astrid looked up from battling the squid homunculus to see Sakura at the monster's mercy. Using her mechanical limbs, she launched into the air and sliced the Moonface clone. But she didn't see the other Moonface clone that leapt from outside her field of vision. The clone brought his fists down on her head, propelling her into the floor.

Sakura tried to fly away, saturated with panic and anxiety. It interfered with her resonance link with the Flight Card, which lost energy and sent her to the floor, right amid a quartet of Moonfaces. Between them, she could see Eriol and Nathan wrestling with the squid homunculus. Astrid struggled to stand after that last attack. The technicians, though unarmed, did their best to wrestle with the remaining Moonface clones.

Sakura gasped in horror as one of the Moonfaces gripped one of the officers. His jaw unhinged like a snake and clamped down on the man's head. The man's flesh was practically sucked off his bones. The horrific sight was too much.

Sakura stood, her wand in hand, with nothing but her survival instincts to drive her. She cast out the Flare Card, enveloping the Moonfaces around her in a firestorm. They disintegrated, but another nearby Moonface re-spawned them. Sakura cast out Spark, only to witness the same futility. She prepared to cast out another Card. Suddenly, a Moonface clone raced forward and kicked her in the stomach. She flew into the wall, the wind knocked out of her. She staggered to her feet, only to see one of the clones pick up the Silver Key box and chime, "Moon!"

"No!" she cried weakly. She raised her wand, but couldn't summon enough focus to send out any Cards. The Moonface clones glanced at her and clicked their tongues in an expression of faux sympathy.

By this point, the squid homunculus had knocked Eriol out of the way and had Nathan up against a wall. Its arms had twirled around his arms and legs, and its beak snapped at him. He grabbed the creature's mandibles and gripped them tightly, cutting himself on the sharp edges. He held tightly, even as the tentacles prised at his limbs. The squid's head thrashed and flagellated with frustration, while the surviving officers looked on in awe of a man fighting a homunculus with his bare hands.

Nathan heard one of them stammer, "How?"

He chuckled, "I'm the Starlight Lancer! This is my power, given to me by Astrid Rachelle, so that I can protect the ones I hold dear." He started to pull the squid's mandibles apart. "And as long as those people exist, there isn't a sorry shit alive who could possibly beat me!" With a roar, he tore the creature in two. Its black blood sprayed across the hangar floor, and disappeared like water on a hot stove.

Nathan marched forward. He hoisted up Eriol and confronted the Moonface clone holding the Silver Key box. Astrid approached the closely-knit group of clones.

"You're beaten, Moonface," she yelled. "Hand over the box."

"No," said the Moonfaces.

Nathan touched his chest and said, "I'm sure the others won't mind me going Victor right now."

"Just give it back, ya Ruskie bastard," snarled Eriol.

One of the Moonfaces checked his watch and muttered, "Three, two, one!"

The roof of the hangar suddenly caved in. A saucer-shaped craft plunged through it. Girders fell from above and crushed the rest of the planes and support systems. Sakura was in such a daze she didn't notice the debris falling directly toward her. Astrid shielded her from the debris with her Valkyrie Skirt.

The Moonface carrying the box chuckled as he strutted toward the ship, which extended a boarding ramp for him. Meanwhile, the rest of him charged Nathan, Eriol, and Astrid. Their efforts were merely for distraction. They didn't re-spawn, nor did they put up much of a fight.

As they fought, the ship soared into the sky and out of sight.

Nathan gazed up at the hole in the roof, and growled with frustration at the loss. He glanced over and saw Sakura, doubled over and hyperventilating. Tears were rolling down her face as she cried, "I lost the key!" Astrid leaned on her knees and panted with exhaustion. Eriol leaned against his staff. Everyone else just sat on the floor in utter shock.

Nathan could still hear chaos echoing through the complex. He nudged Eriol and told him to look after Sakura. Then he tapped Astrid and muttered, "Let's clean up the stragglers."

Neither of them felt terribly enthused at that.

17 | The Blame Game

Bravo's team reached the Regiment headquarters, finding it in ruins. EMTs and rescue teams raced through the wrecked corridors, searching for survivors. They were all on their toes for fear of running into a camping homunculus ready to strip the flesh from their bones. When Bravo arrived, armed with all their Kakugane, the teams moved with far more confidence.

Sakura and Eriol sat in the wrecked infirmary receiving medical treatment. Nathan and Astrid had their Kakugane-powered healing, which Astrid shared when she had recovered. When Bravo and Xiaolang entered, shouldering an exhausted Franklin, Sakura threw her arms around her father. Her tears flowed freely over the man's dirtied shirt.

"I'm back, Sakura," cooed Franklin. She helped him hobble to one of the vacant beds, and the doctors set to work on him.

While holding her father's hand tightly, she turned to Xiaolang and said, "I'm so sorry. They took the box. I let them get away."

Xiaolang's expression softened and he embraced his girlfriend. She was still trembling at afterimages of Moonface's unhinged maw ready to chomp.

Maka, Soul, and Spirit marched into the room. Having heard Sakura's words, Maka snarled, "You let them get both parts of the key?" Sakura pulled away from the blonde and repeatedly apologised. "Sorry doesn't cut it, you damn incompetent!" snapped Maka.

"Oi, lay off her," yelled Nathan, putting himself between the blonde and her target. Soul stepped forward to try and pull Maka away, but the girl was furious.

"You have no idea what you've unleashed," Maka yelled. She glared at Franklin on the hospital bed and said, "Tell them. Tell them what your research revealed."

Franklin pursed his lips with shame. He regarded Bravo with a twinge of anger and explained, "The Silver Key appears to be a magical device, designed to manipulate space and time. With both parts and sufficient energy, it can be used to travel anywhere in the universe, and any*when* in time."

"Theoretically, someone could use this to change the past," muttered Eriol.

Bravo slowly stepped back and rubbed his lips gauchely.

"You knew about this already, didn't you, Costable?" asked Spirit.

Bravo stammered, and covered his chest defensively. At that moment, General Rodrigo appeared at the door and ripped off the metaphorical Band-Aid.

"Yes," he proclaimed. He dismissed the medical personnel, and closed the door behind them. "When we discovered the Silver Key fragment in Antarctica, it came with tablets describing what it did, but not how to activate it. We hoped that it could, at some point, be used as a means to undo the mistakes of our past." He glared at Bravo. "I did *not*, however, sanction Bravo's secret research project." He bowed to Franklin and Sakura. "I deeply apologise for what happened to you," he said.

"We need the Silver Key," growled Bravo. He still crossed his arms tightly and glared at Rodrigo. "You put it on me to find a solution, and I bloody well found one."

"One that alters time?" asked Astrid.

Maka strode across the room to Bravo and bellowed,

"What events were you planning to change? Give the Regiment power over the Reaper? Fix the massive screw-up when you created the homunculi?"

Bravo diverted his eyes evasively as more people accused him and interrogated him. Some even had mixed feelings about the prospect of changing the past. Astrid finally yelled, "Why do you even need to change the past anyway?"

Bravo exploded, "Because of you!" His finger was outstretched at Astrid and his gaze fixated upon her. Then he pointed at Sakura. "And because of you!" The room fell silent. "Two years ago, Astrid Rachelle was sent on a routine mission to clear a homunculus infestation. An idiot raced in and interfered, getting himself killed. And because she *liked* this idiot, she sacrificed a precious Kakugane to bring him back to life."

"Nathan's life was worth saving," protested Astrid.

"And what did it end up as?" asked Bravo rhetorically. "His best friend finding out, his face in the tabloids, a wrecked school, dozens of PTSD cases, and a freaking viral video of an Arms Alchemy activation!" He turned to Sakura. "And speaking of viral videos, did you really think everyone would think that was CGI? Let's not forget the fiasco at Tsukimine Shrine, then also Tokyo Tower that same bloody night! And don't even get me started on the airplane incident!"

"Those people would have died if I hadn't flown in," exclaimed Sakura.

"They would not have been in the mess if you hadn't bought a goddamn book of tarot cards," growled Bravo. He looked at Rodrigo, Spirit, and Maka. "Thanks to them, and the incompetence of the people supervising them, we have been exposed on an unprecedented level. Before long, people will be charging through our organisation. Governments'll regulate us, we'll be put up to scrutiny we can't afford, and then we'll have fucking 'homunculus rights' organisations protesting and flinging Molotov cocktails at us." He glared at Maka. "And you know who they'll be coming after next?" Maka pursed her lips and wrapped her arms around herself. Then Bravo looked at Rodrigo. "We need to fix this! Just one change to the timeline, that was all I'd been planning."

"Could you imagine what sacrifice that would take?" interjected Franklin. His body trembled with horror. "The Silver Key requires energy to run. Guess what kind of energy?" He looked at Soul and Spirit. "It's the same kind that you grow strong on."

"What? Asura Eggs?" asked Spirit.

"No, human souls!" interjected Maka.

"Exactly," said Franklin. "And Shaula has all the know-how to power it."

"Dad, why did you help her?" cried Sakura.

"She threatened you and Touya," said Franklin, his lips trembling. "I couldn't bear to see that happen." He looked at Bravo again, but didn't hold back his anger. "And *you* assured me you wouldn't drag her into this mess."

"I didn't," retorted Bravo. He accused Nathan and Astrid. "These two broke out of security and went to Hong Kong and brought her back."

"Excuse me a sec, *Tristan*," spat Nathan. "While you shitheads were carryin' on in the conference room, Astrid and I decided to act on the intel you had and stopped Moonface from getting the Silver Key. We even brought him back for you to interrogate."

"You wouldn't have saved Doctor Avalon if we hadn't," said Astrid.

"And I wouldn't have needed saving if you hadn't been meddling with the Silver Key in the first place," said Franklin, hopping off the bed and glaring right into Bravo's face. "And I wonder how good your security is if they were able to find out where the Silver Key was? Shaula and Moonface knew exactly where the key was and who *I* was."

"How would they have known that?" asked Xiaolang.

"Moonface mentioned an informant," said Franklin, his gaze still fixed on Bravo. "And since you had intel on the other Key's whereabouts, someone obviously tipped them off and sent them to Hong Kong."

"Might have been DWMA?" retorted Bravo, which earned a vociferous tirade from Maka and Spirit. Soul banged his hand against a bedside table and yelled, "Everybody shut up! It couldn't have been DWMA. And plus, didn't the intel say that Moonface and Shaula could work out where the other Key was just by having one of them. They must've found the other one that way."

Franklin looked at Soul, a bemused expression on his face. He shook his head and said, "That's not right." All eyes fell on him. "There's no way to find one fragment with the other. That was never in any of the scriptures discovered by the Regiment."

"Are you sure, Dad?" asked Sakura.

"I have some magical power too, Sakura," said Franklin. "I studied that key at great length, and I'm telling you there is no way. Who told you that, anyway?"

Everyone looked at Eriol. The Scotsman pursed his lips, and a grin tugged at the corners of his mouth.

"Wait a sec," said Astrid. "If Moonface couldn't use their half, then how did he know the Lee Clan had the other half?"

"Maybe the informant really is in the Regiment," said Xiaolang.

At that instant, Astrid recalled the image of an Alchemic Warrior racing toward them in the hangar.

"Hannah Peterson," she mumbled, her eyes unfocused with amazed realisation.

"She was one of the people guarding me," said Franklin. "I saw Moonface put something in her mouth before I was taken away from Cunnamulla."

"She was a homunculus," concluded Nathan. "And if she was in the meeting when …"

Astrid pointed at Eriol, having put two and two

together. "You're the informant!"

Maka joined her in the accusation and yelled, "You gave that little tid-bit that the Lee Clan had the other half!"

Sakura gasped with shock. "Eriol! You can't have!"

"Busted, I guess," chuckled the Scotsman.

Maka flew into a rage and grabbed the man by scruff of the neck. Astrid too advanced upon him. Sakura charged in, shrieking, "Don't hurt him!" She pushed Astrid out of the way. Maka ignored the girl and landed a punch on Eriol's face. His smarmy smile did not let up even as Maka drew blood. Sakura tackled the girl and yelled, "Leave him alone!" Maka kneed Sakura in the stomach and pushed her away. Soul came to the rescue and held Maka back. Sakura pulled herself up, rubbing her stomach.

Eriol giggled as he looked at the people in the room.

"Look at you idiots," he chuckled. "You have no idea what's in store for you."

Rodrigo opened the infirmary doors and had a security detail take Eriol to the brig. Sakura whimpered as they took her friend away.

"He didn't do this, I'm sure of it," she insisted.

"Oh, shut up, you dumb cheerleader," snarled Maka. "What you think just 'cause you have some magic cards, you have a say here?" Sakura stammered as Maka drew near to her, but the blonde's assault continued despite Soul's pleading. "You're a pathetic, happy-go-lucky girl whose never had a hard day in her life." She shoved Sakura into a wall. "If you hadn't grabbed a random book one day, you'd be flipping burgers at Micky-D's, where you belong!" She shoved Sakura again, and an ingrained reaction kicked in.

Sakura grabbed Maka's arms, holding them to her chest. She then twirled the girl around and pushed her away. She assumed a defensive stance and said, "Leave me alone."

Maka swivelled and rushed Sakura. Xiaolang appeared between them, caught Maka's blow, and delivered a punch to her face. She hit the ground hard.

"My Maka!" cried Spirit.

Xiaolang advanced upon the blonde. Soul moved forward, his hand in scythe blade form, and said, "Hands of my meister." Xiaolang deflected the scythe blade with his magical shield and threw Soul into the wall. Spirit vengefully charged in, almost stepping on Maka, only to be knocked out cold by Xiaolang's volley of punches.

Before Soul and Xiaolang could come to blows, Astrid and Nathan stepped in to break up the fight. Astrid pushed Xiaolang away, while Nathan caught Soul's scythe blade in his bare hand.

"Stop it!" screeched Sakura. The scuffle came to a halt, and they looked at the upset girl. "No wonder those monsters are winning." She buried her face in her hands, unable to find any words to communicate her frustration. Xiaolang's heart melted and he edged toward his girlfriend.

On the other side of the room, Rodrigo gazed at the mess and sighed. Franklin rubbed his face down with his hand, eager to be done with this unwelcome adventure.

"We need to get our systems back up," said Bravo. "We have to find Moonface and Shaula before its too late." He roused Spirit with a nudge of his heel. The red-haired man look up dazed. "We could use some DWMA intel to find them." He marched out of the room before anyone could retort. Spirit staggered to his feet and glanced at Maka, who refused to acknowledge his existence. He gave a sigh and left the room.

Rodrigo remained, and gave Franklin a pat on the shoulder. "I'm once again truly sorry for everything. As soon as we have a plane ready, we'll take you and your daughter home."

"Thank you," croaked Franklin. The two men gazed at the six teenagers in the corner, standing around and either glaring at each other or sobbing quietly.

A worn-out Regiment officer entered the room and saluted Rodrigo.

"Has Lamperouge been detained?" asked Rodrigo.

"Yes, sir," said the officer. "However, he has requested to speak with, and I quote, the six teenagers with attitude."

Rodrigo frowned a moment, before chuckling and glancing at the group. "I think he means you."

Each of them looked confused and intrigued at the same time.

* * *

Eriol sat quietly in his cell, his hands on his thighs, and a pensive smile on his face. That smile widened into a grin when the six people he'd summoned arrived. They stood in front of his cell, tired and worn-out. Sakura was still upset; Maka was irritated; Nathan looked confused; Astrid was exasperated; Xiaolang was furious; and Soul just looked bored.

"Thank you for coming," said the Scotsman. He eyed Maka and said, "Dang, lassie, you got a hook there."

"If you're just gonna call me sexist things, I'm outta here," snapped Maka.

Eriol smiled and held his hands up earnestly. He stood and approached the glass shield. His look was not one you'd expect from a caught double agent. He seemed excited, proud even, to look upon the six of them.

"I have waited a long time for this moment," he said. "Me and my predecessor." He glanced at Sakura and said, "I'm sorry for dragging your father into this. I didn't mean for him to get hurt." He looked at Lee and said, "I apologise about your family being threatened."

Sakura and Xiaolang nodded and accepted the apology.

Nathan stepped closer to the glass and said, "You do know that 'sorry' ain't really gonna cut it. Not with me. I'd like to know why you did it."

Eriol bowed in acknowledgement. He wrung his hands thoughtfully and measured his words carefully. Considering his level of conniving and mastery of word, it was clear he had attained a new high of self-criticism.

"Yes," he enunciated. "Yes, I was Moonface's informant. He didn't know who I was, but I *did* tell him the Regiment had half of the Silver Key. And *yes*, I knew that Warrior Peterson was a homunculus when I met with the Regiment and DWMA. And, **yes**, I used magic to rig a Japanese lottery in order to put Sakura in Hong Kong. I did *not*, however, anticipate that Moonface would escape. Rest assured, I did not know that assault was coming."

"Why did you do it?" Astrid repeated.

"Because I wanted the six of you to meet," said Eriol.

"Six of us?" asked Maka. "Why would we need to meet?"

"So that you might see the common cause you all share, and the good you could do as one," Eriol explained. "I told Sakura the story of Clow Reed and his inspiration to create the Cards she now wields. He wished to emphasise the goodness of humanity and their ability to work together to overcome adversity. He believed this was a better path, rather than –" he glanced at Nathan, "– excising the weaknesses or –" he looked at Maka, "– culling the bad eggs." He took a step back so he could see all of them. "But that was only half the vision. This incomparable sorcerer looked into the future, and saw six lights – beacons in the void. These were to be immensely powerful people who, on behalf of all humanity, would face the coming calamity."

Nathan touched his hand to the glass and said, "That was the vision you showed me?"

"What vision?" asked Astrid.

"I saw something when I shook his hand earlier," said Nathan.

"Of what?" asked Xiaolang.

"Stars, being swallowed by something," Nathan explained. "And I was with five other people, and we all made the bad guy disappear."

"Ridiculous," said Maka, and she stormed out of the room. Soul groaned as his meister marched off, and he shot the others an apologetic glance before following her.

Sakura cringed at the sight, and she turned to Eriol.

"Wouldn't it have been better if you'd just asked?" she mumbled.

"Where's the fun in that, quine?" chuckled Eriol.

Astrid rolled her eyes.

It's always stupid games with this arsehole, she thought.

"Not for nothing, Eriol, but I don't think Maka's on-board," said Nathan. He touched his sternum and shuddered. "Not sure if I am either."

Eriol shrugged, "We'll see."

18 | Meeting of the Minds

As the officers of the Regiment struggled to recover their systems, the upper echelon argued. Much of it concerned how to find Shaula, Moonface, and the Silver Key. That was hampered by discussions regarding how to deal with the treacherous Eriol Lamperouge. Then there was the issue of the communications array, which was still out of commission. Not to mention, all the mirrors in the building were shattered, making communication with the Reaper impossible.

Alone in a corridor, just outside a wrecked lavatory, Maka kicked a wall with frustration. Sweat poured down her brow and she clutched her stomach, knotted with her anger. Soul appeared around a corner and sighed with relief.

"Maka, you shouldn't be wandering alone," he chided.

"What? A poor girl needs a man's help?" snarled Maka.

"Shut up," returned Soul dismayed. "There could be homunculi around, and you wouldn't be able to deal with them without me … or a Kakugane but I'm pretty sure you'd die first."

Maka rolled her eyes, but had to agree with him there.

"No mirrors, so we can't get back to DWMA and ask for the Reaper's help," she moaned. She kicked the wall again. "Goddammit!"

"Maka, calm down," said Soul. He tried to embrace her, but she pushed away and started down the hall.

"For now, it's up to us," she said over her shoulder. "I'm going to the roof so I can try and sense Shaula."

"I'll come and help," said Soul.

"No!" screamed Maka. Soul stopped dead in his tracks. Maka disappeared down the corridor without another word.

Soul groaned and rubbed his face. Usually, he could able to pull Maka out of one of her moods, but this was on an entirely different level.

Obviously, it's her daddy issues, he thought. *But this has been going on since Hong Kong. And when she saw Kinomoto's old man in the dam ...*

Soul pursed his lips at the chill that had emanated from Maka's soul when Sakura hugged her father. He let out a long sigh.

I need Kinomoto for this, he concluded.

He started down the hallway, and navigated the headquarters until he found the brig. Eriol directed him back to the infirmary, where he found Sakura with her father. Xiaolang, Nathan, and Astrid sat nearby. They all looked on edge, and became defensive when they saw him. He held his hands up.

"I come in peace," he said. He edged into the room and approached Sakura. "I wanted to apologise for Maka. She was out of line."

Sakura smiled weakly. Her mood had evidently improved with the recovery of her father.

"It's fine," she said. "She's just stressed, obviously."

"About that," said Soul. He swallowed thoughtfully. "Miss Kinomoto –"

"Sakura is fine," interjected Sakura.

"Okay then, Sakura, I have a favour to ask," Soul went on. "I can tell you that Maka's bad mood is because of you ... Specifically, you and your dad." Soul explained the events behind the death of Maka's mother and her father's subsequent behaviour. When he was finished, he presented his request. "I need you to find a way through to her. She needs to be able to put all this crap aside so that we can all … ya know, do what Eriol said we'd do."

"How do I do that?" asked Sakura.

"Yeah, if Maka clearly hates her so much," added Nathan.

"You can resonate with her," said Astrid. Nathan shot her a confused glance, which she waved off. "You're too dumb to understand," she said snidely, only for Nathan to flip her off.

"Well, *I'd* like to know," said Franklin. "I don't know everything about magic just yet."

While Astrid explained the concept to Franklin and Nathan, Xiaolang, Soul and Sakura convened in the hallway.

"It might be possible," Xiaolang said after some careful thought. "You might be able to get through to her."

"Why can't you do it?" Sakura asked Soul.

Soul shook his head. "She's not pissed at me."

Sakura wrung her hands nervously, and fidgeted under the albino's expectant gaze. She glanced back at her father, chatting with the two Australians who had saved her from the homunculi. She considered them nice people. Xiaolang was, of course, wonderful – the love of her life. Soul was a kind person too, even if his sharp teeth and red eyes made him look a bit scary. And Sakura had said Maka would be cute if she smiled.

Eriol's story had constructed an image in her mind, one in which they worked together as friends to save the world. The thought elated her. She started to wish Maka would be nicer, if only to make that image a reality.

So she agreed.

* * *

Maka paced around the roof of the Regiment headquarters. No matter how hard she tried, she could not extend her senses out further than a mile or two. Even then, what she sensed was sketchy at best.

Gotta find Shaula, she internally growled. She reached out harder, looking for any signature of homunculus or Witch. She found nothing. Her body shook with frustration. She couldn't excise the infernal image of that silly girl hugging her daddy from her head. It stuck there like a wedge in her mental gears, and it would not go away. Then another image entered her mind of her own sleazy papa hitting on that glorified cheerleader, and she punched the railing with an enraged squeal.

Maka's hand seared with the pain of broken bones. She gripped it tightly and sucked in her breath to bare the agony. The fight didn't go her way and tears leaked from her eyes. Now, she couldn't even reach out with her senses to find nearby souls.

She looked out over the land. There was only flat terrain as far as she could see, with a few towns specking the horizon. She had no point of reference for where she was. Never had she felt so isolated.

Except for one time.

Involuntarily, her mind took her back to that moment.

A five-year-old girl in a cream blouse and a red one-piece dress dotted with tears. Her pigtails, held by red ribbons, bobbed rhythmically with her heaves. Alone, she sat on a swing set. She gazed out at the children at play, seemingly unaware of her very existence.

Maka couldn't find even the energy to swing.

She saw a little blonde baby, playing in the sand box with her mother and father. It made her gnash her teeth and grip the swing's chains tightly.

Why isn't Mama here?

Because she died, she remembered.

Why isn't Papa here?

He ran off with that black woman from the liquor store, she remembered.

Maka sobbed harder, such that she didn't notice the

shoes lingering just within her field of vision. She looked up and saw a girl, no older than four, with shoulder length chestnut hair. She patted down her pink overalls and smiled. She looked Asian, but Maka couldn't have cared.

"Whacha doin' here all alone?" asked the girl with a thick New-York accent.

"Being alone," muttered Maka.

The Asian girl looked around with a furrowed brow. Her eyes fell upon the empty swing next to Maka and she hopped on it.

"I'm Sakura," said the girl. Maka didn't reply, so Sakura just said, "My Daddy doesn't like me swingin' alone."

"Where is he?" asked Maka half interested.

"Oh, well," said Sakura, her tone growing solemn. "My Mommy just passed away. And we had the funeral and everything. But he decided to take me and my Big Brother on vacation." She smiled. "He's a good Daddy."

Maka stifled an enraged roar that came out as a low sigh.

"He's probably just here to meet women," she growled. She started to swing. "That's all men are." She swung higher. "They use women up and throw them away." She swung even higher. "They just see women as buckets to dump their loads and forget about them!" Without realising it, Maka released the chains and flew into the air, screaming, "They should all die!"

She face-planted into the dirt. Her tears turned to mud as she pulled out of the ground and spluttered. She continued to whimper, while everyone else continued to play regardless of her cries.

Sakura walked over and stood beside her. She pointed at the other fathers.

"They're not doin' that," she said. "Sounds like they're havin' fun."

"They're just biding their time," snarled Maka.

"Long time to bide," replied Sakura. She looked down at the girl in the mud and intoned, "Maybe you just want that to be it."

"It *is* it!" retorted Maka. "They're all secretly cheating! Just like Papa. And when their wives're dying, they won't even wait for the funeral. They'll be running after the next whore."

"And if you're wrong," said Sakura. "Then it'll mean you just got the raw deal. And then, you'll have to wonder why you did. Maybe it was something you did, and not the big bad world."

Maka grasped at the dirt, looking for some kind of lifeline. Nothing she did made any difference, and she wept. Still, no one but Sakura paid attention. And even then, Sakura seemed almost indifferent.

"What did I do wrong?" Maka finally cried. "Why don't I have Papa? Why don't I have Mama? Why am I alone?"

Sakura shrugged, "You ain't alone. I'm here, after all." Maka gazed up at her. She went on, "I wish I could have my Mommy back. I miss her so much. But I can't get that. It don't mean I can't have anyone else. I mean, I got a bunch of friends, and an awesome boyfriend. As Mick Jagger said, you can't always get whacha want, but if you try, you get whacha need."

"What would I need?" moaned Maka.

"You're here all alone," said Sakura. "How 'bout a compadre? A buddy? Ain't ya got that with Soul?" Maka gasped softly as she recalled the albino who had been her friend for so long. She couldn't believe she'd been taking him for granted so much.

Sakura crouched down and said, "Plus, you're a weirdo. You're quirky." Maka frowned as Sakura smiled and held out her hand. "Because of that, will you be friends with me?"

Maka opened her eyes and the playground melted away. She was back on the roof of the Regiment headquarters. Her right hand was still limp and swollen, and her left was in Sakura's hand.

"Will you be friends with me?" said the girl, this time

with an English accent. She had an earnest smile that Maka couldn't help but return, though she had no clue why. Sakura pulled her to her feet and held her hand tightly.

"Well?" blurted an Aussie accented voice. "Say yes!"

"Nathan!" yelled another voice.

Maka and Sakura looked over to see Nathan, Astrid, Xiaolang, and Soul. Franklin stood a bit further away, beside the roof exit. They all had grins on their faces, tainted a bit by embarrassment at Nathan's outburst.

"What?" replied Nathan. "They're just sitting there."

"You make it sound like a marriage proposal," chuckled Soul.

Xiaolang paled at that thought and quickly pulled Maka and Sakura apart.

"Don't say things to make Sakura question her identity, thank you very much," he exclaimed in jest. Sakura only giggled, as did Maka.

Soul leaned to Franklin and said, "I didn't really think it would work so easily."

Franklin just grinned proudly. "That's my Sakura. She's a girl who makes things happen."

Soul shook his head in amazement, unable to disagree with the man. He then walked over and slung his arm around his meister.

"Feelin' better?" he asked.

Maka nodded. She inhaled sharply as she cradled her hand. Xiaolang quickly procured a paper charm and healed her broken bones. The blonde sighed and leaned back against the railing.

"Sorry, everyone," she said embarrassed. "Just ... all this stuff with Sakura's dad had me worked up. Plus, when Papa hit on you, I just –"

"It's alright," said Sakura. "I was a bit creeped out by it too."

"What? Did your dad actually hit on a girl right in front of you?" asked Nathan. Maka nodded shamefully. Nathan chuckled, much to her surprise. To Astrid, he said, "Well then, you don't get to call me creepy anymore."

"Says the one trying to kiss me all the time," retorted Astrid.

"You too, huh?" Xiaolang jibed.

Sakura slapped his shoulder at the comment, but laughed all the same. Soul hooted while Nathan and Maka jokingly pressed for gossip. Though she would have been happy to continue clowning, Astrid had to stop the conversation.

"Listen, everyone," she said. "Shaula and Moonface're still out there. This fiasco isn't over yet." She turned to Maka. "Did you manage to find her?"

"No, my senses can't reach that far," said Maka. "Even when my mind is clear."

The group grumbled with disappointment. Gazes downturned in thought. Then Sakura had an idea.

"Why don't we resonate again?" she suggested. "When I resonate with my Cards, I can provide them more power and control. Maybe I can resonate with you and boost your range?"

Maka chewed her lip thoughtfully. "That could work."

"I'll get in on that too," said Nathan. He pointed to his chest and said, "This thing makes me damn powerful."

"He's right, it does," said Astrid.

"So I could prob'ly give you a boost too," said Nathan.

"Let's all pitch in," said Soul. "I mean, if Eriol's right and we really are supposed to work together." Astrid and Xiaolang nodded in agreement.

Maka drew a deep breath and held out her newly healed hand. Sakura placed her hand on top. Then Nathan placed his hand below. Soul placed his hand above. Then Astrid on top, and then finally Xiaolang below. They reached out through the aether.

Maka's soul, a blue orb crowned by wings, matched its beating to the pink, feathery energy of Sakura's soul. Then Nathan's shining crimson soul, thrumming a million times a minute, slowed to a dulcet tone. Astrid's soul, in the shape of an ethereal echidna, sung in tune. The beat in Soul's head sped up to match. Xiaolang's focused wolf-like spirit aligned with that of his beloved's mind.

With harmony achieved, their spirits sung louder. Their synchronised, resonating roar burst across the astral landscape, touching every soul they could find. With ease, they traversed the horizon many times over.

Then they saw it: the slick, galling sensation not unlike dining on rotten meat. There Shaula stood, within a needle-like tower, surrounded by a sprawling harbour-side metropolis.

Maka broke the resonance and everyone hunched over. They smiled with delight.

"She's in Centrepoint," said Nathan.

"Where's that?" asked Soul.

"Sydney," said Astrid.

"We should tell Bravo and the others," said Xiaolang.

"No," barked Astrid. Everyone looked at her, quite perplexed. "We tell them, they'll just bicker for hours more. We're working together right now. Why shouldn't we see it all the way through together?"

Nathan grabbed Astrid's shoulders and looked at her.

"Astrid, are you sure?" he said. His hands trembled with nervousness. "I don't know if I can control this."

Astrid grabbed his hands and gripped them tightly.

"You can," she said resolutely. "We have to do this, and we can only do it together."

"Are you serious?" asked Xiaolang, wondering where the Astrid he knew had gone.

"Yes, I am," said Astrid with a cocky grin. "Screw regulations and jurisdictions. Let's get this done."

"How're we going to get there?" asked Sakura.

"The plane we used to get to Somerset Dam," said Maka.

"Let's go then," said Astrid. She locked her gaze onto Nathan, and seemed to transmit her resolve to him. With a deep sigh, Nathan grinned. He then punched the air.

"Let's do it!" he exclaimed.

As everyone entered the fire escape, Sakura and Maka lingered. Maka turned to Franklin and coughed nervously.

"I haven't introduced myself properly," she said deferentially. "I am Maka Albarn. It's nice to meet you."

"Same here, Miss Albarn," said Franklin, shaking her hand.

"I'm sorry I attacked your daughter," said Maka.

"Hey, if she's forgiven you, then no need to apologise to me," replied Franklin with a smile. He then turned to Sakura, who wrung her hands nervously. "You're going to save the world?"

"I don't know," stammered the girl.

Franklin hooked his finger under her cheek and pulled her gaze to meet his.

"I don't think they'll be able to do it without you," he said.

"I agree," said Maka, threading her fingers through Sakura's.

Franklin beamed with unfettered pride and said, "Go, and be my magic girl."

Sakura trembled with excitement and trepidation. She threw her arms around Franklin. Her father returned the hug, before shooing her off to follow the others.

The group walked down the staircase and into the building. After traversing a few floors toward the hangar level, they ran into the face they'd least expected.

"Eriol?" exclaimed Sakura.

"How did you get out?" asked Xiaolang.

"A wizard did it," said Eriol. He glanced at the whole group, and grinned excitedly. "Look at you all, teamed up and everythin'," he chirped. He raised a finger. "But, before y'all get into the action, I think you're missin' somethin'."

"What?" asked Astrid, her excitement overriding her annoyance only slightly.

Eriol pointed to a nearby locker room. The six of them

walked into the room and looked around. They glanced back at the Scotsman with confused expressions.

"On the bench there," said Eriol. "I'll run interference for ya." Then he disappeared down the hall.

Maka grimaced as she looked around the locker room, until she found a bench in the middle. A package resting on it caught her eye, and she walked over to it. There was a gift-card attached to the package with her name on it. Inside it read, "Dear Scythe Meister. From a certain traitor, Eriol." There were five more packages, addressed to Cardcaptor, Coyote, Soul Eater, Spartan Valkyrie, and Starlight Lancer.

Sakura picked up hers and found the pink costume Tomoyo had given her at the airport in Japan. Xiaolang's contained the green costume.

"I thought I'd left these in Hong Kong," she exclaimed.

Maka's contained her blouse, cardigan, checkerboard skirt, and black coat, along with a pair of brand new Converse shoes. She beamed with utter delight.

Soul's contained his yellow and black jacket and his red trousers. He drooled excitedly.

Astrid and Nathan opened theirs and found matching cargo pants, as well as the shirts Ariadne had made for them. Nathan held them up for the rest to see. The star on Nathan's shirt still shone, while the crucifix of Astrid's shirt glimmered in the light. Nathan squeaked with glee at the sight of his red scarf.

"Well, if we're going to save the world, we might as well do it lookin' cool," exclaimed Soul.

"Soul, you're as bad as Tomoyo," said Sakura.

Nathan looked over the top of his shirt and grinned almost evilly.

"In the words of Barney Simpson," he chuckled. Then he yelled, "Suit up!" And he walked off with his shirt.

Astrid groaned.

"It's *Stinson,* you moron!" she cried. She looked at the

others and moaned, "I swear, he does it just to annoy me."

19 | Haka!

The control room of Regiment headquarters had fallen into chaos. The technicians and officers hurriedly repaired the damage incurred by Moonface's attack. They were making progress, much of which seemed for naught, as the leadership couldn't work out what to do. All they did was bicker in the conference room.

Bravo was particularly vociferous against engaging the assistance of other organisations to find the enemy, while Spirit insisted that a mirror be found with which to contact DWMA. The other generals wanted to remove the two men from the decision-making process for their incompetence. Rodrigo stood in the corner and shook his head with dismay, while General Vasuman chuckled.

"Is this a time to laugh?" growled Rodrigo.

"Oh, it's just absurd, isn't it?" chimed Vasuman. "The world's about to end, and all we can do is point fingers. It's just absurd."

The shouting grew so loud that Rodrigo almost didn't hear the beep on the intercom nearby.

"General Rodrigo, we have a problem," said a nervous technician. Rodrigo was sure he could hear a Scottish accent in the background. He and an intrigued Vasuman left the room, and the other generals soon noticed their departure and followed. Their jaws dropped when they saw Eriol standing in the control room, his sun-shaped staff in-hand.

"Lord Lamperouge, you mean to make an enemy of us at a time like this?" exclaimed Rodrigo.

Bravo stepped forward and donned his Arms Alchemy. He clenched his fists and proclaimed, "Let me deal with this joker."

Eriol gazed at a screen nearby. A widget started to beep on the console.

"Uh, Generals … Sirs, everyone in the hangar is walking away," said the technician. Upon a command from Vasuman, he brought a feed from the hangar to the main screen. The repair teams in the hangar had halted their work, and had retreated to the edges of the chamber. Then a group of six marched across the hangar toward the one remaining stealth craft.

One wore a black long coat over a crème cardigan and checkerboard skirt.

One wore red trousers, a yellow jacket, and bobbed to the beat in his head.

One had a green and gold shirt with a star on the chest, and a red scarf.

One had a blue shirt with a crucifix.

One boasted a green suit plated with armour, the face of a wolf emblazoned upon his chest.

One marched in a pink suit, holding a shimmering star-shaped wand above her head.

"What the Hell are they doing?" exclaimed Bravo.

"What I gathered them to do," said Eriol, an infuriating grin plastered on his face.

Everyone watched as the stealth craft lifted away from its moorings and flew into the sky. Only Rodrigo had the presence of mind to say, "Get all communications up. I want to know where they're going."

"So we can bring them back?" asked Bravo, sighing with resignation. "They obviously know where Shaula is." He glanced at Eriol. "Right?"

"Aye, laddie," said Eriol.

"And they'll need all the support we can give them," said Rodrigo. To the technicians, he ordered, "Find out where they're going, and evacuate that area." He gave Bravo a reassuring pat. It did little to assuage Bravo's nerves, as the man could not deter the mental images of another Victor incident. He stood there, immobile, and waited for the Regiment's systems to be repaired.

There's no more planes, so they're on their own, he thought. *And they're going to bust everything wide open now. No way can we cover this up now.*

Eriol moved to Bravo's side and said, "You should take a page out of Sakura's spell book."

"Oh yeah? And what would that be?" asked Bravo, his arms folded.

"Just tell yourself, 'You'll definitely be alright,'" said Eriol. "Works like a charm for her."

Bravo rolled his eyes and wondered aloud, "Pray the day never comes when she eats those words."

* * *

The jet pierced through the skies. It pitched as Astrid twisted the yoke, and directed the plane southward to Sydney. Her GPS readout indicated an ETA of half an hour. It wasn't that much of a hassle to pilot the plane, but Nathan rasping in her ear made it a lot harder than she wanted.

Finally, after the umpteenth time she'd refused, Nathan marched back to his seat with a growl.

"Bitch," he murmured under his breath. Everyone else in the cabin could hear it though.

Soul turned to him and chuckled, "Your girl's a bitch too, huh?"

Maka flared her nostrils and slapped him. Soul quickly retaliated with a slap of his own, and before long the pair were roughhousing beside Nathan.

Sakura looked at the pair in dismay, and wondered how

they could ever work together. She turned to Xiaolang, who fought to suppress his snickers, and said, "We don't act like that, do we?"

Xiaolang stroked her fringe and said, "Of course, not." And he kissed her cheek.

"Cute," said Maka with a faux sneer. Sakura poked her tongue out at her.

Maka's expression softened and she said, "Good job distracting those guards before."

"No problem," said Sakura, saluting with her Star Wand. She cocked her head to the side, and then said, "Maya says thanks."

Soul turned to Nathan and asked, "So, dude, why's Valkyrie such a bitch?"

"Oh, she keeps poo-poo-ing my awesome ideas," complained Nathan.

"What are you? Six?" asked a disbelieving Xiaolang.

Nathan went on, "And I had an awesome idea for our team's name too."

"No, you don't," yelled Astrid from the cockpit.

"It's awesome!" cried Nathan.

"For Christ's sake, Nathan," Astrid exclaimed. "We are *not* calling ourselves 'The Avengers!'"

"Why not?" cried Nathan, while everyone else in the cabin fell over laughing, except Maka.

"Could you be serious for one minute, Grant?" she chided. "We're going into a battle that could very well affect the fate of our world. Not to mention we've disobeyed direct orders, which could get us all demoted or imprisoned. This is hardly the time to be naming ... whatever *this* is."

Nathan's eyes narrowed at her and he said, "Oi, sheila, is it comfortable sittin' down?"

"Why does that matter?" asked Maka confused.

"I'm just surprised the stick up your bum doesn't get in the way," retorted Nathan.

At that, Maka filled with so much rage she almost shut

down. Astrid and Sakura exploded with involuntary laughter. Xiaolang tried to repress his own chuckles, but Soul wore his merriment right on his sleeves.

"Oh, burn! Epic burn, Albarn!" he proclaimed.

Maka's nostril's flared again, this time at Nathan. She shot out of her chair and glared at him.

"I don't need Soul to kick your ass, Grant," she snarled.

Nathan stood to meet her. "Mc-Mac, I could suck the life right out of you."

Maka stuck her nose right in his face. "Suck me, then!" A split second later, utter dread filled her and she backed away. "I shouldn't have said it like that!" she cried, absolutely red-faced. The whole cabin erupted with even more laughter. "Shut up," pouted the blonde as she crossed her arms over her chest.

Sakura sobered first and said, "It's alright, Maka. I understood what you meant. And I agree, Nathan's a big meanie."

"The biggest," said Maka, letting out a brief chortle.

Soul breathed back the last of his laughter and said, "Well, if we're thinkin' team names, Eriol *did* call us 'six teenagers with attitude.' Why not call ourselves the Pow–"

"NO!" screamed everyone in the cabin, to which Soul chuckled gleefully.

Xiaolang, still pink in the face from laughter, and said, "You know what? I think a theme song is better than a name." He turned to Soul. "Soul Eater, I hear you're good with music. Why don't you come up with something?"

"Sorry, Bruce, I left my fifty-piece orchestra in my other pants," exclaimed Soul sardonically.

The group laughed a little longer. Even Maka joined in.

"But Lee's right, we should have a haka," said Nathan.

"What's a haka?" asked Sakura.

"The New Zealand footy team has this dance they do before every game," explained Nathan. "It's a traditional Maori dance meant to scare the enemy into surrender, and they call it a 'haka.' Maybe we should have one."

"Well, Soul, get on it," said Maka with a grin.

Soul grew nervous, and quickly retorted, "Only if I can draw Maori tattoos on your face."

"I'll die first," snapped Maka.

Sakura snapped her fingers and exclaimed, "I know!" She stood and proclaimed, "This should be our haka!"

She stomped the floor twice and clapped. She did it again. Everyone recognised it, and joined in. Before long, Sakura and Nathan were singing Queen's 'We Will Rock You.' The rest quickly joined in.

The group was so caught up in the song that they didn't notice the beeps from the radar. Astrid heard it first, and interrupted the song. She ignored the protests from her teammates and pointed to starboard.

"We got incoming," she announced. The others found viewports and glanced to the right of the plane. Three dots on the horizon quickly turned to metallic birds.

"Homunculi," exclaimed Soul.

"Strap yourselves in!" yelled Astrid. She didn't wait for them, however, and pitched the plane left. The others tumbled inside the cabin as Astrid dove downward then upward in an effort to shake the pursuing monsters. Yet they persisted as irritating beeps on her radar, fixed upon their prey like starving eagles in the Andes. A klaxon sounded, signalling a lock-on alert. "We've been targeted," Astrid announced.

"Sakura, can you shield us?" asked Maka.

Sakura nodded and cast out the Guard Card. She held her wand out to the aft, where Astrid said the enemy missiles were certain to hit. The incoming assault struck Sakura's force field, protecting the jet from harm, but draining her. Her legs shuddered with fear.

"They're flanking us," exclaimed Astrid.

"Oi, Bruce, don't you have any shield magic?" asked Soul.

Xiaolang shook his head. "Only very short range.

Maybe I can use some fire or lightning, but I'd need a clear line of sight."

Maka shouldered Sakura and whispered to her, "You're fine, Sakura. You just need to focus more. Don't be afraid."

"They're too powerful," exclaimed Sakura.

Astrid glanced back and saw Sakura come up empty. She looked at the radar and saw the enemy homunculi fire from three directions. She quickly unstrapped herself and marched to the back of the plane.

"Astrid, who's driving?" asked Nathan.

Astrid looked at Xiaolang and said, "You need a clear line of sight, I'm going to give you one." With a grunt, she wrenched a lever at the rear of the ship, and the aft hatch blew open. The sudden blast of air sucked them out of the jet just as the homunculi's missiles hit, ripping the plane apart in a cloud of fire and smoke.

Xiaolang acted quickly, and summoned a bolt of lightning from his sword. He cleaved two of the homunculi apart. Sakura sent out a blast of fire from the Flare Card, which disintegrated the third. Then she looked down, and saw the eastern coast of Australia rushing up to meet her.

"Sakura, use the Flight Card," yelled Xiaolang over the wind.

Sakura caught his meaning in an adrenaline-fuelled stupor, and procured the Flight Card.

"Become a majestic bird to carry us, Flight," she proclaimed, touching her wand to it. The Card morphed in a flash of light into a four-winged leviathan of the skies. Sakura caught onto the down behind its crest, and grabbed Xiaolang before soaring downward to catch Nathan and Soul.

Astrid and Maka were closer to the ground, and looked up to see the otherworldly bird incoming. Astrid glanced at Maka and yelled, "Having fun yet?"

"Do you have to ask?" retorted Maka.

Soul and Nathan caught them and pulled them safely onto the bird's back. Sakura then held out her wand and resonated with the Flight Card. At her will, the bird pulled out of its nosedive, seemingly without inertia. Then Sakura summoned the Gale Card, which gave Flight a good boost southward.

Nathan pointed ahead, just off from Flight's course, and yelled, "That's Centrepoint!"

Sakura willed Flight toward the spindly tower just on the horizon, and the bird obediently thrust forward. It gained altitude over the houses and high-rises that pockmarked the northern reaches of Sydney. It crossed the vast gap of Sydney Harbour, and encircled the needle-like Centrepoint Tower. The six of them gazed at the central turret, and spotted a lone figure in a spiffy overcoat, looking right back at them.

"Let's go," said Astrid.

Flight vectored toward the tower. When they were near enough, the group leapt off the bird and landed on top of the central turret. Moonface held his arms out wide and exclaimed, "Welcome to the grand opening of the Ultimate Gate!" The broach on his collar and the gibbous shape of his head told them he was a copy.

Nathan looked past him to the strange device at the base of the spire. It was cylindrical, with a mass of wires and cables emerging from it. The cables snaked their way up the spire like technicoloured moss.

"Where's the Silver Key, Slenderman?" he asked. Moonface just shrugged.

"Where's Shaula?" barked Maka.

"Making meals of this metropolis," replied Moonface. "All for the opening to a new world order."

"That ain't gonna happen," snarled Soul as he transformed into a scythe in Maka's hand. Nathan and Astrid activated their Arms Alchemies, and stood at the ready. Sakura raised her wand, and Xiaolang cocked his sword.

"Moon!" chortled Moonface. He subsequently split into twenty copies, each of which drew swords from the sheaths on their hips. They chirped in unison, and then charged forward.

The group raced to meet them.

"Get past them and get the key!" yelled Astrid. She leapt into the air, and spun to cut two airborne Moonfaces to ribbon. She landed, but had to defend herself from three others that came after her from behind.

Nathan blocked the blows of two clones with his gauntlet and countered. He then deflected blows from another to his right and ran the Moonface through with his lance.

Maka swung Soul's scythe form around her body, knocking one Moonface off balance while swatting another off the edge of the roof. She brought the scythe blade down through another, completely bisecting the monster.

Xiaolang blew a trio of Moonfaces off the roof with a windblast, and lopped the sword-wielding hand off another. He unleashed a volley of punches at the homunculus copy before slicing it with an uppercut.

Sakura unleashed a flamethrower from her wand, incinerating a quartet of Moonfaces. She summoned the Gaia Card into her body, imbuing herself with strength to break the kneecap of one Moonface with a single kick. She delivered a few more roundhouse kicks, before finishing the creature off with the Blade Card.

Moonface kept replicating. Yet, with each round of fighting and replication, the group drew nearer to the spire. Moonface appeared to grow nervous and fatigued. Sakura took the chance and summoned a forest of vines to ensnare his copies. She then leapt over the mass of vines and approached the device at the base of the spire.

"Sakura, is the key there?" asked Maka.

Sakura activated the Blade Card and slashed the device's housing open. She peered inside, and her heart skipped a beat. There was no Silver Key, but a timer three seconds from zero, attached to a dozen bars of plastic explosive.

"It's a bomb!" she screeched. She activated the Guard Card without a second thought. The bomb detonated, the sonic boom impacting against Sakura's force field. The tower shook violently, throwing the others off balance. The spire tilted suddenly under the force of the blast.

Sakura flew backward into Xiaolang's arms. Her head spun and her ears rung. With help from Maka and Xiaolang, she managed to regain her footing.

The crumbling spire pitched backwards. Like a felled tree, it toppled, crashing against the upper roof of the turret on its way down into the shopping mall below. They heard a deafening crash, followed by explosions below. Their hearts skipped beats at the thought of all the civilians who had just died.

The remaining Moonface clones, still enthralled in Sakura's vines, laughed hysterically.

"How delightfully devilish of me," the copies chanted in unison.

Astrid dismembered one of the copies, which didn't even flinch, and looked straight into its face.

"Where's Shaula and the Silver Key?" she snarled.

"Blondie there is the one with the soul perception," retorted Moonface. "Ask her." The copy pursed its lip, as if remembering something at the last minute. Behind them, another crashing sound echoed from the ground below. A voracious roar followed it.

Nathan and Maka moved to the edge of the turret and looked down. The six-limbed behemoth left them speechless. It stood at least seven stories tall, armoured in shimmering gold scales. Eight black eyes with luminescent blue irises crowned a maw bearing many rows of sharp teeth.

"What the Hell is that?" exclaimed Soul.

"The perfection of Doctor Butterfly's homunculus

engineering technology, combined with Shaula's soul harvesting device," explained Moonface giddily. "I mean, seriously, suggest a superior soul-stockpiling system!"

Enraged, Astrid cartwheeled around the immobile Moonface copies, slicing their heads off as she moved. When they were all gone, she turned to the others.

"He's still here somewhere," she said. "Nathan, Sakura, you two find him. We'll take care of that thing!"

The rest of the group nodded, and Soul bellowed, "Let's kick some ass."

Maka, Xiaolang, and Astrid leapt off the turret and headed straight down. Gravity accelerated them, and their blades, toward the monster's head.

We have to end this quick, thought Astrid.

20 | Panic!

The four warriors plummeted from the top of Centrepoint Tower, and sunk their blades straight into the behemoth. The creature crashed to the ground under the force of their superhuman inertia, unleashing a shockwave of air and heat that upended cars and sent bystanders flying. It let out a grunt before falling still.

The group moved away and glanced around.

"No way it's that easy," said Soul.

As if he'd jinxed their luck, the behemoth struck the ground with a clenched fist. It pushed itself to its feet and roared.

"Spoke too soon," said Xiaolang. He drew a paper charm and unleashed a barrage of lightning bolts, which dinged harmlessly off the behemoth. It paid them no notice, and took a bite out of the corner of a nearby building. It's mouth lit up with small purple flashes, and Maka gripped her chest.

"Maka, what's the matter?" exclaimed Soul.

"It's devouring the souls of the people!" cried Maka.

"Coyote!" bellowed Astrid, who raced toward the creature. Xiaolang drew another paper charm and summoned a gale to Astrid's feet. She soared toward the behemoth and cleaved across its shoulder blades. The beast roared with dismay and swatted at her. She landed on the other side and ran away. Maka got the same idea and charged forward. She used Soul's scythe form to pole vault into the air. She somersaulted, bringing Soul's scythe blade through the creature's calf.

Atop the toer, Nathan marvelled at their teammates, while Sakura shuddered at the behemoth.

"That kind of coolness should be illegal," said Nathan. He tapped Sakura. "Let's find Moonface!"

They found an entrance hatch in the floor nearby, and passed through it into the viewing level.

Moonface stood in the midst of a cacophony of tubing and humming devices. The sweat pouring down his brow told them he was concentrating very hard. His malicious grin announced that he loved every second of it. Nathan wasted no time and charged forward. With a raucous yawp, he brought his lance down on Moonface. He struck something harder than diamond, and the recoil sent him head-over-heels.

"Tsk-tsk-tsk, I expected more from a larval Victor," muttered Moonface. "But it's good that Shaula's magic holds against you. Nothing can stop me from harvesting the souls in this city!"

"Stop it!" screamed Sakura.

"Never!" Moonface gleefully chirped. He pressed his hands to the pedestal, into which his Arms Alchemy broach had been inserted. He focused all his mental energy into the device.

Suddenly, dozens of energetic bolts blew from cannons linked to the pedestal. They took shapes similar to that of the behemoth. Yet they were much smaller, ranging between half and twice the size of a grown man. They sprawled across the rooftops below. The screams and wails of civilians reached Sakura's ears and she began to pant with terror and panic.

"My minions are reaping, and the Silver Key is charging," muttered Moonface. "When these etheric capacitors are filled, Shaula will activate the key, and the new world shall begin!"

"No!" screamed Sakura. She ignored Nathan's warnings, and unleashed the Flare Card. The air between her and the force field ignited, but the invisible shield did not budge.

The blast launched Nathan and Sakura faster than a bullet from a gun. Dazed, Nathan glanced at Sakura and saw she was unconscious. He grabbed her quickly, and held her above him, just in time to take the brunt of the impact. His back seared with tremendous pain, much like when he had his heart ripped out by his homunculus English teacher.

He finally came to a stop and lay back with a long growl.

"Ouch," he groaned. His Kakugane-induced healing factor sealed his wounds quickly. He was relieved to find his special shirt hadn't torn that much. Then he turned to Sakura, who still lay on top of him. "Sakura, wake up," he urged.

The girl woke with a start and scrambled off him. She staggered around, unable to get her bearings. She blurted things in Japanese, which Nathan couldn't understand. She fell against a wall, covered in disintegrated plasterboard and mortar, and breathed heavily.

"Sakura, calm down, you're alright," said Nathan.

"I can't breathe!" she gasped.

"Slowly," said Nathan, guiding her through an exercise to calm her. She came down from her anxiety attack, only to break down into tears. Nathan moaned, "Sakura, I need you to focus. We've still got a job to do."

"No! I can't do this!" she wailed. "I didn't want this. I didn't ask for this! I'm not a warrior. I do gymnastics at school. I'm bad at math and like music. I didn't want the Clow Cards so that I could fight life-sucking monsters!"

Nathan grabbed her shoulders and held her tightly, but struggled to contain her thrashing. "Sakura, that doesn't matter. You're here, so you have to do it."

"No! I want to go home! Let me go home!" screamed the girl.

Nathan rolled his eyes.

Don't hate me for this, he silently begged any goddesses that might be watching. He then slapped Sakura over the head, and she fell silent.

"Look, I get it," said Nathan slowly, looking right in her eyes. "Two years ago, I was just a regular kid with recurring nightmares about cricket balls. I didn't ask to be brought back to life with powers. And I certainly didn't want to be a soul-sucking zombie boy. But that happened to me, whether I like it or not." He pointed to what assumed was south. "About an hour's drive that way is my home town," he went on. "I have to use my powers to protect my friends there. My friends are probably watching this now, and counting on me to win. So I'm damn well gonna. And it'll be hard, but if I have to, I'll do it without you. You wanna run home, I'll get your boyfriend to come and get you, and he'll take you outta here." Then he picked up the Star Wand that had clattered nearby, and thrust it in her hands.

Sakura looked between the wand and him, flummoxed and overwhelmed.

"If you want to do what's right," Nathan went on, "You'll get your arse out there and kill these things. And you'll goddamn win."

Sakura panted with dismay, "I didn't want the Clow Cards to kill things. I can't believe I killed those homunculi. They're people."

"*Were* people," said Nathan. He stood up and sighed solemnly. "You can protect the people still alive. And that's all you can do."

He neared to the front of the empty shop into which they'd fallen. A sheet of corrugated steel obscured a view of the outside, but they could hear growls of monsters and wails of victims. He looked over his shoulder at the trembling girl huddled in the corner.

"Run if you want," he said. "I won't blame you, but *you'll* blame yourself, trust me."

"How do you do it?" exclaimed the girl. "How do you fight without being scared?"

Nathan scoffed with amazement and held out his gloved hand to the girl.

"Feel my hand," he ordered.

She grabbed it, and felt his trembling within the magical gauntlet.

"I'm scared shitless," he said. "I'd just rather be scared than guilty. Some things we mustn't ever do, even if it means death; and some things we have to do, even if it kills us." He pointed at her fixedly. "Fight or flight. You tell me which is which."

Then he sliced through the steel sheet and burst into the street. The sounds of the monsters' growls gave way to their screeches. With every grunt and yell from Nathan, the monsters' howled more and with greater agony. Their wails grew fainter as did Nathan's yawps, until all Sakura could hear was distant crashing.

She sat there, alone and immobile in the wrecked shop. She gripped the Star Wand, but could not find the energy to stand and move. Every sound she heard from outside drained her more. She clenched her eyes closed and prayed that the battlefield would just go away.

It did.

Sakura opened her eyes and found herself in a familiar field of stars. She stood up and looked around. She didn't see her mother, fuelling a cold floe of disappointment. She looked up and found herself gazing into the face of a man she'd seen in Eriol's mind.

"You're Clow," she gasped.

The bespectacled man of Chinese descent, with long hair and a flowing blue robe, nodded kindly. He held out his hand, and Sakura shook it absentmindedly.

"Thank you for looking after my little kids," said Clow's voice, though the man's lips did not move. "What do you think of them? My Kerberus and Yue."

Sakura stammered a moment, before blurting, "I love them! Of course, I do! They're such wonderful people! And the Cards too!"

"You sacrificed much for them," said Clow. "No one could be more grateful than I."

Sakura clenched her hands around the Star Wand. She trembled with indecision and fear.

"Do you rue the day you found them?" asked Clow.

"No," replied Sakura emphatically. "But I didn't do it so that I could kill monsters. I'd rather just use it to help people in difficult situations."

"Sounds to me like this battle is right up your alley, then," said Clow.

"I'm not strong enough!" cried Sakura. "I couldn't break that barrier, so I can't stop Moonface from controlling those monsters. If I were as strong as you, I'd be able to do it. But I'm not you, Clow!"

Clow crouched to her level and stroked her dusty hair out of her face. He wiped away a tear and said, "Of course, you're not me. I am Clow, and you are Sakura. You have a different power from mine."

"It's not enough," retorted Sakura.

"It is more than enough, if you know what to look for," said Clow. "Do you not remember what Feiwang Lee said?"

Amid her haze of rattled nerves, Sakura recalled standing before Xiaolang's father. There was an altar, with Clow Reed's nameplate sitting separate and solitary from the others.

"He stands alone on this wall because he stood alone in life," Feiwang had said. "Do you stand alone, Lady Kinomoto?"

At that moment, Sakura thought about the people with whom she had entered this battle. Nathan, Astrid, Maka, and Soul were all such nice people, once she got to know them. And Xiaolang was the love of her life.

I'm not alone, she concluded, though it was blatantly obvious.

"Because of that, young one, you stand more powerful than I could ever have hoped to be," proclaimed Clow. The man grinned. "You have one more weapon, don't you? Your ultimate, unbeatable spell."

A fog of indecision still billowed in her mind, yet a shining light had started to shoo it away. With a deep breath, Sakura opened her eyes and returned to the wrecked shop. She stood, her Star Wand in hand, and the Cards waiting at the ready.

"I'll definitely be alright," she said.

* * *

Maka darted around the behemoth, slashing Soul's scythe blade against its knees and tendons. It did slow the beast, but only by a small amount. Any cut she, Xiaolang, or Astrid made sealed too quickly.

"Maka, let's go all out," said Soul.

Maka gauged her surroundings and retorted, "It's too tight here. We'll end up damaging most of the buildings."

Astrid had been listening over the radio. She dodged a swipe from the behemoth and landed on a rooftop nearby to catch her breath.

"You sound like you got an idea," she said. She turned to see a bunch of minions charging her and she quickly decapitated them. Whenever one of them died, she heard a ping from Centrepoint, signalling the re-spawning of her slain enemy.

They're like Moonface, she thought.

"Soul thinks he and I should resonate and use a Witch Hunter attack," said Maka into the radio.

"I've heard of that technique," panted Xiaolang as he magically upended a car on a prone minion's head. "Would be enough to put the behemoth out of commission long enough to do something about Moonface."

"Trouble is, there'll be a bit of collateral damage, and

Soul and I need time to charge," said Maka.

From her vantage point, Astrid looked out over the city skyline. About three streets south, she saw an open area.

"Druitt Street, two streets south," she said. "Go there, and charge up. Coyote and I'll lure it there."

"Copy that," replied Maka. She then raced down the road away from Centrepoint. The behemoth saw her and moved to chase her, only to have Astrid pluck out one of its eyes. Xiaolang slashed through its cheek with his sword. The beast's attention locked right on them.

Maka pole vaulted over a stack of ruined cars, dodged panicked bystanders, and sliced through minions. She caught sight of the Druitt Street sign and saw a three-lane wide road between two antiquated-looking buildings. She smirked with excitement as she raced to the centre of the street and faced north.

"I'm in position," she announced into the radio.

"Hold it, right there!" snarled an Australian man. Maka swivelled and saw a jittery police officer, his gun aiming right at her head. "Drop the weapon and put your hands on your head."

"Get as many people as you can away from here," retorted Maka.

"Drop the weapon!" screamed the terrified man. A minion suddenly pounced on him, and he shrieked as the gold-scaled monster bared its fangs. Maka hooked the scythe blade into the creature's sternum and hefted it off the man. She brought it clear over her head and smashed it into the asphalt. The monster disintegrated before the befuddled man's eyes.

"I'm not your enemy," yelled Maka. "If you're a man, you'll do something useful, like evacuate everyone. Get them as far away as you can!" The confused man looked back up at her, and then glanced at the evaporating minion. The message must have gotten through. He nodded resolutely and scrambled away, barking orders into his radio.

Maka sighed, and focused on her resonance with Soul. Another roar interrupted her, and she saw a dozen minions coming at her. She swung the scythe around to destroy most of them, and the ones she hadn't seen, Nathan swooped out of the air to promptly eliminate.

"What's the story with the tower?" asked Maka.

"Shaula put a force field around Moonface," said Nathan. "It looks like he's controlling all these things."

"Shaula's not there?" asked Maka. Nathan shook his head as he caught his breath. "I can't sense her either. It's as if her signature's coming from every single direction."

"Wanna resonate again?" asked Nathan.

"We're supposed to focusin' on chargin' for a Witch Hunter attack," Soul interjected.

"Witch Hunter?" asked Nathan.

"It's gonna be cool," said Soul, his grin reflecting in the sheen of his scythe blade.

"Where's Sakura?" asked Maka.

Nathan shook his head and sighed. Maka scoffed with dismay and rubbed the bridge of her nose.

"I knew she shouldn't have come along," she moaned.

At that point, Astrid and Xiaolang appeared around a corner, two streets to the north. In hot pursuit was the behemoth, and it was angry. It cleaved through buildings and crushed the asphalt road with its footfalls. Astrid and Xiaolang leapt over the upturned cars and debris, and reached the others before the behemoth fully emerged around the corner.

"Ready with the Witch Hunter?" asked Astrid. Maka nodded, her eyes focused on the advancing monster.

Xiaolang noticed his girlfriend's absence, and inquired. Nathan was about to tell him to go take her home. Suddenly, a soft ping echoed through the streets, and one of the behemoth's arms exploded. It howled in pain, and with its good arm it lunged for the thing that had attacked it. That winged pink blur shot southward. It flew over their heads and landed on an upturned car behind them.

"Sakura!" exclaimed Xiaolang. "Are you alright?"

"Definitely!" replied Sakura. She glanced at Nathan with a grateful nod, and then looked expectantly at Maka. The blonde smiled, and then turned to the behemoth. The monster broke into a run. When it was two buildings away, Sakura unleashed Gale on its legs, tripping it. It hit the ground hard and slid the rest of the way, uprooting the road like paper mache.

Maka stepped forward, her mind honed to the deadliest edge. Soul's reflection looked outward from the scythe blade and winked at the rest of the group.

"You're about to see a real Soul Resonance," he said.

Then he and Maka let out a unified roar. His blade turned silvery blue, and grew to over ten times its normal size. The light mesmerised every onlooker, who gasped as Maka brought the gargantuan blade down, right through the behemoth's head. The monster's body curled upward, spurred by its lingering momentum, until its neck snapped and its body completely detached from its immobilised head. It landed with a crash behind the group, disintegrating in an unceremonious puff of blue smoke.

Soul assumed his human form and stretched, while Maka stood tall. Nathan, Astrid, Xiaolang, and Sakura marched forward and stood in formation.

Moonface was frustrated, and his minions expressed that aggravation with a ruckus of howls and shrieks. They stomped and champed at the six heroes, who just stared back at them, their weapons cocked and ready for battle.

21 | The Battle of Sydney

Puffs of blue smoke burst from the Centrepoint aerie. They began to spread outward through the skies. The six warriors could see they were avian minions.

"That ain't good," said Soul.

Before Astrid could react, she heard a crackle over her radio. An Australian male voice, deep and businesslike, blared through the earpiece.

"This is Inspector Andrew Goodyear of the Sydney Police Force to on-ground units, please identify yourselves," he said.

Astrid glanced at the others, who shrugged.

"This is Astrid Rachelle," she replied to her radio. Eying the army heading out from Centrepoint, she continued, "No time to explain. Suffice to say, we're the only ones in a thousand miles who can handle these monsters."

"We have army and air force incoming," replied the Inspector. "You're saying I should send them home?"

"We could use the help," said Sakura.

Astrid chewed her lip as she looked around. She could see there were still confused and terrified civilians too near to the tower.

"Inspector, we need an evacuation of the Sydney business district," she said into her radio. "Relay this to the army and air force: do not engage hostiles. Get as many people away from Centrepoint Tower as possible. Leave the beasts to us."

"And who are you supposed to be?" asked the Inspector.

"Allies," barked Astrid.

The Inspector sighed, "Support is inbound. Ten minutes."

Astrid tapped her radio off and looked at the team.

"Okay, here's what we do," she began. "We can't touch Moonface, so we need to stall him. Sakura, your domain is the sky. Clip the wings of anything you see."

"Got it," chirped Sakura.

"Nathan, Coyote, you're with me," said Astrid. "We need to get as many people out of these buildings as possible. Kill everything attacking them, and get them out through the underground."

"Understood," said Xiaolang.

"Maka, you have the more accurate soul perception, so find Shaula," Astrid ordered. "Find where the signature is the strongest. Soul, boost her range any way you can."

"Done," said Soul.

"Maka's our ace in the hole! I want a body on her at all times. Got it?" yelled Astrid.

Everyone nodded resolutely.

"Lovin' it," bellowed Nathan, placing his hand in the centre of the circle. "All in!" Everyone threw their hands into the middle and grunted with determination.

Moonface's army flew out of the sky and charged them. Sakura raised the Guard Card, while Xiaolang blew the attackers out of the air with a fire blast. When the attack was repelled, Sakura summoned her wings and bellowed, "Go!" She then shot into the air and went to work on the airborne monsters.

Soul transformed into a scythe and Maka raced forward with him in hand. She swirled the scythe and relieved the incoming minions of their heads. Nathan, Xiaolang, and

Astrid followed closely.

Xiaolang noticed people in the antiquated building to his left, and departed the group. He drew a paper charm and roared, "*Fēnghuá zhāolái!*"

A gust of wind wound its way through the entrance of the building and tripped up the minions trying to block the entrance. He leapt over them, stabbed the lead minion, and placed himself between the horde and the terrified civilians. He was as a green blur, his sword glowing white as he brought it through the necks of the monsters.

Xiaolang turned to the befuddled civilians.

"Are you alright?" he asked. A few nodded, too out-of-breath to speak. "It's dangerous on the streets. Go down through the underground. Understand?"

"You some kind of superhero or something?" asked a boy in his mother's arms. His eyes were alight with amazement.

"No, just a helpful guy," said Xiaolang. He heard howling from the upper levels of the building. He roared at the civilians, "Go! Now!"

He wasted no more time, and launched himself with a windblast onto the second floor. The minion nearest to him met a quick end, and the others turned and cocked their heads in confusion. They snarled with animalistic shrillness and charged him from all sides. He drew a paper charm.

"*Léidì zhāolái!*" he roared. Half the monsters thrashed and squealed under the electric barrage before exploding. One survivor tried to tackle him, but he back-flipped out of its grasp and then lunged forward to embed his blade in the creature's exposed back. He'd dug the sword in with such force that he couldn't pull it out before the next minion attacked. He diverted the minion's punch, and retaliated with an elbow blow, which did nothing against the mechanical creature. It picked him up by the shoulders and threw him through a shop front.

Xiaolang scrambled to his feet, tripping over a finely

dressed mannequin. Out the corner of his eye, he saw a terrified shop owner and a few customers, huddled behind the cash register. One of the shrieking minions flew through the air at him, bearing its glimmering teeth. He crouched to the side and caught it by the neck. He wrested it around and made a shield of it. The second one found itself chewing into Xiaolang's hostage, which melted with a howl.

The second minion shook its head like a dog with an itchy nose. Xiaolang grabbed the supine mannequin and used it as a battering ram against the creature. With a roar, he pushed it out of the shop. He tripped it backwards, and cartwheeled over it toward his sword. With a yell, he wrenched his sword out of the floor and cleaved the beast's head in two. Then he raced back into the shop and ordered the terrified women to get to the underground.

As the women scurried away, Xiaolang looked down the length of the open-plan building. Minions swarmed along its immense length. He drew a few more paper charms, and raced down to engage the beasts.

* * *

Blue plumes of dust, heralding the defeat of avian minions, wafted from above like snow. That much made Astrid feel a little more confident they could hold off Shaula's soul charging. The more of these things they killed, the more people could escape. And it would be only another eight minutes before they had army support to get the people out of harm's way.

This is the first time I'd ever relied on normal human authorities for this, Astrid mused as she vivisected a low-flying avian minion. She flipped in mid-air and stabbed through four more minions.

"No sign of the behemoth," Nathan yelled from across the street as he wrestled with a minion twice his size but half his strength.

Astrid sighed with relief. With her mechanical limbs,

she hurled a truck at a quartet of minions. She turned to Maka and asked, "Anything?"

Maka dodged the blows of a large minion, and then sliced along the length of its arm. She embedded Soul's blade in the back of its head. As the thing collapsed unceremoniously behind her, Maka held out her free hand like a dousing wand. Soul resonated with her to boost her range. And yet, she still felt the consistent reading in every direction.

"She wasn't as hard to find last time," said Soul.

"She's obviously enhanced her soul protection spells," growled Maka as she axed another minion.

"Keep trying," said Astrid.

A sudden smashing of glass and shrill cries drew their attention. Astrid looked up to the building nearby. She could see children cornered by minions on the upper floor. She exchanged glances with Maka, who dealt with another minion before hopping onto the roof of a wrecked car. Astrid raced at her, used her mechanical limbs to jump onto the handle of Maka's scythe. Maka then catapulted her upward to the window.

Astrid rolled through the cracked window, into what appeared to be a bookshop. She slashed up the spine of the nearest minion. She then lobbed the disintegrating corpse at another, disorienting it while she maimed the third.

"Go! Down to the basement!" she chided the kids. A brave adult edged into the action to whisk the kids away.

One of the minions launched Astrid through a stack of bookshelves. She quickly dug herself out from under the heavy pile of books, and raised her blades to shield her from the minion's onslaught. The creature swatted the blades aside and brought its fist down on her head. Astrid darted through the monster's legs, brought her blades through its kneecaps, and then sliced the thing's head off. She moved on to the other minions blocking the exit.

"Everybody move!" she roared, and the shocked crowd

split apart for her. She cut the minions up with her human buzz-saw attack, much to the crowd's cautious delight. "Get to the underground! Now!" she yelled.

An avian minion suddenly burst through the wall and snared a straggler. Its talons dug into the screaming woman, but before the minion could claim her soul, Astrid claimed its gizzard. She then lifted the wounded woman from the floor and shouldered her to the security guard.

Another avian minion charged her from behind, but a lightning bolt struck it, and it splattered against the wall like a bug on a windshield. Astrid glanced outside, and saw Sakura fly past.

"You're definitely getting pancakes later," Astrid chirped.

* * *

Nathan and Maka turned a corner. Minions had covered the narrow street and torn it apart. Agonised wails and horrified screams mixed in with the snarls and growls of hungry monsters.

Nathan held Maka back, and moved to the centre of the road. He held his lance behind him, summoned every ounce of his energy, and pushed it into his lance. The seams in the hull of his weapon cracked, and orange light trickled out. He let out a vicious roar, and then slammed his lance into the road in front of him. The minions' heads promptly exploded like fish bowls at a rock concert, leaving behind flabbergasted city-goers.

"You ain't the only ones who can do cool stuff," said Nathan.

Maka chuckled, which surprised Soul.

"Wow, Maka Albarn impressed by another person," he jibed. "And a cis white straight dude, to boot!"

"Shut up," retorted Maka as she followed Nathan.

They collected every person they could find. Soul retook human form to help pull a car off the trapped leg of a man. Every survivor they found was ordered to look for the underground and wait for the military to arrive. The survivors offered expressions of gratitude.

While Soul and Nathan helped the survivors, Maka searched for Shaula's signature. She recognised a vague direction where the reading felt different, but still couldn't be sure.

Soul heard something that sounded like shells firing in the distance.

"Must be the calvary," he said.

"*Cavalry*," corrected Nathan. "Calvary's the hill where they killed Jesus. I doubt a freaking hill can fire shells."

"Is this important, Skippy?" exclaimed Soul.

Sakura's voice sounded on the radio. Nathan answered, "Go ahead, Sakura."

"Guys, Moonface's unleashed a flying behemoth," she gasped. "I've got my hands full up here, and the army looks like they're trying to fight it. The behemoth is going to the park eastward of the tower."

Nathan looked northward, and saw the tail end of the creature in question. He glanced at Maka.

"I'm still looking for Shaula," she said.

"I'll keep an eye on her," said Soul.

"You sure?" asked Nathan.

"She's my meister," said Soul with a sharp-toothed grin. "Mutha-trucka's got no chance."

Satisfied, Nathan used an overturned car as a springboard and jumped into the building on the east side of the street. He sprinted through the building, cutting down any minion he saw while slicing through walls and dodging bystanders.

He reached the window on the other side of the building and glanced to his right. He saw the flying behemoth through the crowd of amazed office workers. He raced toward the northeast corner of the building, and cleaved through the glass at Mach-level speed. He crossed the distance to the flying behemoth and landed on one of its six insect-like wings. The behemoth's wing beats launched him the rest of the way onto its back, and he brought his lance against the heavily armoured vertebra.

It hardly left a dent.

The behemoth's tail flicked, sending Nathan head over heels. A squadron of avian minions swooped upon him, like a horde of eagles squabbling over a lone spider.

Let's see if I can pull an Astrid, he mused.

He wound himself up, and kept the lead minion in sight. When it was close enough for him to see the hunger in its eyes, he jumped. He spun as he flew toward the bird, and his blade bisected its torso. He brought his blade around and embedded it in the head of the next one. Then he thrust against the third and fourth, skewering them. The last one he grabbed by the talon and dragged it onto the behemoth's back.

In that moment, he allowed himself a momentary lapse in control. His skin turned slightly crimson, and his gauntlet pulsated. The avian minion shrieked as its energy leaked out of its body and into Nathan through the gauntlet. As the thing disintegrated, the behemoth faltered, and it started to fall out of the sky. Nathan glanced forward and saw the green of Hyde Park. It raced upward to meet him, and he quickly jumped from the behemoth's head. He landed on the paved path on the east-most side of the park, just ahead of where the beast smashed into the ground and skidded toward him.

The behemoth opened its huge maw to crunch him in one go. He grabbed the upper teeth with his gloved hand, and braced against the lower jaw with his lance. The monster thrashed in his vice grip, as shells and mortars hit it from all sides. Nathan looked left and right, and saw approaching soldiers firing everything they had at it.

But they might as well have come at it with shovels.

Nathan almost lost his grip on the monster. He released his lance, and grabbed the lower jaw with his bare hands. With a shriek, he wrenched the behemoth's head clockwise, and a loud crack reverberated through the park.

The behemoth disintegrated before the astounded troops.

Nathan leaned on his knees and waited for the deep gashes in his unclothed hand to heal. Then he picked up his lance and approached the nearest soldier.

The soldier studied him up and down and murmured, "You're one of these six fighters we were briefed on?"

"I'm the Starlight Lancer," said Nathan. "Me and five others're takin' out these things. Those things," he indicated the machine gun in the man's hand, "You'd have better luck with nerf guns."

Another soldier approached.

"And I take it your sword there'll do the trick?" he asked sceptically.

"Hey, I just broke that thing's neck with my bare hands," retorted Nathan.

"So what do we do then?" asked the first soldier.

"We got civilians trapped in there," said Nathan, pointing to the city. "We need you to get them out. My team and I will keep these things focused on us."

There was another flash of light from Centrepoint Tower, and another flying behemoth appeared out of the resultant plume. A ground-based behemoth soon followed. Nathan groaned with dismay.

He turned to the soldiers and said, "Do *not* try to fight these things. Just get the people out of here. Okay?"

The soldier wet his lips and glanced at his platoon. The absurdness of the situation set in quickly, and he agreed. Nathan shook the man's hand graciously, and then raced westward, back to the battle. As he neared the fight, his mind wandered to the flying behemoth.

Why did it suddenly fall out of the sky?

* * *

With a swing of Soul's scythe form, Maka knocked a minion across the road as if it were a baseball. Then she carved through asphalt and brought Soul's blade through the legs of another, completely bisecting its body. A flying minion dove from above, its sharp talons vectoring for her head. She braced herself against the screeching bird, which latched onto Soul's handle and hefted them both into the air.

"Maka, watch out below!" yelled Soul.

He resumed human form, save for his hand. He then delved his bladed arm into the creature's torso, ending it. He glanced down and saw Maka falling. She gracefully hit and rolled down a pile of cars. Soul dropped down to meet her, and raised his arm defensively against incoming monsters.

"Any sign of Shaula?" he asked.

Maka closed her eyes and held out her hands. The signature was still the same from all directions.

Soul disembowelled several minions on his own. He kept a weather eye on his meister, and promptly dealt with everything coming her way.

To the east, they heard a crash. Soul glanced down the street and saw the flying behemoth hit the ground.

Nathan must've done it, thought Soul. *Not too bad at all.*

Maka faltered. From within the recesses of her soul, she sensed the tiniest fluctuations in the aether. She looked downward to the ground, just beneath the building across the street from Centrepoint. In that instant, she felt the reading grow stronger in that direction.

"Maka!" yelled Soul, snapping her out of her musing.

She looked over and saw her weapon try to lever a car door open. A family was trapped inside. She raced over and looked at the door Soul was working.

"That door's all deformed," she said. She clambered over to the other side and saw the other door intact, but sandwiched up against another car. "Soul, this side!" Her partner leapt across the car hood. Together, they wedged themselves between the two vehicles and pushed, but it wouldn't budge. A minion leapt onto the other car and snarled at them. They quickly rushed into action and decapitated the thing, and then moved back to try moving the car.

The car suddenly started to move. Maka and Soul opened their clenched eyelids and saw ten more people pulling or pushing the car out of the way. When there was enough space, Soul's hand became a scythe blade, and sliced the door open.

The family scrambled out of the car, disoriented and hurt, but alive and grateful. Maka quickly ordered them all down to the underground. A few soldiers came running through the streets to guide the survivors away. One of troops approached the pair.

"I take it you're these *allies* of ours?" asked the soldier. With a scoff, Maka nodded.

"Leave these things to us," said Soul. "You need to get these people to safety."

The soldier spared a glance at an incoming battalion of gold armoured minions and sighed.

"Do what you gotta do," he said.

Maka grinned. Soul assumed his scythe form in her hand and they raced down the street to face the monsters. Maka twirled, and brought Soul's scythe blade around like a combine harvester through a wheat field. Those that didn't fall at his blade ended up on their backs.

A sudden, massive tremor struck them from behind, and they fell to the ground. Maka scrambled to her feet and held Soul at the ready, as another land-based behemoth stood over them.

"Run, Maka! We don't have enough time to charge," yelled Soul.

Maka glanced over her shoulder, and saw more minions coming from behind. Before she could panic, she noticed, behind the monsters, a pink blur coming in fast.

* * *

A flock of avian minions flew westward from Centrepoint toward the harbour. Sakura felled a few of them with Gale. The remainder pitched toward her.

"Flight, how are you doing?" she asked through the resonance link.

"I can hold up, Master," replied her wings.

"To the deck then," said Sakura. She veered downward ahead of the winged soul suckers. Then she swivelled and unleashed the Flare Card. A superheated plume burst upward from her wand and engulfed the creatures. They quickly re-spawned from the tower aerie and came after her.

Sakura vectored her wings and pulled out of her dive. She darted around the buildings, the avians hot on her tail. She cast out Veil, and a forest of shadowy thorns skewered her assailants. She banked around a tight corner and summoned Forest and Bloom. The minions she saw on the ground were subsequently torn apart by sweeping vines, while the avian minions in her path fell from the sky, their wings caked with pollen.

"Maya, I need you to spread the word," she proclaimed, touching her wand to the Maya Card. Wisps of fractal light flew into every window of every building, and Sakura prayed the people hiding therein got the message to evacuate.

"Master," said Maya. "Got everyone. I mean, it's not like there's a family in the building at three o'clock that's cornered."

Which means there is, concluded Sakura. She pitched toward the building and sent out a Card.

"Carve a path to the survivors, Gaia!" she yelled. A borehole appeared in the side of the building, into which Sakura flew. She summoned Blade and sliced through every minion she could see on her way through, until she found the family huddling in a bathroom stall. A larger minion was reaching for them, its hungry fangs dripping. A black fog suddenly enveloped its head and it floundered futilely to clear its vision. Sakura screeched to a halt and lopped its head off.

She turned to the family, who withdrew from her in

panic.

"It's okay," she said, holding her arms up honestly. She noted the mother's hijab, a soft pink that had been dirtied by minion blood and dust.

They mustn't understand me, she thought.

The father held his wife and son tightly, his eyes fixed on the blade in Sakura's hands. She quickly deactivated the Card, and her sword became a wand again. She tried to make as gentle a face as possible. The boy, whose face was wet with fearful tears, looked directly at her and seemed to recognise her.

"Cardcaptor," he said, though his pronunciation was off.

Sakura smiled and knelt before the family. She held out her wand and said, "Could you hold this for me?" The boy, with a questioning glance to his parents, took the wand. Sakura then drew the Guard and Flight Cards and touched them to the wand. The family squealed slightly as a winged, translucent sphere enveloped them. Then it lifted them effortlessly into the air.

"Take them outside!" Sakura commanded. Flight and Guard obeyed, and set off down the borehole. Sakura sprinted behind them. As the sphere exited the hole, Sakura leapt after them, landing on top of the sphere and descending with it. It impacted the ground and disappeared, leaving the family shaken but unscathed.

A horde of minions were incoming, but Sakura just calmly held her hand out to the boy. With a wary smile, he handed the wand back. Sakura raised it, and activated the Spark Card. A flurry of electric bolts zapped the minions and turned them to dust. Then Sakura led the family through the chaotic street to toward the troops that were incoming from the south.

The mother and father kissed her hands graciously as they went into the soldiers' care. The platoon leader gave her an encouraging salute.

I'm glad I chose to stay, thought Sakura as she saluted

them back. Then she summoned her wings and shot into the sky. She banked around a few corners, zapping and smashing minions where she saw them. Then she saw another land-based behemoth. Maka stood right between it and a crowd of minions vying for her.

Sakura reached out through her resonance link and said, "Alright, everyone, let's go!"

"Yes, Master!" replied the Cards.

Gale blasted Sakura forward, and she swooped down over the minion horde. Shadowy spines, fiery plumes, high-pressure water blasts, and thorny nettles sprung up in her wake to decimate the encroaching army. She cast out Reflect, making a decoy of herself to distract the remaining monsters. With little more minions attacking, Sakura sped toward Maka.

The scythe meister back-flipped over Sakura, who skidded to a halt and raised her magical shield against the behemoth. The beast hit an impregnable wall, giving it a nice concussion. Nathan, racing in from the right, tore through its head with his lance. Xiaolang and Astrid flew in from either side and embedded their blades in the minions vying for Sakura and Maka's necks.

Soul assumed human form, and the five of them made a wall around Maka. The roaring creatures squalled and gurgled as they were cut down, handful at a time, by Nathan's lance, Astrid's Valkyrie Skirt, Xiaolang's sword, Sakura's magic, and Soul himself. Meanwhile, Maka quieted her mind, and reached outward in the direction she'd sensed before.

It does feel different, somehow, she thought.

"Maka!" yelled Soul. Maka snapped back to reality, and saw the flock of avian minions incoming. The others were too caught up in their own scuffles to notice. Maka grabbed Soul's outstretched hand. He transformed into a scythe, and they summoned a Witch Hunter blade in record time. Maka spun in mid-air, flying over Sakura and Nathan, and slicing through the shrieking minions.

Another flying behemoth came at them from down the street. Sakura quickly summoned the Gaia Card into her body, which glimmered dark orange. Then she grabbed Nathan's outstretched hand, twirled him around, and threw him with all her might at the airborne beast. Astrid used her blades as a counterweight, and hurled Xiaolang.

Coyote and the Starlight Lancer flew down the street toward the creature. It bared its teeth, determined to have them in its belly. Its snap missed by fractions of an inch, as Nathan and Xiaolang hooked their blades into the corners of its mouth. Their momentum carried them down the length of the monster, splitting it two ways down the middle. They rolled on the ground and skidded to a stop. The behemoth crashed to the ground and disintegrated.

"Howzat!" bellowed Nathan.

"Not bad at all, mate," said Xiaolang in a poor attempt at an Australian accent.

Nathan grinned, and fist-bumped the Chinese magician. Then he eyed the disintegrating beast. He recalled the other one he'd killed. He had an epiphany, just as a three metre tall minion stomped the ground behind them. He turned and stopped Xiaolang from engaging.

"I got this," he said, handing his lance to the boy. Then he raced forward, sliding between the minion's legs. He leapt up onto the monster's back. He flexed the fingers of his gauntlet, and slightly released his mental control. His skin flashed crimson, and he plunged his hand into the beast's back. The creature started to twitch and thrash as Nathan drew its energy into his body. He felt invigorated and, at the same time, afraid of the pleasure coursing through his stomach.

Xiaolang suddenly felt fatigued, as if his legs had fallen asleep. The minions staggered around and wailed. Then they vanished. Coyote glanced over, and saw Nathan, his skin tinged red and his hair-tips glistening fluorescent green. The boy panted and growled, working hard to regain some kind of control. As if he'd finally moved a heavy boulder into place, his skin and hair returned to normal. He walked over and hefted Xiaolang up.

"Was that your Victor form?" asked Xiaolang breathlessly.

"Yeah, sorry about that," said a guilty Nathan. "You able to walk?"

Xiaolang gingerly released his hand from Nathan's shoulder and nodded silently.

"Any particular reason you did that?" he asked.

"I think I just figured out how to kill these things for good," said Nathan with a grin.

22 | Shaula's Lair

At first, the people of Sydney thought terrorists had attacked. Indeed, that's what the news reported, along with fuzzy video of a fire at the top of the Centrepoint Tower. The feed had been live, and within minutes of the explosion, the Internet was alight with word of an eight-eyed golden monster ransacking the Sydney business district.

Reports soon came in of six people doing battle with the monster. They all looked like superheroes in their various costumes, which would have earned them laughs had people not been running for their lives. Most wondered whether the barista had mixed LSD into their morning soy lattés.

At least, that was the impression to be gleaned from the Twitter feed at Regiment headquarters. Bravo chuckled at that as he rubbed the bridge of his nose.

"They're fighting?" asked a voice.

Bravo turned to see Franklin at the entrance to the control room. The man had a concerned but hopeful expression. Bravo nodded and turned back to the main screen with a sigh.

Franklin approached Spirit, a little unsure about how to deal with the man who had flirted with his daughter. But there were more pressing matters. They both gazed at the control room screen. They saw Sakura and Maka working to fend off a creature.

"My baby girl is winning," whispered Spirit, tears of pride rolling down his face.

"As is mine," said Franklin.

Eriol, meanwhile, moved to Bravo's side and said, "Not a bad idea to team them up, aye?"

Bravo glared at the Scotsman. Unwilling to debate, he sighed, "This is going to get way worse before it gets better."

* * *

At the Kinomoto house, a pot was boiling over on the stove. Touya and Yukito were too distracted by the news to notice. In Sakura's bedroom, a mouthful of chewed cookie fell from Kero's mouth, all over the laptop keyboard, as the flying plush toy watched the live feed.

* * *

The Warrawul dormitory was dead quiet, save for the noise trickling from the television in the common room. At the front of the crowd of students sat Klein, Jessie, and Paul, their jaws ajar with amazement and their eyes wide with worry. But each of them felt pride for their friend, fighting the good fight.

* * *

Death City was in an uproar when word got out that Shaula was attacking another city.

The Reaper chuckled as he gazed at his mirror, showing the action around Centrepoint Tower as it happened.

Kiddo writhed on the floor about the ruined symmetry of the tower, which reduced Patty to giggles and infuriated Liz.

Tsubaki wondered if she was the only one concerned about the civilian casualties, while Black-Star moaned, "Why didn't they invite me? I'm a God, me damn it!"

* * *

Tao Wu hopped off the back of the pick-up truck. He waved the driver away as he started toward town. He glanced around the streets, knowing that the Alchemic Regiment was keeping tabs on him. He didn't mind – he deserved the suspicion. But that didn't stop him from being curious as to their vantage point.

He stopped, startled by the sudden crowd of people outside an electronics store. He looked over the shoulders of the amazed people and saw one of the television screens. A newsfeed showed shots of a battleground in the middle of Sydney. Golden giants eerily familiar to the boy snarled at the camera.

Then he saw the bright lance that occasionally haunted his dreams.

With a grin, he thought, *Go for it, Nathan!*

* * *

A hidden facility lay beneath the Alexandria Kalinin Memorial Aged-Care Home. Within that secret Regiment facility, Shu Wu huffed after another hour of physiotherapy. The nurse shouldered her to a chair and let her rest.

After a minute of panting, Shu looked over her shoulder and saw the nurses crowded around a television. She saw the battleground of Sydney. Homunculi clones – certain to have been perfected from Doctor Butterfly's work – smashed and rampaged through the city.

Before Shu could break down, she saw the four mechanical limbs of the Spartan Valkyrie. With an excited gleam in her eyes, she bellowed, "Kick their arses, Astrid!"

* * *

Masaki Kinomoto stood in the study of his home, completely aghast at the television. At first, he thought his eyes were deceiving him. But with every frame, he came to realise that it really was his granddaughter, flying through the air.

"You weren't joking, Touya," he said.

* * *

In a mansion in Canberra, Ariadne sat between her mother and father. Their hands gripped each other's, while their eyes took in every frame of Nathan, fighting with monsters in the middle of Sydney.

"So, this is what he does instead of study," said Henry, his tone deadpan but his smile elated.

* * *

Meiling dropped her phone at the sight of her Twitter feed. She raced into the living room of her penthouse in downtown Hong Kong, and switched on the television. Her mother and father entered the room, and they sat down to watch the breaking news of a monster attack in Sydney.

Feiwang nervously turned to his stoic wife and asked, "Is this what you foretold?"

"Not quite," replied Yelan, her stoic face hiding the nauseating cocktail of fear and excitement in her gut.

* * *

In an underground bunker, a tall, pale man sneered at the television feed. His eyes narrowed through the holes of his butterfly mask.

"Grant, you damned hypocrite," snarled Papillon.

* * *

Tomoyo's phone overflowed with messages from concerned friends, all of whom were watching the same news feed. But the girl and her mother could hardly be concerned with their electronics. Their eyes were glued to the screen, which displayed images streamed straight from Australia.

Only one thing gave poor Tomoyo any relief: Sakura

was wearing her costume – including all the cameras hidden therein!

* * *

A flash of energy reverberated through the aether, and dinged against Maka's soul. She looked away from her freshest kill toward the place she'd sensed the fluctuating signature. The sensation came a second time, far stronger and clearer than before.

Astrid swooped in and cleaved through a minion vectoring for Maka's back.

"Maka, what's the matter?" she asked breathlessly.

"I think I've found Shaula," said Maka, pointing to the ground beneath a building across from Centrepoint. She reached out once more, and clearly detected the Witch's unique stink. "Yep, I've definitely got her," she said confidently.

Nathan's voice blared over the radio, "Guys! I think I know how to kill these things all together."

"What is it?" asked Astrid.

"It involves going Victor," said Nathan, a little sheepish. "I tried it on a big guy just then. I got really close to the spine. I felt like there was a core or something that was linking me to the others."

Xiaolang's voice butted in, "The others around it started to lose their energy when he did it."

Sakura landed nearby, a confused look on her exhausted face. She tapped her earpiece and said, "That didn't happen over here."

"These things were fine all around us," said Soul.

"Then we might need to go bigger," said Maka. "Nathan, try it on a behemoth."

Nathan chuckled, "Good idea. But I'll need a hand getting to the spine."

Maka and Astrid exchanged glances and ideas without speaking. It was Soul who finally spoke up and said, "Skippy, Bruce, and the Cheerleader get the behemoth then. Spartan, Maka, and I'll go after Shaula." Maka glanced at Sakura, who nodded confidently. She sprouted wings and flew down the street.

Maka led the way into the department store, under which she was sure Shaula was hiding. The place was infested with minions, who gurgled and shrieked as Astrid and Maka cut them down. Astrid carved a path under Maka's direction, until they broke into the underground.

"She's near," murmured Maka, crinkling her nose at the stench of Shaula Gorgon. She glanced down the passages, and picked the path to their left.

"You sure, Maka?" asked Soul.

"Positive," said Maka. "And so help me, Soul, if you say only fools're positive, I'll hurt you."

"Whatever you say, fool," retorted Soul.

Maka rolled her eyes and glanced at Astrid, who wore an odd expression. When Maka asked, Astrid just said, "Nothing. It's just really bizarre watching this from the outside."

"Wanna see your head from the outside?" snarled a voice behind them. A tall homunculus emerged from the shadows and pounced on Maka. Astrid countered an attack from another homunculus coming from the other direction. She diverted the thrusts of his knife and ran him through with her blades. She then stabbed the other homunculus through the head before it could bite Maka's head off.

Astrid pulled Maka to her feet.

"You okay?" asked Soul.

"Fine, just not used to dealing with homunculi," said Maka.

"Also, too busy looking for Witches," said Astrid. Then she eyed the passage through which the homunculi had come. "Speaking of which …"

Maka held out her hand and sensed Shaula's signature from the dark passage. She led the way, Astrid close behind and sniffing for homunculi like a bloodhound. A faint glow trickled through the blackness, and it grew brighter as they neared a corner.

They found themselves in an abandoned sewer shaft, a remnant of an old structure long since demolished. A tangle of pipes plunged into the room from the concrete slab above. They hummed as they funnelled glimmering blue energy into a core in the centre of the chamber. Within the glass core, they could see the two halves of the Silver Key, coiled around each other in a double helix that pulsated as if alive.

"Beautiful, isn't it?" murmured a voice that made Maka's hair stand with rage. Soul's scythe form shuddered. Astrid flexed her mechanical limbs.

A leather-clad woman skulked from behind the core. Her neck-length purple hair glistened in the blue light. Her red-cyan eyes radiated triumphant, righteous anger.

"Shaula Gorgon, I presume?" muttered Astrid as she cocked her four blades.

"Screw pleasantries," snarled Maka. Her eyes fixed on the core, and she brought Soul's blade against it. They struck the glass casing hard, but their blow made no dent.

"Too bad, sugar," said Shaula sassily. "Your scythe boy would have better luck penetrating your hoo-hoo than that glass."

"Then we'll just take you out," bellowed Astrid. She and Maka lunged forward and brought their blades against Shaula's body. The Witch leaned backward, as if doing the limbo, and artfully dodged the honed edges of Soul's scythe and the Valkyrie Skirt. She swivelled in mid-air. She parried the butt of Soul's handle with her elbow and stopped Astrid's blades with a shield of black light. The magical shield glimmered bright purple as Astrid struck it multiple times.

With a shrill yawp, Maka brought Soul's blade around for an uppercut. Shaula darted out of Astrid's path and blocked Maka's blow with her shield, causing it to glow brighter. But Maka had more up her sleeve. She brought her head forward, crushing Shaula's nose with her forehead and bruising her jaw with a clenched fist. She hooked Soul's blade against Shaula's midsection, and hurled the Witch against the wall with savage force.

Shaula slumped on the concrete floor, seemingly beaten. Maka didn't feel like gloating. Neither did Soul. Their soul wavelengths matched perfectly, and they charged forward as one, Soul's blade at the ready to cleave the Witch's head in two. At the last nanosecond, Shaula's hand appeared between them, her palm sprayed. Her magical shield flashed with bright purple.

"*Tseghai!*[12]" growled the Witch.

With a high-pitched crash, a bolt of black lightning enthralled Soul and Maka's bodies. They flew away from Shaula and smashed against the core. With a chuckle, Shaula floated onto her feet.

"Suck it, bitch!" she bellowed.

Astrid scrambled to her feet and charged forward with an immense war cry. She slashed and swiped at Shaula, only to glance against her magic shield. The barrier, directed by the Witch's palm, glowed brighter and brighter as she nonchalantly parried and blocked Astrid's every attack.

"Seriously, are Alchemic Warriors *this* stupid?" she asked over Astrid's continued shouts and lunges. Astrid came at her with a frontal assault, and the Witch harrumphed, "I guess they are." She held out her palm.

Astrid deactivated her Arms Alchemy before impacting Shaula's charged shield. Her momentum carried her within reach of the Witch, and she grabbed Shaula's outstretched arm and twisted it behind her back.

"Stupid is a stupid does, *bitch*," she whispered into Shaula's ear. Then she threw the Witch against the wall.

The small of Shaula's back impacted the palm of her hand. The pent-up energy in her shield suddenly unfurled

---

[12]   Witchese Language: "Absorb-Invert"

onto her, shooting her across the room and headfirst into the opposite wall. The Witch hit the ground, motionless.

Astrid pulled some cable-ties out of her pocket and restrained the Witch, and then raced to where Maka and Soul lay in a crumpled heap on the floor. She gently slapped them awake. Maka looked to be concussed, and staggered as she stood. Soul gingerly moved his sore joints, but his head was clear enough to notice Shaula's motionless form.

"She won't be coming to for a while," said Astrid with a satisfied grin.

"Let's kill her now," grunted Maka.

"Wait," said Astrid, eying the core. "I don't know whether she has some kind of lock on it. We kill her, we could lose the ability to shut this thing down."

The trio glanced at the device. They moved around it, studying any distinguishing feature they could see. Maka noticed a tablet computer hooked to the device, and she tapped a widget to bring up the control screen.

"Looks like they'd accrued enough souls to activate the thing," said Maka, a bad taste in her mouth considering the people who had died.

"Why didn't she do it, then?" asked Soul.

Maka studied the read outs closer. "It only has enough energy to go back twenty years. If they wanted to do more, like wipe out DWMA or the Regiment, they'd have to go back even further."

Soul noted the energy gauge on the screen and said, "They ain't gettin' any more souls, it looks. Means we won, right?"

"Not until we shut this thing down," said Astrid. She glanced at Shaula, who was still out cold. Then she turned back to Maka and asked, "Is there a shutdown command?" Maka didn't respond. Astrid called her name, but Maka was fixated on the console.

"Maka, what is it?" asked Soul nervously.

"Twenty years," Maka whispered. "This is good for

twenty years of time travel."

"Wait, Maka, what are you thinking?" asked Soul. He tried to pull her from the terminal, but Maka shoved him off.

"I can go and save Mama!" she yelled. "I can go back in time and warn her about the cancer before it gets too bad to treat. And I can go and stop Papa from cheating!"

"You can't! Think of the people who died to charge that thing," retorted Soul. "You think your Mom will like it that she lives because of a mass murder."

"I can warn her about Shaula too!" replied Maka. "Hell, I can kill Shaula back in the past before any of this. If it works, none of those people will have died."

Soul grabbed her by the shoulders and shook her.

"I can't let you do this," he pleaded. "You'd be no different from her. It's not right."

Maka gritted her teeth. She pushed him away and barked, "I have a chance to fix the wrongs in my life, and I won't let it slip away!" She lunged for the terminal, only to be lifted out of reach. She turned and saw Astrid's mechanical limbs, having hooked under her jacket. She struggled futilely in Astrid's grasp.

"The dead are dead," said Astrid, her gaze fixed on Maka's red-rimmed green eyes. "And no matter how bad you want to change it, you'll screw up so much more trying." She hooked her finger under Maka's chin and forced eye contact. "Believe me, I know what it's like," she enunciated.

By then, Shaula had started to stir. She looked over at the trio and giggled weakly. Though blood drizzled down her head, she found the energy to grin manically.

"A tempting idea," she murmured. The trio glanced at her. "I wonder whether man has ever wished to go back to the very beginning, just so he could walk around paradise with a naked woman again." The three rolled their eyes. Shaula went on, "But the program is in place. Moonface cannot be stopped. Once enough souls are collected, the

Ultimate Gate shall open, and you will not even be a memory."

As if she'd jinxed her luck, the apparatus started to shudder. At first, they thought the device had activated. Astrid checked the gauge and noticed the reading falling. The whine of the core faltered and started to decline. Shaula's eyes shifted between the core and the feeding conduits above. Her grin turned to panic, and then to dismay.

"No," she whispered. "It's not possible! Moonface can't have!"

Astrid beamed at Soul and Maka. "They did it! Nathan's plan must have worked!"

The core's glow flickered as its energy readings dropped lower, until it finally hit zero and the light went out. Shaula screamed with rage, and struggled against the cable ties binding her. Astrid glanced her way and sneered with delight. The Spartan Valkyrie sauntered toward the Witch and cocked her blades.

"Your plan is dead, and now so are you," she proclaimed. She thrust her blades toward Shaula's heart, but they clanged against concrete. Shaula had disappeared in a flash, and a purple iridescent scorpion scampered down a grating nearby. Enraged, Astrid slashed the grating open and plunged her blades as far down into the pipe as they would go. She found nothing.

"Damn it!" she yelled. "She got away!"

Maka fell to her knees and punched the ground with disbelief and frustration. Astrid slumped her shoulders and sighed away her fatigue and disappointment. Only Soul stood tall with his red irises focused on the inert core.

"But we still won," he said. He placed his hand on Maka's trembling shoulder, and looked into her eyes. "We'll get her some day, but here, we won."

Maka smirked and nodded reluctantly. She glanced at Astrid, who huffed, "Long bloody day!"

23 | The Behemoth Falls

Sakura soared down the street, and landed near Xiaolang and Nathan. She embraced her boyfriend.

"So, what's the plan?" asked Xiaolang.

"You said you needed to get to the spine of a behemoth," said Sakura. "The tower spawned one that's heading north."

"We'll have to slash its neck open first," said Nathan.

"What're we doing standing around here?" exclaimed Xiaolang. "Let's go!"

Noticing Sakura's fatigue, as well as his own, Xiaolang glanced around and saw a car that had been barely scathed by the battle. He raced over, slashed the door open, and hotwired it. The trio climbed into the vehicle, and Xiaolang peeled around the corner and drove north.

"Since when can you drive, Xiaolang?" asked Sakura.

"California," replied Xiaolang.

"What? Did Astrid teach you?" asked Nathan slyly. "What else did she teach ya?"

Sakura's eyes bugged out while Xiaolang's face went blood red.

"What're you implying?" asked Xiaolang.

"What do you think I am?" retorted Nathan facetiously.

"No! Don't say that kind of thing!" yelled Sakura. "Xiaolang's *my* Number One!"

"Yeah, but I'm implying that you weren't his first one," jibed Nathan.

Xiaolang looked over his shoulder and screamed, "Could you be serious? Your city is being attacked, for God's sake!"

"And I'm in a car drivin' to the fight," retorted Nathan with a chuckle. "What? Would you rather I asked 'Are we there yet?'"

Sakura and Xiaolang let out a chuckle and shook their heads with disbelief. They turned their attentions to the city outside. They crossed an intersection, and Sakura bellowed, "There! Turn right!" Xiaolang jerked the wheel, and the car tilted as it swerved to go down the adjacent street. In the back seat, Nathan's head banged hard against the window.

Xiaolang looked over his shoulder with a smug grin and asked, "You alright back there?"

"Get stuffed," retorted Nathan.

Xiaolang brought the car to a stop half a block short of the behemoth. The massive beast rampaged through buildings, and snarled with frustration at finding no prey. As the car came to a halt, the beast sniffed their scent, and directed its eight hungry eyes in their direction. The trio scrambled from the car and stood before the beast.

"You focus on getting yourself ready," said Sakura. "Make sure you can change back once you finish that thing."

"Got it," said Nathan.

Xiaolang and Sakura raced forward. Sakura sprouted her wings and took to the skies. Xiaolang launched himself into the air with a gust of wind, and fired a barrage of lightning at the creature, which stumbled backwards. Sakura summoned the Gaia Card, and willed a spire of rock to sprout from the ground into the creature's gut. Then she and Xiaolang landed on its exposed shoulder blades and prepared to slash its neck open.

Two boulder-like paws came out of nowhere and

knocked him off. Sakura caught him with the Gale Card. They raced down the street to gain some ground against the creature, which had become preoccupied with protecting its nape with one arm as it chased them eastward.

It's onto us, Nathan realised.

At that moment, he heard someone yell over the din. He glanced to a nearby alley and saw a group of soldiers. A few survivors stood with them. He raced over to them.

"Starlight Lancer?" asked the lead soldier. He noted the lance and gauntlet.

"Yeah, we're tryin' to kill these things," said Nathan. He glanced at the rattled survivors and said, "I'm sorry we haven't done a better job." It did little to keep down the images of cricket balls streaming through his head.

The lead soldier glanced around the corner at the behemoth and sighed incredulously.

"You're doing a much better job than we are," he said. "I'm Sergeant Jones. We're just getting the last survivors we could find. But that thing'd cornered us. Any chance these things'll stop soon?"

"We've got an idea on how to stop them," said Nathan. He explained the plan in brief. Jones glanced at the behemoth again, and noted the claw covering its nape.

"You're gonna have to get its hand out of the way first," he said.

Nathan looked around and pondered a moment. His mind, exhausted as it was, couldn't come up with any solution.

"Can't we just tie it down?" asked one of the survivors.

Jones glanced at the little boy, then at Nathan, and grinned. "There's construction going on at Martin Place. They've got a tonne of steel wire. You and your buddies tie it up, we hold it down, and you do your thing."

Nathan thought quickly, and his eyes brightened. He tapped his radio and said, "Guys, I've got a plan. Sakura, get over here. Xiaolang, keep the behemoth busy."

When Xiaolang received that message, he rolled his eyes with dismay. His legs were shaking with fatigue, to say nothing of his mental state. Never had he used so much magic in one day, and the strain beared down upon him. He darted out of the behemoth's way as it lunged for him, and he scrambled into a nearby building.

Thankfully, the creature was obsessed with him, and it tried to reach through the building to get him. Its claw smashed through the concrete and mortar of the building's lower levels, and already Xiaolang could hear the building rattle. He sprinted down the building's entrance passage and scrambled up a stairwell. He leapt and jumped as the creature's sharp claws punctured through the concrete wall, and they narrowly missed him. He burst out of the stairwell into an abandoned office. He raced toward the window, through which he could see the top of the behemoth's spined head. He covered his crown with his forearms and plunged through the glass, passing right in front of the behemoth's face. He relished the surprise he saw in its eight eyes. He brought his sword across two of those eyes, and completely destroyed them.

His speed carried him into the building on the opposite side of the road. He rolled to maintain his momentum, and raced through another abandoned office. He slid down the elevator shaft and ran out into the street. His victory against the beast had given him a second wind, and he punched the air with delightful triumph.

"Xiaolang," said Sakura through the radio. "Nathan and I are in position. Lure him north to a street called Martin Place."

"Roger that," replied Xiaolang cockily. He turned to the creature, which rubbed its damaged eyes and squalled. Then he bellowed, "Hey, stupid! Come and get me!" The behemoth snarled and lumbered after him. He raced north, leaping over cars and darting around the behemoth's one-handed grasps. When he was close enough, he nipped the golden claws with his sword, which served to distract it from the pink-clad girl standing on a rooftop ahead. Brown energy imbued her body, and she held a length of heavy steel wire in her hand.

Xiaolang skidded to a halt when he heard the beast roar with anger. He turned and saw the wire fastened around its wrist. Sakura welded it on with the Flare Card. The behemoth removed its claw from its neck, and brought it down on where Sakura stood, but the girl had already jumped out of the way. Nathan then leapt out from a roof on the other side of the road, and coiled another length of wire around the behemoth's free wrist. Thinking quickly, Xiaolang unleashed a fireball that welded the wire together.

"Do it now!" yelled Nathan as he landed nearby.

In the adjacent streets, hordes of civilians and soldiers pulled the wires with all their might. The behemoth was no match for them, and whined as it struggled in their thrall.

"Xiaolang! Let's go!" yelled Sakura. The pair nodded resolutely, and raced forward.

Sakura drew a Card. "Knock its feet out, Aqua!"

Xiaolang drew a paper charm and proclaimed, "*Shuǐlóng zhāolái!*"

Torrents of water shot from Sakura's wand and Xiaolang's sword. It knocked the behemoth's legs out from under it, and it toppled forward. The pair kept running, dashing through the creature's legs. They didn't even wait for it to hit the ground, before they launched themselves back the other way. Sakura summoned her Blade, while Xiaolang's sword glimmered in the sunlight. With a unified roar, they cleaved through the armour and flesh of the behemoth's nape, exposing a pulsating blue device.

"Do it, Nathan!" screamed Sakura.

The Starlight Lancer soared through the air, onto the back of the struggling beast. The behemoth pulled desperately against its steel chains, but the people held it tight. Sakura released vines and shadows to bind it harder.

Nathan gazed upon the core of the behemoth, and

flexed his gauntlet. In that moment, he had a vision of Ariadne's hand, hanging out of the stomach of a mechanical snake. The memory, and what it signified, gave him strength. He plunged his hand into the behemoth's core, eliciting a panicked cry from the thing.

In an instant, he felt as if he were connected to every minion attacking the city. He could see through their eyes, and smelled their desperation – Moonface's desperation. And thanks to his intrusion, the minions could no longer feel anything but Moonface's terror.

Up in the Centrepoint Tower aerie, Moonface was mortified, aware of the precipice upon which his doom now hung. He desperately tried to withdraw his Arms Alchemy from the control pedestal, but it wouldn't budge. He couldn't escape the force field around the device either. He was completely trapped.

Nathan heard Moonface's panicked wails through the link and cockily murmured, "Complain all you want, you son of a bitch!"

Then he released his mental controls. His skin turned deep crimson, and his hair shimmered fluorescent green. Every single minion across the city seized and screamed. Their bodies glimmered with red light, which melted their golden carapaces. In the tower aerie, Moonface gave a devastated wail of "Moon!" before shrivelling into a black corpse and eroding away.

Across the city, minions fell and disintegrated, and they did not re-spawn at the tower.

The behemoth upon which Nathan stood was the last to finally go, leaving the crimson-skinned man kneeling on the street. He clutched his heart and panted to push his Victor form down, but it had become more difficult than ever before. He sensed elated people drawing near to him, and he bellowed, "Stay away!"

His mind swam with the image of Moonface's final doom. Finally, the monster that had hurt so many people – including Tao and Shu Wu – was gone. The pleasure it gave him kept him from reasserting his control. He could sense energy trickling into him from the people just at the edge of his drain range. He desperately wanted them to come closer.

Nathan, said a voice, echoing softly through the fugue. *Nathan, we've won. You can come back to normal now.*

He listened to the voice. The ever-present image of a cricket ball, stained with his sister's blood, spurred him on. He matched his breathing to the ebb and flow of the voice, until he found a way out of the treacherous sea. He clambered onto an island of wrecked asphalt, and looked around. Sakura stood right in front of him, her hands clasping his. Nearby, Xiaolang leaned against his sword and sighed away his own exhaustion. A crowd of soldiers and civilians emerged from the nearby streets.

With a pant, Nathan released Sakura's hand and fell onto his backside. He panted in long slow breaths. Every part of his body ached.

He heard footsteps, and looked over his shoulder. There was Astrid, Maka, and Soul. They all looked completely beat. Maka was concussed, and leaned against Soul for support.

"You did it?" asked Astrid, out of breath.

"Yeah," said Nathan. "You get Shaula?"

"She got away, but we got the key," said Soul. He held up his jacket, wrapped around the two halves of the hated device.

"I think we won," intoned Xiaolang.

"Yeah," rasped Nathan. He fell onto his back and moaned, "What a long bloody day!"

The flabbergasted bystanders surrounded them. Their confusion lingered like a stench. Astrid, Maka, Soul, Sakura, and Xiaolang withdrew nervously, unable to look away from the wall of people enclosing them. Nathan hardly cared as he pulled himself to his feet and addressed the people they'd saved.

Sergeant Jones pushed his way to the front of the

crowd. He shook his head with bewilderment and asked, "So, what're you six supposed to be?"

Nathan yawned.

Astrid and Maka exchanged nervous glances.

Sakura gripped her wand close to her chest.

Xiaolang held his Number One close.

Soul stole a glance at Nathan's shirt and Sakura's costume.

It's as good a name as any, he thought.

Then he stepped forward.

"I'm Soul Eater," he proclaimed. He pointed at Sakura. "That's Cardcaptor." He pointed at Xiaolang. "He's Coyote." He pointed at Nathan. "He's the Starlight Lancer." He pointed at Astrid. "She's the Spartan Valkyrie." He pointed at Maka. "We call her Scythemeister."

Then he held his head high and said, "You can call us the Star Warriors."

24 | The New World Begins

Plumes of smoke billowed from the centre of Sydney for the rest of the day. EMTs, fire fighters, police, and soldiers worked tirelessly to find any remaining survivors of the attack. The media had gone absolutely bananas over the incident, now being referred to as January-Twenty-Six[13]. People were stoked over the attack of magical creatures, more so over the six extraordinary heroes who fought the beasts.

Of course, if anyone saw the so-called Star Warriors, huddled together behind an ambulance just outside Museum Train Station, they would have been less than impressed. Soul had dislocated his shoulder and Maka needed seven stitches in her head. Astrid had twisted her ankle at some point. Sakura held an icepack to her forehead while Xiaolang had icepacks on both shoulders and knees. Nathan, seemingly unscathed, concealed an Earth-shattering migraine.

The entire team was worn out, and were grateful when a Regiment aircraft arrived to transport them out of reach of the press. As they watched the smouldering skyline of Sydney drift away, they all sighed with minds nearly blank.

---

[13] January 26 is Australia Day, celebrating the anniversary of the arrival of the First Fleet at Sydney Cove. It has similar significance to American Independency Day.

Bravo emerged from the cockpit. He opened the case containing the two halves of the Silver Key. They lay inert as strips of ornate metal. The man clenched his fists at the torment of such power just barely outside his grasp. Then he looked at the six warriors.

They cleaned up my mess, he thought.

Bravo glanced at Maka, who sat beside the key case with a vacant expression. He stood before her and said, "Thank you for your hard work, Miss Albarn." Maka nodded weakly. Then Bravo moved onto Soul, who managed the slightest grin.

Then Bravo looked at Xiaolang and said, "You fought extremely well, Coyote. And I hope this won't be the last time the Regiment works with the Lee Clan." Xiaolang nodded.

Bravo then knelt before Sakura and said, "I apologise for dragging your father into this. I'm also sorry for throwing all the blame on you. None of this was your fault, Miss Kinomoto."

Sakura croaked, "Thank you, Mister Bravo." And though she didn't look like it, she was definitely glad Eriol had rigged that lottery.

Then Bravo turned to Astrid and Nathan. His chest ached with shame and awkwardness. He finally forced himself to speak.

"I didn't do right by you," he said. "Either of you."

Astrid pursed her lips, but remained silent. The image of Bravo's accusations was still fresh in her memory. There was also the nagging fact that Astrid's affections for Nathan set in motion the whole chain of events Bravo had wanted to prevent. Those thoughts kept her from disagreeing with the man.

Nathan, on the other hand, stood and wrung his hands remorsefully. He recalled the ecstasy of drawing all that energy out of Moonface and his minions. He shuddered at the powerful hunger he had felt within. Images resurfaced of Papillon's younger brother disappearing behind the teeth of the newborn homunculus.

"Bravo, I won't use my Arms Alchemy until the Regiment can undo what's happening to me," he said. "I don't want to be like Victor … Or Chouno."

Bravo placed his hand on Nathan's shoulder and said, "We'll figure out a way. I promise you."

Soul spoke up, "So what happens to us now?"

Bravo harrumphed, "Secret's out. The world now knows about DWMA and the Regiment, not to mention the reality of magic. This world is about to change in a major way. And you six are at the centre of it all." He scratched his head with dismay as well as intrigue. "I guess what happens is … either you become celebrities, or outcasts. It's for the people to decide."

* * *

The skyline of Manhattan simmered with noise, and yet felt completely empty. Maka's vacant green orbs scanned the area. A person might have walked down that street, or a cab might have driven by. She hardly cared. Her brain was too much of a frazzle, thanks to the hearings and testimonies she'd had to give over the last few weeks.

It wasn't just her. Her five cohorts lounged about the room, proverbial steam rising from their overworked heads.

Soul and Nathan had quickly thrown off their ties, jackets, and shoes, which lay in a pile beside the door. Only Sakura had any presence of mind to pick-up after the boys. Even she couldn't stay on her feet, and had propped her knees up on a coffee table and rested her head on Xiaolang's shoulder.

Nathan tried to relax, but his recurring flashbacks had held off sleep. Heavy bags weighed down his eyelids.

Astrid chewed her nails in the corner, pondering her testimony over and over again. She knew there was nothing left to say, and yet her brain would not stop going over every single nanosecond of her life. She rose with a sigh and started to pace. When that did little to help, she walked toward Maka, and together they gazed out the window.

"How many weeks've we been doing this?" she grumbled.

"I feel like we were in Sydney only yesterday," intoned Maka. "I never thought these secrets would come out. I couldn't imagine it ever happening."

"I did," chuckled Astrid. "But I imagined the whole world would blow up. I wasn't expecting to have to testify before the United Nations." The ladies chortled incredulously at the idea.

Maka gazed at Sakura, dozing on the couch. With a smile, she said, "It was good of Sakura's friend to hire all those lawyers for us."

"Yeah, not even the Regiment had anything like that," said Astrid. "We never needed it. I should thank Missus Daidouji in person."

Maka gazed at Astrid pensively. She recalled the moment, in that abandoned sewer, in which the scarred woman had stopped her from using the Silver Key. Her curiosity overwhelmed her. She glanced around at the others, deciding a more private venue would be suitable.

"I need to powder my nose," she said, tugging at Astrid's sleeve. Astrid caught Maka's meaning and followed her to the adjoining bathroom. Then she faced the scarred woman. "Back in that hole, you stopped me from using the Silver Key. You said you knew what it was like to want to change the past. What did you mean?"

Astrid tightened her jaw and shifted her gaze. She tried not to touch the scar on her nose, but the fight did not go her way. She glanced at the door, noting Maka had locked it. She beckoned the blonde closer, and started to whisper.

"I was in kindergarten," she said. "It was my first day, actually, and my Mum and Dad had come to see me off. The weather was bloody miserable. Absolutely raining cats and dogs. I remember I wore yellow galoshes. They squeaked like Hell while I stumbled through the wreck of my school. Mud and broken glass all through the halls, wrecked lockers, bodies everywhere. And … I thought I'd found one of my classmates in all the chaos. And …" Astrid started to pant, her skin blanched. "When I saw his face," she stammered, wincing at the memory. "And he had my mother's head in his hands … he'd eaten her." She touched her scar. "That *thing* gave me this scar. It was then that I was born an Alchemic Warrior. And for so long, I rued that goddamn day … until I met Nathan. And I almost lost him so many times, most of them because of my own anger and regret." She finally forced herself to look at Maka, whose eyes and mouth were wide. She sniffed back her tears and said, "More than once I thought I'd sell my soul to undo that day. And if that were enough, I'd do it in a heartbeat. But it isn't, is it?"

Maka thought about how many people had died, their souls sucked out of their bodies by Moonface's minions. It was obvious that even a single soul sacrificed to change the past was too much. But hundreds would be an atrocity.

Damn good way to end up an Asura Egg, she thought.

"Thank you," she said, looking right into Astrid's red-rimmed eyes. "Thank you for stopping me."

Astrid beamed. "Soul seems a decent guy, and a wise one too. You should listen to him more."

Maka rolled her eyes. "He's an idiot most of the time."

"So is Nathan," retorted Astrid.

Maka giggled in reply.

A knock on the door snapped them out of their laughter.

"Astrid, Maka, are you alright in there?" asked Sakura through the door.

"Yeah, we're fine," said Maka. "We'll be right out."

* * *

Another week passed.

The six had spent their time couped up in a hotel room

in downtown Manhattan, awaiting the United Nations' decision. Of course, the Internet had already run rampant with viral videos and tweets regarding the existence of Death City in the middle of Nevada, as well as the revealed double lives of countless Demon Weapons, Alchemic Warriors, and magic users.

Thankfully, the combined resources of the Lee Clan and Daidouji Industries, along with a generous donation from one Masaki Kinomoto, kept the focus on the Star Warriors. Each of them had their own Facebook page and brand, provided by Tomoyo Daidouji. Every time that girl showed up, she acted like a thousand fan-girls all rolled into the ultimate groupie. Sakura loved it; Maka was annoyed by it; it made Xiaolang and Astrid very uncomfortable; and Soul and Nathan couldn't stop marvelling at their combined coolness factor.

One day, Tomoyo burst through the door with Bravo, Eriol, and Spirit in tow. They each wore excited yet cautious expressions.

"Turn on the TV," said Eriol.

Sakura struck the remote and tuned the TV to the station as instructed by Bravo. The news broadcast announced an imminent speech by the United Nations General-Secretary regarding the incident in Sydney. Each of them sat down and grew tense as the elderly man unfurled his speech on the podium.

"The last few weeks have triggered a major shift in our world," he announced. "Troubling, challenging, and even bizarre facts have come to light. New threats have appeared, as well as new possibilities. And no way forward is immediately apparent. Regarding the existence of the Alchemic Regiment, of this entity known as the Reaper and his organisation of shape-shifting individuals, and of those who wield supernatural abilities, the United Nations General Assembly cannot make a decision as of yet.

"Therefore, a period of inquiry is to be established. The nature of these organisations and the abilities of their participants will be ascertained with utmost transparency. It will be determined how they may be a danger to the world at large, and how much of a benefit. At present, I believe they will be the latter.

"The reason for this is the six individuals who, seven weeks ago, heroically and courageously defended thousands of innocent people in Sydney, Australia. These aptly-named *Star Warriors* are to be commended. They are the best evidence for what these newly discovered societies might offer our world. It is for that reason that I have recommended to the governments of Australia, Japan, Hong Kong, and the United States of America, that these individuals be honoured, and all resources necessary be allocated for their continued defence of our world."

The man stepped away from the podium to raucous applause and furious clicking of cameras. With a relieved smile, Bravo switched off the TV and glanced at the others. Spirit gave his daughter a hug, while Eriol gave Sakura and Xiaolang an encouraging pat on the shoulder. Astrid glanced at Nathan, who still wrung his hands nervously.

"You know what that means, Grant?" asked Bravo. "Not only do you have all the Regiment's resources, but the world's. We'll figure out a way to reverse the Black Kakugane."

Nathan let out a relieved smile, while Astrid gripped his hand tightly and rubbed his shoulder soothingly.

Soul rubbed his eyes and yawned. He wiped away the drool from the corner of his mouth and said, "So, that mean we get to go home now?"

* * *

The six stood beside the Cherry Hill Fountain in Central Park. A large area had been cordoned off for them to get some fresh air following weeks in confinement. Meanwhile, motorcades were being prepared to escort them out of the city and back to their own countries.

Sakura glanced at the others despondently.

"It'll probably be a while before we see each other again," she thought aloud.

"I doubt that," said Maka. "There's gonna be tons of threats to the world. And they'll call us to save the day."

"Now that is a cool idea," said Soul.

"Well, if it's all the same to the world, I'd like a holiday," said Nathan.

"Second that," said Xiaolang.

Astrid harrumphed, "Since I'm babysitting Nathan, I likely won't get a holiday ever again."

"I love you too, Astrid," said Nathan facetiously.

While Astrid grabbed Nathan in a headlock and punched his head vengefully, Maka, Soul, and Xiaolang chortled. Only Sakura had any empathy for Nathan and calmly urged Astrid to release him. Nathan rubbed his head, and graciously bowed to Sakura for her help.

"You know what, I don't think we've had a group photo yet," said Sakura.

A few minutes later, Tomoyo had set up her DSLR camera. The six stood in front of the fountain and waited for the paparazza to configure the camera to just the right settings. Then she issued demands in Japanese, which Sakura translated.

"Nathan, she says you're too tall," she said, prompting Nathan to move right to the back and crouch down. "Maka, you're too tense. Loosen up," translated Sakura, and Maka took a breath. "Soul and Astrid, come in a little bit more and don't scowl," said Sakura. They obeyed reluctantly. Only Xiaolang, who had taken a position next to Sakura and Maka, didn't feel entirely out of place. Of course, he'd had to deal with Tomoyo's hobby for much longer than the others.

Tomoyo was finally ready to take the photo.

"Smile," she said with a poor English pronunciation.

Nathan glanced at the people in front of him, and his grin widened evilly.

Tomoyo proclaimed, "And cheese!"

At the last second, Nathan threw his arms around everyone and yawped.

* * *

The eyes of the Reaper's mask slanted with disappointment. Soul and Maka stood on the dais before him. The former had his hands in his pockets, and wore an aloof expression, while the latter was erect and tense.

"Daw, why couldn't you have brought me some of those Anzac cookies," moaned the Reaper.

Soul laughed, "They were really good!"

Maka sighed, "What about this whole mess, Lord Reaper? Are you really fine with civilian organisations auditing us? What if they decide to shut us down? What about all the parents of our students, who thought their kids were at a school for the gifted?"

"Meh, I was bored of all the top-secret mumbo jumbo anyway," replied the Reaper. "For the first time in a long while, I can just be honest. It's kinda refreshing, really." Maka rolled her eyes with dismay. "Maka, dear, don't worry. You did an amazing job! You and your new friends saved so many people. You both should feel good."

"I know I do," said Soul. He wiped away his drool. "Star Warriors ... Don't ya just love that?"

"Of course, you would," muttered Maka. "You think every idea of yours is cool."

The Reaper chuckled and dismissed them.

"Go and take some time off," he said. "Party with Black-Star and Tsubaki. Kiddo might even have you over for mojitos."

Maka smiled reluctantly, and bowed as she left. The Reaper watched the pair leave. Kiddo, who had been standing beside the mirror, glanced up at his father.

"Father, please be honest," he pleaded. "Are you sure this is alright?"

"Kiddo, m'boy," chirped the Reaper. He turned and

addressed his son. "Of all the worlds in the cosmos, this one is unique."

"How so?" asked Kiddo.

"If ever we get into a pinch, our stars aren't that far away," the Reaper said, his cuboid finger outstretched. "As dear Sakura would say, 'We'll definitely be alright.'"

Kiddo shook his head incredulously. Knowing his father was in far too good a mood to debate, he turned and left the room. The door closed with a thud. The Reaper then turned to the mirror, and an image of Eriol appeared in its frame.

"Is this good, Lamperouge?" he droned.

Eriol pursed his lips and said, "For now."

* * *

Tsubaki donned an oven mitt and pulled the baking tray out of the oven. The aromas of tomato, pasta, and browned melted cheese filled the kitchen. Maka watched from the dining table and wrung her hands fretfully.

"I feel bad about you doing all the cooking, Tsubaki," she said.

"C'mon, Maka, it's a woman's job to cook the food," said Soul. Of course, it was only to provoke a reaction from the blonde, and it was quite successful in the end. Tsubaki only chuckled at the mayhem as she set the lasagne on the dining table.

"Oooh, this smells delish!" exclaimed Patty as she neared her hands to the steaming dish. Liz quickly swatted her hand away.

"It's hot, you silly girl," snapped the elder sister.

Kiddo blushed at the sight of the figure of eight Tsubaki had left in the cheese topping. In his eyes, it completely made up for the odd number of pasta layers.

Black-Star started cutting out slices for everyone, while Tsubaki served a simple salad. Then they sat down and started eating.

"You know, I really can't wait until we can do this with

your new friends," said Tsubaki.

"I think that'd be real cool," said Soul. He nudged Maka, who beamed.

She thought about Astrid and Sakura. They both seemed so nice, and yet so powerful, *and yet* so inseparable from the men in their lives. She glanced at Soul and thought of her relationship with him. Until she met them, she hadn't realised just how much she depended on him, and how happy that made her. Thanks to Sakura, she knew how valuable he was. And thanks to Astrid, she knew that all her pain had been worth it.

"We'll definitely meet up again soon," she thought aloud.

* * *

Nathan woke just as the jet hit the tarmac at Canberra airport. Astrid had to pull him along, even though she completely understood his reluctance. It was back to a treatment cell with him, until they could remove the Black Kakugane. He was not looking forward to the white walls of a padded room again.

"Look alive, Grant," said Bravo as they walked through the secured corridors of the airport terminal. Nathan glanced at him, and then looked in the direction of his outstretched finger.

At the end of the corridor stood six people. Klein, Jessie, and Paul wore grins of pride and excitement. His parents, Henry and Blythe, wore inscrutable expressions. Overflowing eyes crowned Ariadne's smile.

Nathan and Astrid glanced at Bravo, completely dumbstruck. The man chuckled and motioned for them to go. Nathan burst forth and threw his arms around his little sister. His friends stepped forward and group hugged him, completely red-faced with amazement at his achievement. While they gang-hugged Astrid, Nathan turned to his parents. He couldn't tell if they were horrified, joyous, irritated, or all three. Then Blythe walked forward and embraced him tightly. He cautiously returned the gesture. Then his father walked forward and shook his hand, before gauchely hugging him.

Bravo looked on from a distance. His heart ached but he managed to keep his own tears at bay.

Please God, let them be wrong about him, he thought with dismay.

* * *

Xiaolang approached the vault, in the lower basement of his family compound. The damage incurred by Moonface had long since been repaired, and the very floor beneath his feet thrummed with protection spells. His stomach churned with discomfort.

"Mother? Father? Are you sure this level of security is necessary?" he asked nervously.

"Given what has been unleashed, yes," said Yelan stoically.

Xiaolang shuffled uncomfortably.

"I hope you don't blame me for it," he said softly.

"Not at all," said Feiwang. "It was inevitable, quite frankly, that this kind of revelation would come. But we need to be ready, my son."

Xiaolang eyed the vault, containing the Lee Clan's half of the Silver Key, as well as many other magical treasures. They were beyond dangerous. And now that so many more people knew about them, it was clear they needed to be kept out of the wrong hands.

There was especially one artefact, hidden within, that preoccupied Xiaolang.

"Did you ever determine who made that counterfeit Sealing Staff?" he asked.

Feiwang fell silent, while Yelan shuddered. Their alarm wafted from them like a shockwave from a volcanic eruption. Xiaolang wondered if he really wanted to know. The staff of Alice Axilotl made his skin crawl, so he could only imagine how it made them feel.

His father turned to face him, a worried look in his eyes.

"Before I tell you, you must swear something," he said sternly.

"Yes, Father?" said Xiaolang.

"Swear that you will do anything for Kinomoto," he proclaimed. He jabbed his finger at his son. "Swear that you will go to Hell for her."

Xiaolang's eyes widened. His father had never asked him something such as this before. Of course, he couldn't imagine why. The answer was obvious.

"I will go to," said Xiaolang, his shoulders back and chin held high. "I swear to God, I will go to Hell for Sakura."

Feiwang pursed his lips, satisfied with the response. He then leaned down, and whispered into his son's ear.

Xiaolang's eyes widened in shock.

* * *

Sakura sighed with exhaustion as she stood before the Daidouji mansion. Her security detail, courtesy of Tomoyo's mother, led her through the gates. Finally, she had some time away from interviews and meetings with the Japanese government. She had wanted to spend the night with Yukito, Touya, and Franklin, but Tomoyo had important news for her.

Kero floated beside her, though he flew near her shoulder, wary of the security guards from whom he was used to hiding.

"This is totally weird," he muttered to her.

"Everything is," replied Sakura.

The guards led her through the mansion until they reached Tomoyo's room. Tomoyo dismissed the guards, and Sakura breathed a sigh of relief, as if to scream, "Freedom!" She regarded her friend, whose eyes were glimmering with excitement like nothing Sakura had seen before. Tomoyo grabbed her hand and dragged her into her workshop. Six sizing mannequins in different configurations lined one wall. The other wall was packed with large computer displays, presenting different designs and patterns.

"Now that I have all their measurements, I can commence my magnum opus!" exclaimed Tomoyo.

"All whose measurements?" asked Sakura nervously.

"Isn't it obvious?" asked Tomoyo. "Your team! I'm gonna be the Star Warriors' official costume designer!"

"What?!" screamed Sakura.

"Oi! Don't forget Kerberus!" exclaimed Kero. "Next time, I'mma flyin' into battle. Pah! That albino reckons he's so cool. That Aussie wanna go? They'll all bow to the awesomeness that is me!"

Tomoyo clapped her hands together and shrieked, "Oh, this is going to be delightful!"

Sakura withdrew into a corner and buried her face in her palms. Her cheeks burned with embarrassment. And yet, in the depths of her heart, she could not shake her own excitement.

Being a Star Warrior is awesome, she thought.

Epilogue

A faint wave rippled across the length and breadth of the universe.

In the gap between the tenth and eleventh dimensional membranes, that infinitesimal fluctuation awakened an entity. Its very being was instantly alert and it searched in panicked, almost manic fervour for the source of the signal. Yet the wave was too minor to isolate, even for an existence of such magnitude as it.

The entity trembled with disappointment and frustration. But it willed itself to return to slumber and conserve its strength. They would surely give it another chance to sniff them out.

Such was their nature.

About the Author

Craig Stephen Cooper grew up in Wollongong, New South Wales, Australia. At a young age, he quickly developed a flare for the dramatic, an obsession with various video games, and an aptitude for expressiveness.

In response to his desire to develop video games, his parents allowed him to study software engineering under a tutor while still in primary school. At the same time, he took dance lessons after school. He later decided drama was a path better suited to his love of storytelling, and studied speech and drama during high school.

While completing a Bachelor of Computer Engineering, he underwent practical and theory examinations for an Associate Diploma of Performance Art. During his Doctor of Philosophy in Telecommunications, he taught speech and drama to primary school children. As a member of the Fellowship of Australian Writers, he has presented workshops on storytelling and poetry, drawing on his speech and drama studies.

Cooper conceived of *The AXOM Saga* while on a train from Fukuoka to Nagasaki in Japan. Under encouragement from his friends, he wrote the stories with a passion to equal his first novel, *Final Flight of the Ranegr.*

He also dabbles in video game and mobile app development.

About the Illustrator

Tessa Eden grew up upon the shores of Australia's sunny beaches, frolicking in the sand and exploring the beautiful underwater world. Her father being a software engineer, and mother an illustrator, it was natural that she would grow to combine the two, becoming a digital artist. She now spends her days painting digitally, and creating 3D animations and CGI for animation studios in Sydney.

9 780645 175394